Fee pressed her lips softly to her baby's brow and closed her eyes. Her lips trembled slightly, then she said in a low, clear voice. "I'm a single mom. There isn't anyone else except my sisters and their husbands. My kids are all I have."

"You're…what?" Brody still wasn't sure he was hearing her right. "But Robert—"

"Robert's gone," Felicia said softly, meeting his eyes. There was no mistaking the anguish he saw there. "I never thought I'd hear myself say this, but…I'm divorced, Brody. My husband had an affair. He left me and the kids a year ago. My marriage is over."

Over… The word carried such finality. Brody knew how it felt to lose someone before getting married; he could only imagine how heart wrenching it would be to go through the agony of divorce. His heart went out to the beautiful woman before him—then nearly stopped when she dropped her next bombshell.

"He ran away with an actress…from that TV show *Itsy-Bitsy.* You know, the one about the swimsuit models? The title is supposed to refer to their bikinis, but I think it's a statement about the producers' minds!"

"Robert did what?" It would be, Brody realized, the undisputed scoop of the year. The journalist's insides were swirling with such a rush of thoughts and feelings, he very nearly missed what came next.

"He ran off with that starlet Tiffany Diamond. He'd treated her one afternoon at the hospital when she came in with a twisted ankle. I'm a single mom. And," Felicia said, speaking with the complete and utter conviction of one who had gone through gruesome torture and had no intention of going through such tribulation again, "that's the way it's gonna stay, because I promise you this: I will *never* fall in love again!"

Our **Giggle** Guarantee

We're so sure our books will make you smile, giggle, or laugh out loud that we're putting our "giggle guarantee" behind each one. If this book fails to tickle your funny bone, return it to your local bookstore and exchange it for another in our romantic comedy line.

Romantic Comedies from WaterBrook Press

SUZY PIZZUTI
Say Uncle...and Aunt
Raising Cain...and His Sisters

SHARI MACDONALD
Love on the Run
A Match Made in Heaven
The Perfect Wife

BARBARA JEAN HICKS
An Unlikely Prince
All That Glitters
A Perfect Stranger (Spring 2000)

ANNIE JONES
The Double Heart Diner
Cupid's Corner
Lost Romance Ranch (Summer 2000)

THE SALINGER SISTERS

The Perfect Wife

—THE—
SALINGER SISTERS

The Perfect Wife

A Romantic Comedy by

SHARI MACDONALD

WATERBROOK
PRESS

THE PERFECT WIFE
PUBLISHED BY WATERBROOK PRESS
5446 North Academy Boulevard, Suite 200
Colorado Springs, Colorado 80918
A division of Random House, Inc.

ISBN 1-57856-138-8

Library of Congress Cataloguing-in-Publication Data
MacDonald, Shari.
    The perfect wife / Shari MacDonald. — 1st ed.
            p.   cm. — (The Salinger sisters)
        ISBN 1-57856-138-8
        I. Title.   II. Series: MacDonald, Shari. Salinger sisters.
    PS3563.A2887P47   1999
    813'.54—dc21   99-14976
                                                              CIP

Printed in the United States of America
1999—First Edition

10 9 8 7 6 5 4 3 2 1

To Verna Mae Strong

Thanks for shattering all the mother-in-law stereotypes,
for loving me as your very own child,
and for raising, with Bill,
the one I now call "the most wonderful man in the world."
I am eternally, gratefully, and lovingly in your debt.

The Salinger Sisters Series

Acknowledgments

Thanks to my dear editorial trio—Lisa Tawn Bergren, Traci DePree, and Carol Bartley—for your support, advice, wisdom, and friendship; to Phil Christensen and Erin Healy for baby stories that made me laugh till I choked on my Diet Coke; to Dr. Kim Heggen for medical advice (and for being my first "let's pretend" friend); to the ever-hysterical Lindy Warren for the "wrong dress" story; and to my beloved Craig—not for keeping me sane but for loving me in the midst of my craziness. I adore you.

One

Brody Collins stared without flinching into the perfectly crafted mirror over his equally flawless bathroom sink. "You," he growled, shaking one finger at his stone-faced reflection, "are one lucky man. Do you realize that, Collins? One lucky man indeed."

The sour-faced chap peering back at him did not even blink. He did not give the appearance of one who felt lucky, Brody noted bitterly. If anything, his two-dimensional counterpart looked decidedly bored. Which was fitting because, of course, that's exactly what Brody Collins was. Bored. Bored with work. Bored with the city. Bored with life.

Bored with himself.

Leaning forward to get a closer look at his pathetic personage, Brody eyed his reflection critically. One lip curled up in an involuntary sneer, noting with a sense of detachment just exactly what he was bored *with*. From his cool blue eyes and close-cropped hairstyle to his upscale, casually formal, could-be-on-his-way-to-an-Easter-egg-hunt-or-dinner-with-Steven-Spielberg business attire, he was the personification of L.A. chic.

He shot his image one last look of disgust, then turned deliberately away. What was his problem this morning? Brody was predisposed to finding other people irritating, but he didn't usually start out the day by finding fault with himself. Chalk it up to the fact that he hadn't been sleeping well lately. As the editor of *California Dream* magazine, he certainly had nothing to snivel about. On the contrary, he had all the advantages that made grown men's mouths water.

He had power. The aftershocks caused by the features and reviews printed in his slick, color-infused publication reverberated from Hollywood to New York and far beyond.

He had prestige. As the controlling force behind the magazine with the fastest-growing circulation in the nation—and as an eligible single male called upon to both work and socialize with some of the most glamorous women in the entertainment and fashion industries—Brody Collins was living the dream of red-blooded American males everywhere.

He had wealth. In addition to the countless perks that came with his highly coveted position—worldwide travel, lucrative profit sharing, even a generous clothing allowance—Brody was one of the most highly paid editors in the business. Not that he cared. Though he made his home in one of L.A.'s most expensive and exclusive communities, Brody had little interest in the accumulation of possessions. As a result, his upscale condominium was sparsely furnished—"Neo-Empty," his younger sister Abby cheerfully dubbed it. The few work associates and Hollywood contacts who'd actually set eyes upon his domicile had interpreted from its sparsity a trendy social/political statement about the pointlessness of materialism and had praised Brody for making what they tearfully proclaimed to be "a stand for all of humanity." If that was what this particular segment of humanity wanted to believe about him, Brody figured—and if that belief made them look upon him and his publication even more favorably—he certainly wasn't about to correct them. Which was why he didn't bother to mention that shopping for home furnishings and objects of decor, for him, fell somewhere between having his teeth cleaned and getting audited by the IRS.

No, he was lucky all right. His latest story coup simply confirmed it. He couldn't wait to see the look on the face of his publisher, Nicholas Fortunata, when he explained that *California Dream* had snagged exclusive rights to cover the wedding of "Rent-a-Yenta" Lucy Salinger, L.A.'s much-beloved local matchmaker.

Brody snorted derisively at the mere thought of it. There was no accounting for taste…or intelligence—the general public was apparently willing to read about anything. Pinochle-playing pit bulls, aliens squatting in the Mojave Desert, Elvis and Queen Elizabeth's love child. Thank goodness, unlike the national tabloids, his publication hadn't stooped quite so low…yet. Nor was *California Dream* known for inventing fictional stories; at least this Salinger woman truly existed. Having seen her himself thirteen years prior, he knew that much for a fact. Though whether or not her much-publicized romance was the fairy-tale-come-true the public desperately wanted it to be…well, that remained to be seen. Brody's lips twisted into a silent manifesto of doubt.

Not that he begrudged Lucy Salinger her success. When it came right down to it, in fact, he was cautiously pleased on her behalf—and on behalf of the girl she had once been. Ever since his years at L.A.'s George Washington High, where Lucy had been a lowly freshman during his senior year and had occupied a locker two pea-green hallways from his, he'd picked her out as one of the sharper tacks in the student-population box.

This was, of course, a judgment based more on general impressions than on irrefutable fact. His acquaintance with Lucy then had been very slight. Today, if it were not for the facts that her image had been plastered on the pages of every local publication and her guileless face had grinned back at him from his television screen as a feature on virtually every national news magazine—from *Inside Scoop* to *Timeline* to *Good Day, Americans!*—Brody would have been unable to pick her out of a crowd if his life depended on it.

He failed to see any real newsworthiness to her story. As far as he could tell, Lucy Salinger was simply a good businesswoman with a successful venture under her admittedly charming belt. But ever since her engagement had been announced the previous summer—on what Brody cynically suspected must have been a slow news day—her romance had stuck in the public's mind. Lucy Salinger and her company, Rent-a-Yenta, had grown in popularity. Everyone from Seattle to Sarasota wanted to read about the adorable matchmaker and the "perfect match" she'd found for herself through her own dating agency.

It was romantic. It was captivating. It was inspiring.

It was rubbish, Brody concluded with an edge of superiority: maudlin, mawkish, slushy, sentimental rubbish. But rubbish sold, especially the sentimental type. And this particular rubbish was going to sell more than a few copies of *California Dream*—so who was he to complain?

He still couldn't believe his good fortune. As much as Brody liked to believe he was responsible for his own success, he couldn't deny the truth of the statement "It's not what you know, but who you know that counts," particularly as it related to his career. During his tenure as editor of *Dream,* he had on occasions too numerous to count found himself on the receiving end of favors by directors, producers, actors, photographers, and fashion "names" who expected good publicity from Brody in return for their kindness. For the most part, except where it grossly conflicted with his weakened-but-still-existent journalistic integrity, Brody had been happy enough to oblige. This time, however, his benefactor was none other than Deke "the Geek" Jurgensen, 1988 president of the Washington High Chess Club and a former reporter for the *Washington Bulletin*, for which a seventeen-year-old Brody Collins had once proudly served as senior editor.

Though Brody had grown up in L.A., it wasn't often that he ran into old high-school acquaintances, certainly never by chance. Los Angeles was too heavily populated for that. But after work just two nights ago, at an ATM on Wilshire Boulevard, the impossible had occurred. That was before the Rent-a-Yenta exclusive had surfaced. Before Brody had a local celebrity piece of any particular substance lined up for next month's issue of *California Dream*. In fact, it was exactly this problem that was weighing heavily on his mind as he left work that evening and stopped at the nearby cash machine.

Brody had just slid $100 cash into his Tommy Hilfiger wallet, folded it neatly into thirds, and crammed it into his back pocket when the encounter occurred. As he turned back toward his Lexus, he nearly crashed into a pointy-nosed, slightly balding man whose face lit up at the sight of him.

"Well, if it isn't…Bro-dy *Collins!*" the bespectacled man crowed, making it sound as though he were announcing Brody's entrance to a game-show audience. *Ladies and gentlemen, our next guest hails from right here in Los Angeles. He's a graduate of Cal State–Berkeley. His hobbies are rubbing elbows with the rich and famous and alternately avoiding and extricating himself from relationships with women who want a commitment! Won't you please give a warm welcome to our next guest: Bro…dy…Collins!*

Momentarily distracted by his irritation at the fact that the man had failed to remain outside the invisible ATM "boundary lines," Brody stared coldly at the perpetrator of the verbal assault.

He was religiously devoted to keeping photos of himself out of *Dream*. But that didn't stop the local papers and dubious news publications like the *National Interrogator* from printing images of him socializing at press functions and cocktail parties with wide-eyed starlets and statuesque glamour queens. He dreaded these rare moments when "his public" recognized him. Thankfully, such incidents were fairly rare.

"Excuse me, *friend*," he said, sounding decidedly unfriendly. "We at *California Dream* appreciate your patronage, but I'm afraid I'm in a bit of a hurry. So if you'll excuse me?" He turned deliberately away.

His pointy-nosed fan was far from deterred. "Don't tell me you don't…" With his lanky legs, he make a quick jog to the right and planted himself squarely in front of Brody. Two beady, black eyes bored into Brody's, then widened in genuine surprise. "You really don't know who I am!" the man gloated. A thin-lipped grin spread across his reptilian face. "Ooh. Brody Collins. Big-time editor! People say you're quite the interrogative journalist, and I can see why!" He waggled his eyebrows exaggeratedly, his enjoyment obviously immense.

Brody felt his ears burn. He would have liked to dismiss the little lizard as the raving lunatic he almost certainly was. But as much as he hated to admit it, the guy did look slightly familiar. Brody racked his brain. He must be a director or producer, or perhaps a screenwriter. With those looks he certainly wasn't an actor. Though he certainly was *acting* inappropriately, making dopey, grinning faces as he was, like some socially inept teenager…

Brody's eyes opened wide.

"*Geek?*" He stared. "I mean, uh…Deke? Deke Jurgensen?"

Far from being insulted, Deke's mood had actually improved as Brody made the connection. Brody wouldn't have thought it possible for the man to look any happier, but to his amazement the lizard smile widened into an alligator grin. "That's my name!" Deke said with the enthusiasm of a birthday-party clown. "Don't wear it out!"

No danger there.

"Well, Deke. Good to see you, man." Brody smiled stiffly, shook Jurgensen's clammy hand, and began to glance about for a means of escape. The fact that he himself had been considered a bit nerdy in high school was a fact that Brody had tried with great effort—and a fair degree of success—to forget.

"I suppose you're wondering what *I've* been doing all these years!" Deke cheerfully thumped Brody on the shoulder.

"Well…" *Not really.*

"I'm in sales. Computer sales. Booming business. *Booming.*" Deke looked around helplessly, as if searching for some way to illustrate how "booming" business truly was. Stumped after several seconds, he curled his right hand into a bony fist and halfheartedly smacked it into the palm of his left hand, effecting more of a *slap* than a *boom.*

"That's, um, great."

"I don't suppose I need to ask what *you've* been up to, Mr. Big Editor Man." Deke threw him a knowing glance.

"I don't suppose."

Brody's indifference was completely swallowed up by the magnitude of Deke's enthusiasm. "That's right," he said, kicking one hip out jauntily to the side and resting one hand casually upon it. "I'd say the ol' *Bulletin* staff hasn't done too shabbily in the world. What with you and me and, of course, Lucy…"

"Who?" Brody blinked at Deke. "I remember a couple of Lucys at Washington, but none of them were on my newspaper staff."

Deke smiled at him patiently, clearly pleased that his reporter's memory was proving superior to Brody's. "She was a couple of years younger than us. Remember? She joined the paper when I was a junior."

"I was gone by then, Deke," Brody informed him coolly, something small and petty within him not letting him leave without setting the record straight. Jurgensen's smug attitude was insufferable. "I graduated. You were two years behind me."

Deke appeared flustered. "Well...whatever. You worked with her sister then. Felicia. On the yearbook. You remember her, don't you?"

There, Deke was right. Brody clearly remembered Felicia Salinger from Mrs. Warburn's seventh-period class: the second of four sisters; tallish, but not tall; attractive, at times even breathtaking. Felicia had been an average-to-good student who had served on the yearbook staff with Brody during his senior year. He'd even had a crush on her earlier in high school. But what Felicia's existence had to do with the subject at hand—the accomplishments of Washington High alums—eluded him.

"Of course I remember her," he said, revealing nothing of his former feelings for the effervescent Felicia. "Nice girl. Smart," he noted, seeing that Deke expected him to comment. "I believe she married some older student right after graduation."

"Some older student?" Deke licked his pale lips. "Felicia Salinger married money!"

"You don't say." Brody did his best to hide his discomfort. As a teenager he had hoped that Felicia would end up with a nice guy. Someone like him. That was not entirely correct. What he'd really hoped was that she would end up with him, Brody himself.

"Right." Deke nodded eagerly. "I heard a rumor that the guy was a bit of a jerk. But his family had the bucks, and the word is he was headed off to med school about the time Felicia married him. He's probably some hotshot surgeon by now, like on TV." But as the man spoke, Brody's mind was already working out the meaning of his earlier words.

Wait a minute. Felicia Salinger…Lucy…Salinger?

Brody had gripped Deke's scrawny arm. "Hold on! You mean, the Lucy on the *Washington Bulletin* staff was Lucy Salinger? The *Rent-a-Yenta*?"

Brody smiled at the mirror as he recalled the moment it had dawned on him. He had been aware that he and Lucy Salinger went to the same high school—simply because he was aware of everything that had to do with Fee. It hadn't occurred to him until then that his own particular personal connection with Lucy—though admittedly a weak one— might somehow work to his advantage.

"That's right." Deke's eyes narrowed. He appeared disconcerted that Brody was so much more excited about Lucy's success than his own. "She's getting married too, you know," he said weakly.

Duh. "So I hear." Brody forced himself to smile warmly.

"My sister's going to the wedding."

"She's what?" Brody gaped. Though Lucy Salinger had announced her engagement almost a year earlier, the date and location were among the most closely guarded secrets on L.A.'s social scene.

Deke blinked at him, apparently stunned to have elicited such an extreme response. The effect Brody's excitement had on him was much like that of sunlight on a house plant— slowly he turned to face Brody head-on, grinning toothily. "That's right. Jody's an old friend of Lucy's."

Brody shook his head ever so slightly. For months, he'd had one of his best reporters on the story. She hadn't been able to get her hands on so much as a catering menu, much less anything as helpful as a time or location.

"So when's the big date, Deke?" Brody spoke casually.

Deke looked first to the right, then the left. He licked his thin, dry lips and leaned in toward Brody. "Two weeks from Saturday," he whispered conspiratorially.

"Great, great." Brody tried to demonstrate only the vaguest interest. "Isn't that nice for her?"

"You don't fool me, Collins," Deke said nasally. He sniffed. "I know you want the scoop. And you can have it. But it'll cost you. It'll cost you big." The cliché fell easily from his lips, as if he'd practiced the words often and had spent years waiting for fate to bring him the opportunity to utter them.

Brody sighed. There was no use in denying that he wanted the information. Customarily, he was a master at the poker face. But this time Jurgensen, of all people, had caught him unguarded.

"Fine, Deke. What do you want?"

"I want a thousand dollars and I want to be credited as your source."

Brody grunted. "Who do you think you are? Bob Woodward?"

"Perfect!" Deke lit up at the mention of the *Washington Post* reporter. "And this is Yentagate!"

"Right." Brody held up the first two fingers of each hand and shook his jowls in his best Richard Nixon imitation. "And I...am not...an idiot," he spat out.

"Well..." Deke frowned at his feet. "What then?"

"Fifty bucks."

Deke's head shook. "Come on, Collins. I know you can afford more than that. Besides, I want credit."

"You want what?"

"You know. Credit. A byline. *Fame*. The chicks love to see a guy's name in print."

"Chicks?" The last time Brody had heard women called that, he'd been in high school himself. And he'd probably heard it from the same geeky lips.

Deke glared back at him, pink faced but resolute.

"Oh, all right." Brody sighed again. "At the end of the article, we'll put 'additional reporting by Deke Jurgensen.'" His reporter would kill him, but Brody was in charge, after all. And without Deke's information, there wouldn't be a byline to get mad about.

"I think," Deke said, brightening, "that I'll sneak into the wedding myself and do some of that 'additional reporting…'"

"No," Brody said sharply. "A hundred bucks, 'additional reporting by,' and a promise from you that you'll keep outside a two-mile radius of the wedding at all times. Also I want the time, date, and location, as well as Lucy Salinger's home telephone number. That's the deal. Take it or leave it." Brody knew that the Rent-a-Yenta office was deflecting all requests from the media, and Lucy's home number was unlisted.

"I don't know how I'll get all that," Deke complained.

"Oh, come on. A fine reporter like you?"

Brody found it hard to believe that anyone could miss the river of irony in his voice, but apparently Deke had. The man puffed out his chest.

"You'll have it within twenty-four hours," Deke whispered in his best spy voice.

And to Brody's immense surprise, he actually had. When he'd gotten home from work the next evening—after waiting at the office until seven, hoping to hear from Jurgensen—he'd entered the security code for his voice-mail system and immediately recognized his former schoolmate's nasal intonations coming from the telephone receiver.

"I got your home number from Information," Deke said sotto voce. "It seemed safer this way. I didn't want to risk the facts getting into *the wrong hands.*"

Lord, save me from sources with an overdeveloped James Bond complex. Brody was almost disappointed when Deke failed to say, "This message will self-destruct in thirty seconds."

He was not, however, disappointed with the actual information his source provided. It was exactly what Brody had asked for: date, time, location, and phone number. Wasting no time, he began punching buttons on his sleek black cordless phone.

"Hello?" The voice on the other end was breathless, as if its owner had rushed to answer.

"Hello, Lucy? Is that you?" Brody kept his voice confident, even.

"Ye-es. Who's this?" She sounded more curious than suspicious.

"It's Brody. Brody Collins. From Washington High? The *Bulletin*?"

There was the tiniest of pauses. "Brody Collins. You mean, from *California Dream*."

Brody gave Lucy his warm, throaty chuckle. "You know where I work? That's amazing. I'm honored, in fact."

"It's my job to know people, Mr. Collins," she said evenly. "I'm acquainted with several of the local celebrities in your social circle."

"I'm sure you are." In fact, Brody himself had reported on several of the matches with which Lucy had been credited, including that of a Hollywood director, a blues musician, and a popular shortstop for the Angels. "I have to say, even back in high school I always thought you'd be a success." That much, at least, was the truth. Brody always found that it served his best interests to be as honest as possible.

Lucy, for her part, was not taking the bait. "Excuse me, but...how did you get this number?"

"As a matter of fact, I got it from an old *Bulletin* associate of ours."

"A...who?"

"Deke Jurgensen."

"Jody's brother? Why would he—?" Lucy stopped short. "Wait a minute. You're calling about my wedding," she accused. "Aren't you? You found out about it from Deke! He must have gotten my number out of Jody's address book or something; she'd never have given it out on her own. Oh, this is just rich!"

Brody laughed again, heartily, hoping to put her at ease. "Well, to tell you the truth, as one *Bulletin* reporter to another—"

"We never worked on the *Bulletin* together," Lucy said sharply. "You graduated before I ever joined the paper."

"No, we didn't work together," Brody admitted, deciding to try another tack. "That's true. I guess I knew your sister Felicia a lot better." All right, now he was stretching the truth a bit. But technically, he did know the older Salinger better, at least in the sense that they'd actually shared at least one class. And he *had* had a major crush on Lucy's elder sister during his sophomore year. Not that Felicia ever had the time of day for him; she never even seemed to notice that he was alive.

"You knew my sister?" Something changed, almost imperceptibly, in Lucy's tone. "One of Fee's old boyfriends, huh?"

Brody gripped the phone tighter. "You could say that." *I'm a boy. I was her friend. Almost. At least, I could have been...*

"Interesting," Lucy mused.

In the silence that followed, Brody considered his next approach. For some reason, the mere mention of her sister's name had caused Lucy to back off of her hard-nosed attitude. Perhaps the best thing to do now would be to go in for the kill. "Actually, you're right about me calling on behalf of *California Dream*. It's no secret that people are interested in your story, Lucy. And as a former reporter yourself, I'm sure you understand the need to—"

"I was in ninth grade," she interjected, but Brody no longer sensed outright hostility in her voice. Rather, she sounded vaguely amused...and perhaps slightly intrigued. "Hardly a hard-core reporter."

"All right," he said matter-of-factly. "So we're not exactly family. I'll cut to the chase. You're obviously good at your job, Lucy. And I'm good at mine. I want your story. And I'm willing to give you whatever terms you require to get an exclusive."

"I've already rejected all offers from the papers and television programs," Lucy informed him. "Including yours."

"I'm aware of that," Brody said. "But I'd like a chance to change your mind. I'm prepared to offer you a fee of—"

"Please," she said with the slightest trace of irritation in her voice. "I don't need money. I couldn't care less what you offer me."

Brody thought about this for a moment. It wasn't the first time he'd heard such a statement. But it was the first time he'd heard it spoken with a conviction that made him almost believe it.

"We can give you absolutely the best coverage," he tried again.

"I don't need—or want—any publicity," Lucy told him firmly. "I assure you, I've already had more than enough."

"Of course," Brody said soothingly. "But...but..." He searched his mind for an argument that might sway her. "Think about the *romance*," he said dramatically. "Think about all the women who are touched by your story. Think about the hope your wedding can give them...is already giving them. Do it for those women." Brody hoped he sounded more convincing than he felt. "Do it for love."

To his surprise, Lucy actually seemed to consider this. "Do it for love, huh?" Brody thought she now sounded more playful than perturbed.

"That's right."

"Humph," she grunted. "An old boyfriend of Fee's, huh?"

Brody mumbled something unintelligible, hoping she would interpret the sound as a sort of affirmation.

"We-ll…" Lucy managed to draw the word into two syllables and extend it over several long seconds.

She was toying with him now, Brody could tell. *Women*, he complained silently, rolling his eyes heavenward.

"I *suppose* it wouldn't hurt for you to come."

Brody opened his mouth to offer his thanks.

"But," Lucy interjected before he had a chance to respond, "I have a few conditions for you, Mr. Brody Collins of the *Bulletin*."

I'm sure you do. Here we go.

"Of course," he managed to murmur amicably.

"First of all," Lucy told him crisply, "I don't want you to take any photos during the ceremony."

"But—"

"I mean it. I don't want this to turn into a circus. We're already paying a photojournalist to cover the day for us, and my future brother-in-law is going to be running around with a camcorder. That's already one too many cameras for my taste, but Alexandra—that's my future sister-in-law—insists that we let her husband, Wallace, shoot a video. I'm not going to let one more photographer on the loose during the ceremony."

"But—" Brody tried again.

"I will, however," Lucy said sweetly, "allow you to take photos during the reception."

"Thank you. That's very—"

"Provided," Lucy continued, "that you don't get in any of our guests' faces. Particularly the famous ones. If," she said noncommittally, "there are any. Which I'm not admitting that there are."

"Understood. If I could just—"

"And you're the only representative from *California Dream* I want to be there," Lucy went on. Brody reached into the freezer and pulled out a microwave dinner-for-one. For a moment, he considered laying the telephone down on the smooth Corian countertop while he prepared his pitiful meal. The way she was going on, he doubted Lucy would notice if he was listening or not. "Unless, of course, you're not prepared to take the photos yourself," she was saying. "In that case, you can bring one photographer, but that's it."

"Fine." He was rapidly approaching the point of being willing to make any concession, just to get her off the phone.

"All right then," Lucy said cheerfully. "I guess that about sums it up. I'll mail an invite to your office. I assume it's in the book."

Brody grunted his affirmation. There hardly seemed to be any point in trying to form a complete sentence anymore. He pulled the mini-lasagna from the cardboard box and ripped off its flimsy protective plastic covering.

"Great. Then I'll tell Fee you're coming—"

"No…wait! Don't!" Startled, Brody dropped the brick of lasagna onto his foot. "Ow-ww!"

"What is the matter with you?"

"Nothing, nothing." He stared, dismayed, at the frozen block of pasta and marinara on the floor. "I just wanted to surprise Felicia—uh, Fee—that's all." The last thing he needed was for the sisters to discuss the subject; once Lucy discovered that he'd never dated Felicia, he was certain she'd retract the invitation. Besides, he had no intention of actually attending the function himself; he'd send one of his underlings to do the job. The fewer people who'd be watching out for him, the better off he—and *California Dream*—would be.

"Mmm. Surprise her, huh?"

Brody suspected it was a good thing he hadn't actually eaten dinner yet. Listening to Lucy's sickening-sweet tone would have made it hard for him to keep the meal down.

"Well, far be it from me to spoil a reunion between high-school sweethearts!"

Spoken like a true matchmaker.

"Thanks," Brody grunted. It would make sense that a woman like Lucy Salinger would be caught up by the thought of two old flames meeting again after thirteen years—star-crossed lovers, crossing paths one last time. If Felicia wasn't married, and was actually on the dating circuit, who knew what her matchmaker sister would be tempted to do? Thankfully, he wasn't in a position to find out.

"I'll see you at the wedding then," the bride-to-be chirped and clicked off the line a moment later.

Brody didn't bother to correct her. *Yeah, right, you'll see me at the wedding.* A guy like him, the editor of *Dream*, had better things to do with his time than run around covering every puny little social event in the city. That's what he had reporters for.

The faintest wave of contrition washed over him, but Brody easily shrugged the feeling off. Lucy wouldn't even know the difference. She had no idea what Brody looked like these days, and for that matter, he guessed, neither did Felicia. Perhaps he had misled Lucy Salinger just a bit. But he would abide by her requests. He hadn't outright lied. And any misunderstandings that had occurred…well, it was all for the good of the magazine.

As he prepared for work the next day, Lucy's words still echoed in his head.

An old boyfriend of Fee's, huh?

I'll see you at the wedding…

Still, he managed without too much effort to dismiss the annoying feelings of guilt that stubbornly continued to raise their tiny, unattractive heads. He was, after all, only doing his job, he reminded himself sternly. His boss, Nick Fortunata, would be pleased with the maneuver. The achievement would result in increased visibility for *California Dream* and even more power, prestige, and wealth for Brody.

That's right, Collins, you are one lucky man... The words echoed through his brain. But as he combed through his dark, dripping hair and poked a toothbrushful of fluoride-enriched paste past his lips, Brody could not bring himself to gaze again at the look of emptiness worn by the shadow of the man he once had been and, at some deep level, wanted desperately to believe he still might be.

Two

"I am…the fattest…bridesmaid in the world!" Felicia Salinger Kelley's wail of frustration echoed throughout her tastefully furnished room at the swanky Hollywood Hills Hotel. Planting her hands firmly on her hips, she glared daggers at her reflection in the mirror.

"Well, let's not call *The Guinness Book of World Records* just yet." Felicia's sister Catherine peered critically over Fee's shoulder. Her thick golden mane had been pulled up in a sleek French knot, and her blue eyes sparkled in light of the challenge at hand. "I mean, yeah. Your days of being a waif are long over. Whose aren't? Join the club. But that isn't necessarily a bad thing. Look at yourself."

"I'm looking, I'm *looking*. That's the problem."

"You're strong and shapely—"

"Shapely, huh? Is that the politically correct term for 'fat' these days?" Fee sulked.

"I'm serious." Cat nudged her in the ribs. "There are more important—and much wiser—things to focus on than being skinny. So you're not going to grace the cover of one of those ridiculous fashion magazines this year—"

"Try *ever*," Fee grumbled.

"Hey, now…" Catherine threw out a pouty lower lip and batted her bright eyes exaggeratedly. "Does somebody need

19

a hug?" She wrapped two long, graceful arms around Fee's neck and squeezed fiercely.

"Augh! Back off! You're choking me!" Half gagging, half chortling, Fee managed to extricate herself from her sister's crushing embrace.

"Ha! Made you laugh!"

"Hardy-har-har. So you did." Fee's smile faded. She squeezed her right eye shut and glanced back at the mirror with her left. "But now what?"

"I'm thinking," Cat reassured her, tapping a front tooth with one French-manicured nail. "I'm thinking."

Eight months after giving birth to her third child, Fee thought she'd done a pretty decent job of pulling herself together today. Her sleek dark hair—recently cut in a swingy, stylish chin-length bob—was tucked behind one ear. Her gentle gray eyes were outlined in a soft charcoal liner that she had applied with a careful hand, making her look wide-eyed and youthful, and her subtle copper lipstick—compliments of her youngest sister, Daphne—was a perfect match for her golden skin tone, brought on by time spent outdoors playing with her children under the bright Southern California sunshine.

Fee's eyes scanned downward. At her throat hung the simple, classic strand of pearls Robert had presented to her on their first wedding anniversary—not as expensive as the gifts that had followed over the years, but still her favorite piece of jewelry: this, despite the fact that its sentimental value, too, had long since faded. Even her gown appeared flawless from this angle. Soft folds of shimmery pale blue silk fell from her shoulders, tapered in at the curve of her waist and filled out visibly, but not unattractively, at the hips by childbearing, pooling gracefully around her feet. Fee smiled weakly. From the front, all was as it should be.

The smile melted away as quickly as it had appeared. So why couldn't she get her dress properly fastened in back?

"Oh, for crying out loud…" Spinning around for perhaps the thirtieth time that morning, Felicia twisted and contorted her body in an attempt to wrest the offending zipper into its proper position. "Come on, come *on*," she growled. "What is the matter with you, you…you—" She sucked in her breath, tucked in her stomach, and made one last valiant effort before letting the air out in a rush. "Augh!" Her arms fell to her sides in defeat. Incredibly, there simply wasn't enough fabric to cover the skin of her back. There was no denying the horrible truth any longer: the elegant, custom-made bridesmaid gown did not fit her. The most important event of her sister Lucy's life was just two hours away, and Fee was going to be stuck watching from the sidelines.

Cat raised one thin, perfectly shaped golden eyebrow at her. "You done?"

"Yes, I'm *done*." Fee let out a dramatic sigh. "I never should have had those popcorn balls with the kids two nights ago."

"Honey," Cat said, surveying her back critically. "This is way beyond popcorn balls."

"Thank you very much," Fee said icily. "But I'll have you know, I've been eating sensibly for a year and exercising *faithfully*," she said with force, adding under her breath, "more or less" before her volume went up again on the last two words: "—for months."

It was true. In the years since she'd given birth to her second child, Clifford, Felicia had carried around ten extra pounds that she'd seemed unable to shed. During her latest pregnancy, she'd been much more careful about how she ate. And she'd been working off the extra weight slowly but surely ever since Gabe's birth in August. All this at the insistence of her three maddeningly meddlesome, and infinitely loving, siblings:

ultra-organized eldest sister, Catherine "Cat" Salinger-Riley, president of the Salinger/Riley Advertising Agency, which Cat owned and operated with her husband, Jonas; crazy youngest sister, Daphne Salinger, who worked as an account executive at Salinger/Riley and dated Jonas's younger brother Elliott; and, of course, Fee's free-spirited, professional matchmaker sister, Lucy Salinger, soon-to-be Lucy Howard, following her wedding that very afternoon to Campbell Howard, the handsome behavioral psychologist who had finally captured the young romantic's heart.

Related by blood, bonded by life, the Salinger sisters were as close—and as different—as four women could be. While the girls were growing up, family had been important to them, having lost their mother to leukemia when they were still quite young. But in recent years, following their father's death from a heart attack, the four were closer than ever before. It was this sense of sisterhood, of community, that had prompted Cat, Lucy, and Daphne to comfort, fiercely support, and stand by Felicia over the past year, following her abandonment by her husband, Robert. They were determined to see Fee through her crisis, and they had done exactly that: encouraging Fee to dig deep within herself and find the inner strength she needed for the sake of her children—Dinah, age ten, and Clifford, seven—as well as for her own emotional health. They'd challenged her to take care of herself physically, emotionally, and spiritually for the first time in years. They'd coached her through the birth of her third child, which without their help she would have had to go through alone. As a result, this time around, both during her pregnancy and after having Gabe, Fee was in much better shape than she'd been in for a long time. The undertaking had brought her great pride. She'd done it because she valued herself, not because she felt shamed into it, as she so often felt with Robert. And to her surprise, that attitude shift had led to positive results. Fee felt good. And she thought she looked pretty good. But had she just been fooling herself?

A loud rapping at the hotel room door startled her. "Hey! You guys in there?" Fee grimaced as she clutched at the fabric of her dress. "Please don't tell Daphne," she begged Cat in a loud whisper.

"Um…you're not exactly going to be able to keep this a secret," Catherine quietly pointed out. "It's impossible to hide. You can't walk down the aisle like this."

"Gee. You think?" Fee said dryly.

"Yeah, I think. Sorry, toots, but I'm fresh out of ideas. Maybe Daph can help. She's the creative one."

"What's going on? Are you guys whispering?" Daphne demanded through the door. "Are you two still alive? We're all waiting for you up in the H. B.'s suite."

Felicia turned wide eyes upon Cat. "H. B.?"

Cat nodded soberly. "Hysterical Bride. I was at Lucy's this morning and she's a bit—how shall I put this?—high strung. We might not want to inform her about your little problem just yet."

"Did you hear me?" Daphne shouted, getting louder now. "Gabby and Velma are already up there," she said, mentioning the two friends who were also serving as bridesmaids. "What's the holdup?"

The holdup? Just that I'm going to need help "holding up" my dress…

Felicia stared helplessly at her image in the mirror. There was no escape.

"Everything okay in there?" Daphne called.

Felicia took a deep breath. "Sure," she mumbled. "If you call complete and utter humiliation okay."

"What's that you say?"

"Fine," she called back a bit too loudly.

Daphne remained silent for a moment. Felicia bit her lip. Cat stood quietly waiting.

"All right, Fee," Daphne said a bit more firmly this time. "I know something's wrong. Open the door." She waited a moment, then continued, "I took kick-boxing lessons with you, you know. I could knock this baby in if I tried." Felicia pictured her little sister on the other side of the doorway, arms folded, bright eyes snapping, determination oozing from every pore in her five-foot-four-inch frame. Daphne was a firecracker, that much was certain. And though she wasn't exactly a control freak, like Cat had a tendency to be, she wasn't one to let a little thing like a locked door stand in the way of what she wanted.

"Please. You'll just break your foot," Fee told her disapprovingly.

"Too bad, since it's Lucy's wedding day. Guess you'll just have to live with that on your conscience."

Might as well, Fee thought soberly. *Lucy's already lost one of us as a bridesmaid. Might as well have a whole row of limping, half-naked sisters in the audience...*

"Fee...?" There was no mistaking the warning in her tone. "Cat? You in there? Am I the *only* reasonable sister present? I'm gonna count to three. One...twooooooooo..."

"Oh, all right, Bruce Lee," Fee sighed. "I'm opening up now. Don't kick, or you'll take out my appendix." Right now that sounded less painful than her actual predicament. Reluctantly, she released the lock and opened the door to her sister, who stood on the threshold, grinning like an idiot, wearing an exact replica of the dresses covering Cat's body and not quite covering Fee's.

"Hi-*ya!*" Daphne quipped, making her greeting sound like a martial-arts cry and lunging forward in a dramatic karate chop.

"Hi-ya, yourself," Fee muttered and backed away from the door, holding the back pieces of her dress together with one hand.

The younger woman seemed not to notice her awkward stance, but simply gave Felicia a nod of approval. "Ooo-la-*la*. Hey there, glam queen! You're looking migh-tee-fine. You, too, Kit-Cat."

Cat wrinkled up her nose at the mention of the childhood nickname she despised. "Thanks loads."

Felicia laughed in spite of herself. "You don't look so bad yourself, Daph." Her sister did indeed look quite elegant—and uncharacteristically demure, despite her martial-arts entrance—in her bridesmaid's gown. Typically, Daphne had a style all her own. "A living, breathing fashion experiment," Lucy called her. But today, Daphne's wild, chin-length auburn curls were more or less tamed, and had been pulled up in a crown about her head. Her makeup, too, was toned down from its usual bright red lipstick and colored eye shadows. Muted earth tones gave her a more subdued look, and her earlobes were adorned with simple silver studs instead of the dangly "peace" symbols Daphne had been favoring lately. Fee could not hide her surprise. "You look so…uh…"

"Normal?" Cat supplied helpfully.

"Well," Fee admitted, "now that you mention it…"

Daphne waggled her dark eyebrows at her and grinned wickedly. "Looks can be deceiving," she warned, then poked one foot out from under her elegant skirt to reveal well-worn Doc Martens boots and red-and-white striped tights that made Fee think of the lead character from Clifford's *Where's Waldo?* books.

"Nice," Cat deadpanned.

Felicia gaped for a moment, then snapped her mouth shut. At least the skirt was long enough that the offending apparel would barely show during the ceremony, which was a lot more than she could say for her own back and bra strap. She closed her eyes and tried to push back the thought.

"What's the matter?" Daphne stepped forward protectively. "You sick?"

"No. It's much worse than that." Fee turned to reveal the offending patch of bare skin.

"What?" Daphne shrugged. "It's your back. I've seen it before."

"Yes, but there will be people here today who haven't seen it, and I'd really rather they didn't, if you get my drift."

"You mean, you can't zip up?" Daphne frowned. "Oh, for crying out loud. Is that what all the fuss is about? Here. Let me."

"Daphne," Cat assured her, "trust us, it's not going to work." But she stepped back to let the youngest Salinger try her hand.

Obediently, Fee turned around and let her sister fumble with the zipper. "All right, but you'll see. It's not going to close." After several minutes of trying, Daphne was willing to concede the point. "Whew! That," she said, shaking her head in amazement, "is a bummer."

"That," Cat echoed primly, "is the understatement of the day."

"Don't you have anything you can wear over it?" Daphne's eyes scanned the room.

"What? Like my overcoat? Your leather jacket? Maybe a hotel tablecloth? I'm sure no one would notice that."

"Shh. I'm thinking." Daphne chewed on one rough, unmanicured thumbnail. "Velma had on a crocheted shawl when she got here," she suggested hopefully. "Maybe we could safety-pin you up in back, and you could wear the shawl over your shoulders?"

"With this formal silk?" Fee shook her head. "I don't think so." She stared down at her figure. "Daph, how could this happen in just two weeks? The dress was a little loose before, but I didn't ask the seamstress to take it in. And even if she did, why would any seamstress worth her beans compensate by that much?"

"That's pretty bad," Daphne admitted. "I can't believe she did such a rotten job. If it helps to hear it, your dress isn't the only problem. Cat's gown fits perfectly, obviously. And so do mine and Velma's. But Gabby's is at least an inch too big all the way around. I mean, she can wear it and everything," she said dismissively. "But it was supposed to be a size—" She stopped abruptly.

"What?" Fee grumbled. "What is she, a size three? Size zero? Perhaps a negative one? Spare me the details and get me a pound cake." Despondent, she threw herself onto the bed and considered ordering room service. If this was the reward her good behavior had earned her, it was time to resume drowning her sorrows in sweet, gooey mounds of Mud Pie.

Daphne ignored her request. "Wait a minute. Did you check the label when you picked up the dress?" she demanded.

Fee shrugged. "Why would I? It was on the inside of the door when I got here; I assumed that Lucy dropped it off, or one of the hotel staff brought it up. Obviously, it's mine. Who else but one of us bridesmaids would be wearing formal blue silk on a Saturday afternoon in April?"

"Don't you get it?" Daphne grabbed her sister's arm. "Gabby's dress is too big." Cat was grinning now too. Felicia glared at them both.

"I'm afraid that," she said with the tone of one who had long suffered, "is more information than I need on the 'wee bit of a thing,' but thanks for sharing."

"And your dress is too small!" Cat cried triumphantly, throwing both arms in the air.

Fee's eyes narrowed. "Again: a point that I really didn't need to relive at this moment. But your support is overwhelming."

Daphne's lips turned upward at the corners, hope giving way to certainty as her mind worked out the truth of the situation. "You goof," she said fondly. "You didn't gain weight. You're wearing the wrong dress."

"I'm—" Fee's frazzled brain began to process what her sister was saying. "You mean, you think they got switched?"

Cat nodded as she walked over to the garment bag hanging on the door. "Bingo!" she cried triumphantly, turning over the attached tag as proof. "'G. P.' Gabby Palermo. There you have it."

Daphne shook her head in reproach. "Good grief, Fee. Does everything have to be your fault? Did you even consider the fact that this was someone else's mistake, and not a reflection of something you did wrong?"

"Well…no," Fee admitted, rolling over on the bed and smoothing out the wrinkles in her dress. Perhaps she wouldn't call room service or Guinness just yet.

"You know, you're not always to blame," Daphne said matter-of-factly. "Man, Robert really did a number on you, didn't he?" She opened the door to the closet and reached for the overcoat Felicia had stored there. "Come on. We're running late. If we don't get up to Lucy's suite, and pronto, she's going to kill us."

Obediently Fee grabbed her makeup bag, keys, and purse, then followed her sisters out the door while they headed off for the elevator. As they walked, Daphne threw the coat over Felicia's bare back.

"Have you seen Jonas and the kids?" Fee asked. It wasn't often that she was able to enjoy a social event without spending every minute worrying about what trouble her children were getting into. Today she had gladly entrusted them to their Uncle Jonas's care and was feeling a shade guilty at the sense of freedom she was enjoying, especially since her brother-in-law had little experience in dealing with children in general and infants in particular. At the thought of her eight-month-old, Gabe, Felicia's stomach tightened, and she felt an intense longing to hold her baby.

Daphne pushed the Up button on the elevator. "Yeah, Elliott's helping him," she said, her lips curving into a smile at the mention of her boyfriend's name.

"I see. The blind leading the blind, I take it?"

"Exactly. He's bringing them up to Lucy's suite in a little while, though, so they can kiss you good luck before the ceremony." Daphne rolled her eyes. "I think he just wants to kiss Cat."

"Probably."

Cat beamed.

Felicia pursed her lips. "No details, please." The elevator doors opened, and the three of them stepped inside. As Daphne pushed the button for the next floor, Fee tried to remember the last time she'd been kissed. Though she wasn't sure, she guessed it had been on the night Gabe was conceived. Prior to that evening, Robert had been cold and distant for months. Yet he'd seemed genuinely remorseful during the holidays and had paid extra attention to Clifford and Dinah…and, to Felicia's surprise, also to her; she hadn't understood why at the time. But she had welcomed her husband's affections.

Unfortunately, in the following weeks, Robert resumed his previous pattern of behavior: spending more time playing golf and hanging out with fellow doctors from the hospital than he did with his family. Soon long workdays turned into regular late nights. Eventually Robert confessed to Fee that he'd had several "emotional affairs" over the years and that Christmas he had been struggling with guilt over his desire to take his latest relationship to a physical level. He'd eventually stopped trying to fight his urges and began a full-fledged affair with a starlet early the next year. By that time, Fee was already pregnant. News of this fact had been the final straw as far as Robert was concerned. By March he was gone. In August Gabe was born. Now eight months old, Gabe was the new love of Fee's life, along with her two ongoing loves, Dinah and Clifford.

Faced with the end of her marriage, Fee had believed that she had failed her husband in some crucial way. She had tried so hard to be exactly what Robert wanted. But in the end, she could not deny the hideous truth that he simply wanted something—or rather, someone—else.

Ironically, after all those years of turning herself inside out trying to please him, Fee had come out of her marriage no longer knowing who she was in the deepest part of her soul. Ever since, she'd been trying to get reacquainted with herself once again—to be kind to herself. To be her own friend. To her surprise, she'd found that she really did like herself— the same Fee whom Robert had ceased to love. And she had reconnected with the Source of strength she had somehow lost touch with through the years. Though she believed with all her heart that her husband should have stayed with the family, she clung to the hope that God would somehow bring good out of the disaster that had turned her life—and the lives of her children—upside down. So far, she was still waiting.

"Hey, did you meet Cam's cousin last night at the rehearsal dinner?" Daphne asked, nudging her arm.

"No," Fee said suspiciously. "Why?"

"Apparently he saw you and was *veeeeeerry* interested," her sister confided. "He asked about you, if you were single and all that. I heard it from Jonas who heard it from Cat who heard it from Lucy. Sounds like he's gonna ask you out. He didn't strike me as the greatest prize in the world," she admitted. "But first impressions can be deceiving. You might want to give him a chance."

"Anyway," Cat added gently, "it would be a date. You haven't been on a date since the divorce came through, not since Robert left."

"You haven't," Daphne pointed out ruthlessly, "been on a real date since high school. We—Lucy and Cat and I—think that maybe it's time for you to get back out there."

Suddenly the elevator seemed very small indeed. Felicia fought off the feelings of claustrophobia that threatened to strangle her. "Well, I'm not interested," she said vehemently, pushing her hair back behind her ears almost violently. When the doors opened, she could not get out of the elevator fast enough. She threw a quick look over her shoulder and saw Daphne and Cat staring after her, mouths gaping.

"I'm serious," Felicia told them with conviction, marching down the hall toward the Hysterical Bride's door. "Maybe I don't *want* to be 'back out there.' Did you ever think of that? For the first time in a long time, I'm beginning to understand what I want. I want a good life for my kids. I want to spend time with my family, the ones I love. I want to be growing in my faith. I want a career that I enjoy, that will give me enough money to take care of my family." As they neared Lucy's door, she reached out and rapped soundly with the knuckles of her right hand. "And I also know what I *don't* want," she said with the enthusiasm and conviction of a gubernatorial candidate proclaiming her running platform, "and that is another man in my life. I'll tell you two one thing: There is no way I'm going to fall for some guy at this wedding!"

"Famous last words," Daphne said with a grin, ever the optimist.

Felicia opened her mouth to launch a protest, but before there was time for even a single word to form on her lips, Lucy had flung open the door, shrieked at her sisters in hysterical delight, and smothered the three of them in an enthusiastic bear hug that made Fee reflect favorably on her soon-to-be brother-in-law, Campbell, and—for the moment, at least—drove all negative judgments about men completely from her mind.

Three

"Yes, Kevin. Of course I realize it's a Saturday. But David called in sick—I don't know, pneumonia or something—and I really need someone to cover this event." Pressing the telephone receiver to his ear with his left hand, Brody gripped a No. 2 pencil fiercely between the fingers of his right hand and twisted it sharply until it snapped. He looked in disgust at the piece of yellow-painted wood and lead and threw the useless utensil into the trash can by his feet. He reached for a new pencil from the cup filled with presharpened writing instruments, kept there at his insistence by his secretary, June, and now—during June's maternity leave—by his sharp-tongued twenty-three-year-old sister, Abby. Aside from his computer and rack of file folders, the cup was the only other object that resided permanently on his desk. There were no knickknacks or mementos, no wooden frames with cropped photos of gurgling babies or smiling girlfriends for Brody Collins. Everything was orderly and clean. Just the way he liked it.

"I understand that you have plans with your family," he said crossly into the receiver. "But I have plans with the designer and the printer. We're on deadline, you know." What was the problem with working on a weekend? He was in the office almost every Saturday, and when he demanded it, so was June…and now Abby. Why couldn't the guy budge and give

33

him one crummy afternoon out of his life? Especially after all the prime assignments he had thrown Kevin's way. Some days, Brody reflected testily, it just didn't pay to be an editor: not even a respected, well-paid, influential editor of one of the most popular magazines in the nation.

He half listened, half fumed as his reporter ran through a list of reasons why he could not accept the last-minute assignment: It was the one full day he and his wife got to spend together with the kids...they'd made a promise to their children...family plans were sacred...blah-blah-blah. *Family plans.* Brody felt a flare of irritation at the thought. What on earth was so important that it couldn't be rescheduled? A trip to the zoo? He had a news flash for his reporter: The elephants, giraffes, and monkeys would still be there next week. A visit to the ice-cream parlor? Ooh, now *that* was time sensitive.

Brody could almost feel his blood pressure rising. He had occasionally wondered if he'd made a wise choice in choosing not to marry and have children. But if he ever had serious doubts, this quelled them. A feeling of self-righteousness arose within him. No sir. You wouldn't ever hear of Brody Collins shirking his duties because of a trip to Mr. Cheesehead's Pizza Parlor. Go to the park or go to press? It was a no-brainer. Where was this man's sense of responsibility? Where were his priorities? His sense of loyalty?

"I appreciate your predicament," Brody said levelly, though he really didn't appreciate it at all. "But who am I supposed to get to cover this wedding?" He obviously couldn't send a female reporter; the invitation was addressed to a man, and he'd already requested that his scheduler assign a female photographer to the piece. And *not* covering her wedding was not an option, no matter how much he wished that was the case; for the past two weeks, every local paper and several national news magazines had been printing pre-wedding stories about

Lucy Salinger and her business. The woman was the most high-profile personality in the romance business since Cupid.

"Do what? Cover the wedding *myself?*" Brody sat up straight in his chair. The thought was appalling. He couldn't remember the last time he'd written one of those fluffy society pieces. That was what he hired people like Kevin for. "You've got to be kidding." But Kevin wasn't laughing, and neither was Brody. With David out sick, Kevin unavailable, and the rest of his male reporting staff out on other assignments, there really wasn't anyone left but him to attend the festivities.

"Fine," he grumbled into the mouthpiece. "I'll deal with it then. You go have"—he gritted his teeth—"fun with the kids. I'll see you on Monday. And…what?" His scowl deepened. "Thanks a lot, but I don't intend to have a good time at the wedding. Huh? No, I will *not* catch the garter. Good-bye, Kevin." Forcefully, he slammed the telephone back into its cradle.

His sister's cheerful voice broke into his thoughts. "Talked to Kevin, did you?" Abby asked innocently. Brody looked up to see her slight, five-foot-three-inch frame leaning against his office doorway, arms folded, her stance so casual it had to be posed.

Slowly, deliberately, he tipped back his chair and clasped his hands firmly together, forming a steeple point with his two index fingers. "Ye-es," he said, knowing what was coming. "You know I did."

"And is he taking the assignment?"

Brody glowered at her. Drat that Abby! How could she stand there looking so guileless when she was thoroughly enjoying being a thorn in his side?

"No, he did not take the assignment…just as you predicted, sister *dear.*"

"Hmm." Abby patted her hands together. "Imagine that."

"Abbs, if you're going to give me another lecture about having a life, and letting my staff members do the same…"

The young woman cracked a smile. "Fine. No lecture, Big Brother, since you obviously already have my words of wisdom memorized. But…" She obviously could not resist making a comment. "Can you blame him? He's got two children under the age of eight. Kids demand attention, you know."

"I demand attention too," Brody groused. "Doesn't mean I get it. Anyway, *we're* working today. Why shouldn't he?"

"Don't be such a Scrooge. Everyone's entitled to a little fun. Especially Kevin. After all he and his family went through this last year…"

Brody frowned. "Uh…what exactly did they go through?"

"You're not serious?" Abby folded her arms across her chest. "You don't know? Their youngest was diagnosed with leukemia. It's in remission now."

"Oh." It was all he could think of to say. Brody couldn't remember the last time he felt so ashamed of himself. "Honestly, I didn't know." Brody saw himself as driven, but he certainly wasn't unfeeling. "Why doesn't anyone tell me these things?"

"They do. You only hear what you want to."

"Abby," he growled. "You make me sound like a two-year-old."

"Poor widdle Bwody," she cooed, slipping into baby talk. "Does him want me to get him some milk and cookies?"

Brody ignored the taunt. "No, but since you mentioned food, a bite of lunch would be good, if it's not too much trouble." Abby liked to make Brody think that everything was trouble. Months ago, when she'd asked him to give her a job while she took time off from school to decide what she wanted to do in life, Brody had considered his only sister a godsend. He'd spent years training June and did not look forward to starting the process all over again. At least with Abby he had an assistant who was already accustomed to his various quirks, and he to hers.

Abby had a mouth on her, and that mouth was always and forever spouting opinions about life in general, and his in particular. More than once Brody had questioned the wisdom of bringing the lovably irritating woman-child onto his staff and into his professional inner sanctum. "Get something quick though," he continued his order, "from the restaurant downstairs. I'm gonna have to take off in the next half-hour. Looks like I'm covering this wedding myself. And none of that tofu stuff you keep trying to pass off on me," he grumbled. "Just a burger or a sandwich. And no sprouts, for crying out loud."

"Yes, boss." Abby saluted cheerfully, did an about-face, and disappeared from view.

Brody watched her go, feeling partly irritated and partly relieved that he seemed not to have seriously offended her. He put up with a lot of teasing from his little sister, but she certainly put up with a lot of grief from him too. For that matter, so did Kevin. All the staff put up with a lot from him. Brody Collins was a difficult man to please, and he was the first to admit it. But just because he was a tough bird didn't mean that he didn't care.

He sighed. He cared more than he liked to admit. Though he pushed his staff to their limits, he never would force anyone to cancel personal plans in order to take an assignment. Even he wasn't that heartless, and he was sure his reporters knew it. Or they wouldn't turn assignments down so readily. Still, on Monday, he'd apologize for giving Kevin a hard time. A peace offering for Kevin's kids might be a good idea too. He was an excellent reporter; Brody didn't want to lose him.

He tried to remember what Kevin had: a boy and a girl? Two boys? Both girls? Oh well. Abby would know, and if she didn't, she'd find out from June. He'd have her pick up something cute and inexpensive to help smooth things over. He didn't know what was hot on the toy market these days; it had been years since he'd paid attention to the trends—five years, in fact, since he'd relinquished editorial control of *Child's Play* magazine to his friend Adam Bly. *Child's Play* was Brody's first independent business endeavor, and its success had earned him both financial stability and critical acclaim before the age of twenty-five. With features on baby care, parent care, and everything in between, *Child's Play* had been a stretch for a childless man like Brody, and he had risen to the challenge. Of course, that was back when he still planned to one day have children himself...before Brody had learned that he might carry the gene that caused Huntington's disease and, if he did have children, he stood a fifty percent chance of passing the condition on to any child he fathered. Before Lana, his girlfriend of a year and a half, had dumped him and his questionable genes, leaving him with a ruined life...and a shattered heart.

But that was a lifetime ago. Though Brody still owned the majority of *Child's Play*, he trusted Adam to run it on a daily basis and got involved only where big decisions were concerned. Today, most of his attention was consumed by *California Dream*. Zeroing in on the lifestyles of the wealthy and prestigious, *Dream* was popular internationally and gave readers a behind-the-scenes look at the parties, the fashions, and the personalities that made California, for many, so incredibly appealing.

The change suited Brody just fine. While shallowness and materialism went against the values he had been taught as a child—and were admittedly difficult to reconcile with his childhood faith in a God he still believed in, at least in theory—the surface-only approach to peoples' lives made it easy for him to maintain the professional detachment that was such an integral part of his work. Admittedly, the work was less rewarding than his work at *Child's Play,* but it was less painful, too, during those post-Lana weeks. It was also a huge step forward professionally and more than paid the bills. He was in an enviable position in the magazine-publishing industry, and he knew it. Most men and women would give their eyeteeth for his job. So why wasn't he happy? He should be on top of the world. There was no reason to let a little thing like ennui get in the way.

Besides, Brody told himself, it probably wasn't his job at all that was making him feel so restless. He was just working too much, and that was making him feel disconnected. It had been years since he'd dabbled in a hobby—or since he'd done anything with real meaning to it. Perhaps if he took up an outside interest he'd feel better. He still had that project car in storage: a Ford Falcon that he'd bought months before and hadn't laid eyes on since. Or perhaps he could try something altruistic, like feeding the hungry or cleaning up a polluted beach, as Abby had often suggested that he do. She was forever reminding him that he had been given so much already, it was time to give something back. Tithing ten percent to the local church he attended on holidays wasn't enough, she insisted. Occasionally, she took a different tack, telling him his efforts would not only benefit others, they would certainly also help to relieve his stress—which, he had to admit, he had plenty of. But all that meant one thing. Brody needed to give of himself.

The thought made him nervous.

It didn't have to be anything that would make him uncomfortable, though, he reassured himself. Picking up a little litter here, a few hours dishing out soup at a local shelter there… It was the perfect solution. He might even be able to find a few local politicians who'd be willing to join in for the sake of their public image, make a story out of it.

Pleased with the economy of the idea, Brody grabbed his day planner and jotted down a few quick notes. He was still writing when Abby poked her yellow-haired, ponytailed head in the door.

"Soup's on!" she said brightly and held out a Tupperware bowl that appeared to contain exactly that.

Brody sniffed the air like a bloodhound. "Soup?" He raised one shaggy eyebrow. "What happened to my burger?"

"A Type-A personality like you doesn't need that much cholesterol," she said primly, stepping toward him. "You've already got plenty of stress. Like you need clogged arteries on top of that?"

"Abby, the only thing causing me stress right now is you."

"Don't argue with me, Bro," she ordered. "And don't make any snotty comments either. This is my lunch, which I brought from home. I called downstairs and they said it would be at least twenty minutes before they could have anything ready for you. You said you had to leave before that, so…I'm making a sacrifice. I'll pick up something for myself at the restaurant after you leave—on your tab," she said with a grin.

And you're the one making a sacrifice? Brody resigned himself to the inevitable. "Okay, soup. Fine. What else?"

"Yogurt…half a bagel…" Abby dug through the brown paper bag and pulled out a second Tupperware container. "And applesauce."

"Applesauce?" What kind of professional ate applesauce for lunch? Surely he hadn't heard her right?

"Applesauce."

Brody made a mental note to give the girl a raise. Clearly she wasn't making enough money to allow her to eat properly.

"Yum," he said dully. "And since you're feeding me baby food: How about zwieback biscuits? Or maybe a little Ziploc baggie full of Cheerios? Have you got any of those in there?"

Abby moved as if to snatch the meal away. "No one's making you eat it. You can try to make it until the reception without fainting. I just hope your stomach doesn't start growling in the middle of the ceremony. Of course, you could always stop at Burger World on your way to Hollywood Hills. I just hope you don't run into heavy traffic on the freeway. It sure would be a shame to be late, or—worse—to miss the wedding altogether…"

"All right, all right." Brody waved her back as if shooing away a pesky bug, but Abby managed to grab away the soup and bagel and made as if to exit the room with them.

"No, no." A sigh. A flutter of eyelashes. She was the perfect martyr. "I wouldn't want you to *force* yourself."

He glanced at his watch. The irritating girl was right. He didn't have time to pick up anything else, and he'd had nothing but a blueberry muffin and a cappuccino for breakfast. "Wait! You win. I humbly apologize," he called after her, knowing full well that Abby was immensely enjoying her little game. She eyed him doubtfully. "Seriously. I looove soup. And I'm sure any soup you made is especially wonderful…Sis."

"It's from a can," she said darkly.

Brody kept his pasted-on smile cheery. "That's what I meant. I'm sure your soup-from-a-can is the best soup-from-a-can in town."

"Laying it on a bit thick, don't you think?"

He ignored the comment. "What kind is it?" Brody reached for the meal. He hoped she'd bring it to him, but with Abby he could never be sure.

Smirking, Abby walked back over to Brody's desk and put the plastic bowl and shiny custard-colored bagel back down in front of him. "Crow," she said meaningfully.

"Mmm," Brody said, playing along. "My favorite. Though I must say it's an acquired taste."

"Well, you've certainly had enough opportunities to acquire it."

"Hush, child. Respect your elders. Have you got a spoon?"

Abby pulled one out of the brown paper bag, along with a paper napkin with little pink hearts printed on it. "Careful you don't choke on the big chunks. Crow has a tendency to stick in one's throat."

"No kidding." Brody sank the silver utensil into the broth and spooned some of the fragrant liquid past his lips. As it turned out, it wasn't "crow," but a savory beef barley that made his mouth water. He swallowed quickly and reached for another bite. Nodding smugly, Abby backed out of the office and left him to finish his meal in peace. For this, Brody was truly grateful. As much as he adored his pesky sister, he had little time left for chitchat. He had less than ten minutes now to get out the door.

As he slurped his soup indelicately, Brody reviewed what he knew about the Salinger woman. Her wedding was set to take place at the stately Hollywood Hills Hotel. So clearly she had both good taste and a fair amount of money. He could only guess whether the funds for the posh affair came from her own business venture; an inheritance from her father, the late L.A. advertising mogul Edward Salinger; or Lucy's husband-to-be, a behavioral psychologist. He guessed it was probably a combination of all three.

The interviews he'd seen of her—which had consisted of comments no more revealing than "I'm very happy" and "I truly appreciate everyone's good wishes"—as well as his own experience speaking with her on the phone had led him to believe that Lucy was a levelheaded, no-nonsense sort of woman. One who seemed to know exactly what she wanted.

He could not help but think such single-minded determination would have served Lucy's sister Felicia also. Ever since his conversation with Deke, Brody had found his mind unexplainably drifting back to his former classmate. He could think of no other reason for Fee to come to his mind so often in these last days than his guilt at lying to Lucy about their relationship. Though he hadn't thought about her in years— had, in fact, deliberately tried to forget about her while he was still a teenager—memories were coming back to him in great detail.

Fee was the adorable, boy-crazy cheerleader who dated all the most popular guys; Brody, the withdrawn, too-intelligent-to-be-considered-cool editor of both the school paper and yearbook. He had first met her when they were sophomores. They sat next to each other in advanced placement English. She'd been lovely then, as he recalled, braces and all. Week after week, she'd sat next to him, her shiny hair hanging like a dark curtain between them, except when she tucked it back behind her ear. At those moments, Brody was able to sneak sidelong glances her way, catching glimpses of her finely arched nose, dark eyebrows, one shell-like ear, and sweetly curving lips that from time to time graced him with the gentlest of smiles.

He'd spoken with her on numerous occasions. But, while Felicia was kind and polite, she never expressed even the slightest romantic interest in him. He had been saddened by this, but not surprised. A late bloomer, Brody's growth spurts had not occurred, and his better-than-average looks had not surfaced until well after graduation.

Felicia, on the other hand, was picture perfect and had no problem finding dates. It was *keeping* boyfriends that proved a bit more difficult. Week after week, Brody had listened furtively as she talked with friends at nearby desks about her hopes that she would be invited to the prom or Spring Fling by Phil, Bill, Danny…whoever was the guy du jour.

Brody had watched, amazed, as she set her heart on one self-absorbed lout after another. Her relationships rarely lasted longer than a month or two. For some reason, she was drawn to popular "bad boys" who did not value her, and they had treated her accordingly.

Brody had looked on sadly at first, then in disgust. He had no idea what would make a girl actually pursue a guy who would mistreat her. It was, however, none of his business. By the time he was a senior, working with Felicia on the school yearbook, he had almost completely buried the feelings he once had for her.

A bit agitated, Brody pushed his empty soup bowl away, tucked the half bagel into his pocket, and reached for Abby's applesauce. As he spooned the spicy fruit pulp into his mouth, he tried to refocus his thoughts. There was no reason to waste his time thinking about Fee. It would be easy enough to identify her; no doubt she would have some role in the wedding, as the bride's sister. Hopefully he would be able to avoid her, since he'd misled Lucy on the phone about their relationship.

He wasn't actually worried, though, about being found out. By the time he spoke to Felicia at the reception, any threat of discovery would be long past. He would have his story. For her part, Lucy would be so caught up in the details of her wedding, she'd probably not even be aware he was there, much less have any real interest in throwing him out on the street. No, if he hadn't been unmasked as a villain yet, chances were he was home free. Who knew? It might even be interesting to talk with Felicia again and see how life had treated her.

Despite his initial unwillingness to attend the wedding, Brody found himself growing increasingly curious. What would Felicia look like after all this time? Would her dark, shiny curtain of hair still be the same? Her eyes as soft and gentle? As—

"Ow!" Brody jerked back abruptly as he poked himself in the chin with a spoonful of applesauce, then watched with dismay as the mashed fruit fell from the utensil and landed with a *splat* on the sleeve of his jacket. "That's…just…great," Brody muttered under his breath.

"Nice job, slugger. What do you do for an encore?"

Brody glanced up and found himself under the scrutiny of Carmen Cantrell, the red-headed photographer who often worked weekends for *California Dream*. He'd forgotten that she was taking this assignment today. And Carmen was a difficult woman to forget under any circumstances. Not that the average man would even want to. She was breathtaking. "You want I should spoon-feed you?" Carmen suggested, her voice low and sultry.

Brody raised one eyebrow. There was no mistaking her tone. He had never actively pursued the woman—though being a single man with a pulse and a healthy libido, the thought had crossed his mind more than once—but Carmen had never let a little detail like that keep her from expressing her obvious interest in him. And while he had no intention of getting seriously involved with any woman at this point in his life, Brody could not help but feel flattered by the attention.

Occasional flirtation with the woman seemed harmless enough. For one thing, Carmen wasn't actually one of his employees; she was simply an associate, and that put them on somewhat equal terms. Besides, he got the distinct impression that a long-term relationship was the last thing Carmen was after, which made him feel both cautious and safe. He wasn't interested in having a sexual affair; his conscience and morals would not allow that. Though his church attendance—at a local nondenominational Christian congregation—was sporadic, he still ascribed to traditional Judeo-Christian ethics.

At the same time, there was no denying that he longed for female companionship, particularly the companionship of a woman who would be incapable of hurting him. That description fit Carmen to a *T*. She was clearly gorgeous, and she was just as obviously shallow; there was no way she could reach Brody—or hurt him—on a deep level.

His parents hadn't raised him to be a swinging-singles type. But considering his family's medical history and the risk of passing on Huntington's disease, Brody was certain that no woman of real worth would ever want him. And he was beginning to wonder if shallow, flirtatious pseudo-relationships with no commitment were better than no relationship at all. He and Carmen had been flirting aimlessly for a while. Maybe he'd follow through on the impulse to ask her out to dinner once or twice.

"Hey, Carmen. I'd forgotten you had this gig today," he admitted, wiping applesauce off his sleeve with one of the napkins from Abby's paper bag.

"Such flattery." Carmen approached him with a smile that expressed quite clearly that she didn't need his—or any other man's—compliments to reassure her that she was worth remembering.

"What are you doing here? I figured I'd meet up with the photographer at the wedding."

"I called earlier to confirm the time of the assignment, and Abby told me she thought you'd be covering it. I thought maybe we could ride together," she suggested.

"Abby said…?" Brody sighed in exasperation. "Honestly, I don't know what to do with—"

"You bellowed?" The girl poked her head in the door.

"You just knew Kevin wasn't going to take the assignment, didn't you?" Brody locked his eyes on hers. "How does it feel to know that you're always right?"

Abby pretended to consider this for a moment. "I dunno," she said, stroking the graceful curvature of her chin. "Why don't you ask my brother? He's always right too. Or so he claims."

"Sounds like a brilliant guy. Maybe you should try listening to him once in a while." Brody rose from his chair and stepped around his desk, pausing briefly to consider his reflection in the glass that covered the framed still life hanging over his credenza. He would have liked to dress more formally for a wedding, especially this one. Thankfully he'd worn a white oxford shirt and fairly presentable jacket and dress pants to the office that morning. There was certainly no time to go home and change now.

For no particular reason, he wondered what Felicia Salinger would see when she laid eyes on him that afternoon. The grumpy workaholic Abby made him out to be? Or would she have forgotten him completely? Had he changed so much in all those years? He hoped so. If all his efforts had come to anything, he bore little resemblance to the shy boy he had once been. Oddly enough, though, he was beginning to feel a bit self-conscious. Brody bit back a laugh. Now *that* was funny. Mr. Take Charge, Brody Collins, feeling less than confident? He couldn't remember the last time that had happened.

Wow, Collins. You really need to get out in the field a bit more if something like a little wedding is able to rattle you.

Brody stopped briefly to grab a tie out of his desk drawer, then moved to Carmen's side and took her by the elbow. "Shall we?" he said, noticing her eyes sparkle at his harmless touch. But oddly enough, he found that his thoughts were still more occupied with the dark-haired, gentle-eyed, high-school student he'd once known than with the voluptuous redhead at his side.

Brody gave Carmen a brisk smile, then turned away and stepped through the door.

Oh well. Only a few more hours before the ridiculous wedding would be over. Then he could get back behind his desk where he was most comfortable, put all these irritating distractions behind him, and forget about those troublesome Salinger sisters once and for all.

Four

As soft as a baby's breath on his mother's cheek, breezes whispered through the young leaves and graceful branches that arched overhead. Around the borders of the hotel courtyard, earth-colored stucco walls soaked up the warm spring sunshine while red-tiled roofs offered up spots of bright, cheerful color among the green bowers waving to the gathering of onlookers below. From every corner of the garden, pink-faced geraniums nodded in their copper planters, and bougainvillea vines offered up hundreds of fragrant blossoms—their heady perfume adding to the ambiance of the romantic celebration.

Fee tightened her grasp on the nosegay she clutched between her fingers: creamy white Virginia roses, fragrant purple lilacs, white hydrangea blossoms, and delicate lilies of the valley wrapped tightly in a smooth ivory silk and organza ribbon. To her right stood Catherine, her golden hair and pale blue eyes giving onlookers every reason to believe that the exact shade of the dresses had been chosen to make the most of her glorious coloring. Beyond Cat were Lucy's dark-haired assistant Gabby, looking perfectly comfortable in the tiny dress that had driven Fee to the verge of an emotional breakdown, and Velma, the stout, sixty-three-year-old mother figure who had long ago taken Lucy under her wing.

On either side of the aisle, Felicia's children—Dinah and Clifford—stood like miniature sentries. A flower girl for the second time in her life at age ten, Dinah was the consummate professional: keeping one eye on her little brother, lest he should fail at his duties as ring bearer, and at the same time watching Lucy—who, she had earlier announced, looked "just like a fairy princess"—and hungrily soaking up every detail of the magical event. For his part, Clifford looked bored but had so far managed to remain fairly close to his assigned mark. Whereas Dinah had kept her white pinafore, patent leather shoes, and ivory-colored tights impeccably clean, Clifford had at some point before the ceremony knelt in a bit of mud while engaging in his favorite hobby: catching bugs. To his utter delight, the hotel's gardens were—quite literally—crawling with them. Fee had wiped the muck off as best she could, but the boy still looked rather unkempt. Knowing her son, though, Fee was aware it could have been a lot worse, and she was simply grateful that at that moment neither one of the children was screaming or bleeding.

To Felicia's left stood Daphne, her Doc Martens and crazy tights blessedly hidden by a swath of blue silk. And beyond Daphne was the bride—drawing every eye, just as she should—arrestingly beautiful in her halter dress of duchesse satin and silk crepe. Lucy's thick dark curls were woven into a braid along with a string of pearls, all of which had been doubled up and securely fastened with pins just above the nape of her neck. "You look like you've got a loaf of challah bread on your head," Daphne had quipped, which was, in the strictest sense true, but did nothing to detract from the bride's elegance and grace.

Next to Lucy waited her groom, Campbell, his bespectacled gray eyes filled with tears, his strong, handsome face hiding none of his anticipation and joy. Beyond him, Fee noted, a

small army of groomsmen watched with exaggerated seriousness, like a row of schoolboys, looking both dapper and
uncomfortable in their rented "monkey suits." For a moment,
she tried to remember which of the monkeys was the cousin
who had expressed an interest in her, but the thought was
easily pushed to the back of her mind. She'd sworn off men
for a lifetime, she reminded herself. Being delighted for her
sister was one thing; welcoming another one of those hairy
creatures into her own life was a different matter altogether.

"Dearly beloved," the minister began, his clear baritone
cutting cleanly through the afternoon air. "We have come
together in the presence of God to witness and bless the joining together of this man and this woman in holy matrimony.
The bond and covenant of marriage was established by God
in creation, and our Lord Jesus Christ adorned this manner
of life by his presence and first miracle at a wedding in Cana
of Galilee…"

Fee felt a tiny lurch of her heart as the words spilled from
the officiant's lips. It hadn't occurred to her that the words of
the standard Protestant ceremony Lucy and Cam had chosen
would be the same ones that were spoken at her marriage to
Robert twelve years before. Nor, if she had known, would she
have suspected that she would find this to be so disturbing.
All day she'd managed to put her own personal tragedy behind
her. But suddenly she felt overwhelmed by melancholy upon
hearing the holy promise spoken once more, knowing all the
while that the man she had loved had purposely chosen to
walk away from the covenant he once had made with her and,
she had naively thought, with God.

For that rude awakening, she had only herself to blame.
Robert had told her he was a Christian when they first started
dating, and at the time Felicia was so thrilled by the fact that
he seemed to care for her, she hadn't for a moment challenged

his claim. It wasn't long, though, before she realized that Robert's occasional visits to church were made solely for her benefit and that he considered himself a Christian only in a societal sense. To him it was the same as saying he was an American who loved apple pie, and it required just as much personal commitment and sacrifice. To Fee's dismay, once the marriage license was signed, her new husband no longer felt motivated to sit through what he called "boring" church services, particularly when there was a perfectly good football or basketball game on television to amuse him.

For years, Fee had begged Robert to come to church services with her and, later, the kids. Eventually, she had given up fighting the losing battle. Urging Robert to come with her seemed only to drive a deeper wedge between them. There had been nothing else to do but pray for her husband…and she did, fervently. That was one of the things that made it so hard to accept Robert's eventual decision to leave her, Dinah, Clifford, and Gabe. She'd prayed for God to touch Robert's heart. Intellectually, Fee knew that Robert had free will and could walk away from both her and his Creator. That, however, did not change the fact that on a purely human level she wished God could have—would have—stepped in and forced her husband to do the right thing. Nor did it keep her from feeling dismay and anger because he had not done exactly that.

"It signifies to us the mystery of the union between Christ and his church, and Holy Scripture commends it to be honored among all people…"

Fee felt her cheeks flush hotly. Though she could not have taken her marriage vows more seriously, the fact of her divorce made her feel as though she were standing in front of the five-hundred-plus crowd with a scarlet *D* sewn onto her breast. She consoled herself with the words from 1 Corinthians, which she had memorized months before: "If a woman has a husband who is not a believer and he is willing to live with her, she must not divorce him…. But if the unbeliever leaves, let him do so. A believing man or woman is not bound in such circumstances; God has called us to live in peace."

Felicia clung uneasily to those words. She believed Paul had written them to individuals who had become Christians while already married to an unbeliever. She wasn't yet sure if such grace applied to believers who had found themselves yoked to non-Christians as a result of their own poor choices. But little comfort was better than no comfort at all. Besides, she knew that God was about mercy and kindness and not condemnation. He would love her no matter what—plus she had her children. That's where God's grace felt truly real to her.

She had to admit, though, raising three children alone was hard—the hardest thing she'd ever done. She would manage, of course. People bounced back from divorce all the time. Well, she thought wryly, maybe *bounced* wasn't exactly the word. *Crawled,* perhaps, *scraped* themselves from the floor, or *rose*…like a phoenix from the ashes. Fee sighed. The point was, they survived and she would too.

The hardest thing these days wasn't missing Robert, though a part of her still did and, she suspected, perhaps always would. The divorce had been final months ago, and Felicia had accepted its finality. But not long thereafter, Robert had announced his intention to marry a pert young starlet named Tiffany, whom he had met early that year at the hospital where he worked, and who apparently had no problem with football on Sundays. Though Fee had once harbored hopes of reconciliation, Robert's determination to marry again had made her realize that he truly was gone for good.

No, she had decided, the hardest parts these days were the loneliness, the sense of failure, the difficulty of doing all the work of raising the kids on her own. Felicia constantly found herself feeling exhausted and beaten down—and she hadn't even started working outside the home yet, which was something she was going to have to do if she wanted to maintain some sort of adult relationships. But what she wanted most anymore was simply peace. The days of wishing for romance were over. At this point in her life, her greatest wish was not for a passionate date with some Fabio type, but for reliable cleaning services and around-the-clock, backup childcare. Now that would be a dream come true.

Unfortunately, it was even less likely to happen than the date with Fabio. Still, it would be nice to have a little help now and then…

"The union of husband and wife in heart, body, and mind is intended by God for their mutual joy," insisted the minister, "for the help and comfort given one another in prosperity and adversity…"

"Help and comfort." You preach it, brother, Fee thought fiercely. Maybe her sisters were right. They'd been urging her to hire someone to come in and help her with the housework and with caring for Gabe. If she got a part-time job as she intended, she might be able to swing it. It would get her out of the house anyway and back into the world of adult conversations and friendships. Her sisters assured her it would be good for her, as well as for the kids. She knew they were probably right. Dinah and Clifford were both in school now; they wouldn't even know she was gone, especially if her work hours were flexible. Still, she hated the thought of entrusting sweet little Gabe to anyone else's care, even if just for a few hours at a time.

At the thought of her eight-month-old son, Fee felt a twinge of longing and immediately turned to sneak a peek at his tiny, adorable head. There he was, just where she had last seen him just minutes ago. Smack-dab in the center of the front row, cradled in the arms of his devoted Uncle Jonas, Gabe was slack jawed and snoring, oblivious to the festivities around him, praise be to God.

For several long moments, Fee lost herself in musings about her little Boy Wonder: his long, handsome lashes and head full of soft, thick hair…the way he had begun to prowl about the living room while clinging resolutely to various pieces of furniture…his advanced ability to play pat-a-cake endlessly and wave bye-bye to his aunties at only eight months old.

Clearly, the child was a veritable Einstein.

At that moment her baby stirred, lifted his head from Jonas's strong shoulder, and blinked sleepily at a couple in the row behind them. Fee pushed back the urge to run to him; Gabe was doing fine in Jonas's capable hands, she told herself. She bit back a grin as Elliott made a preemptive strike, picking up Messy Mouse out of Gabe's diaper bag and waving it in front of the child's face in order to capture his attention before he began to loudly protest his lack of activity. To Fee's relief, Gabe responded immediately by beaming at Elliott and reaching out one pudgy fist for his favorite toy.

She shook her head in wonderment. Gabe was her little miracle. Fee remembered the day, eight months before, when he had come into this world under the watchful eyes of her three birthing coaches: Cat, Lucy, and Daphne. Robert hadn't been there. He was already off traveling the globe with his then-current love interest. As a matter of fact, there hadn't been even one male—excluding Gabe, of course—at her younger son's birth. Even Fee's doctor had been a woman.

Men, schmen, Fee thought disparagingly as she glanced around the crowd full of them. Who needed 'em anyway? She couldn't think of a single man who could turn her head these days. Not Robert. Not Cam's cousin. Not…

Not…

Well, hello there!

Felicia blinked, refocused her eyes, then blinked again. Sitting directly behind Jonas was a man so attractive, so utterly appealing, she simply could not help but look twice. Though she could not place the stranger, she had the uncanny feeling that she really ought to know him. Racking her brain, she pored over every detail of the man's appearance: His hair was a soft, light brown; his eyes a startling blue; his shoulders broad, leaving a vague but undeniable impression of strength. Without moving a muscle, he managed somehow to ooze confidence. Fee judged him to be hands-down the most attractive male present. This despite the fact that he did not seem to be enjoying himself. As the minister spoke, the man shifted uncomfortably in his seat, looking like he wished himself miles away. From time to time, a deep furrow appeared between his thick dark eyebrows, and he glanced around, jotting down notes on a small spiral tablet he held in the palm of one large hand.

Though the man was clean-shaven, she could already see just a hint of shadow above his upper lip and across his strong cheeks and jaw line. His clothes were expensive looking and reflected his obvious sense of style: white, button-down oxford shirt, camel-colored jacket, and simple navy tie in a perfect knot at his masculine throat.

"The voice of my beloved," the minister intoned, quoting from the Song of Songs. "Look he comes, leaping upon the mountains, bounding over the hills. My beloved is like a gazelle or a young stag. Look, there he stands…"

Felicia swallowed hard.

Who on earth was that guy? And where had he come from? She'd thought she knew most of her sister's friends. Maybe he was a relative of Cam's? No, no…he was seated on the bride's side. Obviously he was here to honor Lucy. He must be one of her celebrity acquaintances, Felicia thought. No doubt that was why she recognized him.

The man continued to scribble in his little notebook; Felicia continued to watch. For reasons she could not explain, she felt strangely comforted by his presence. Perhaps it was simply that he gave her something else to think about besides the fact that her own marriage had failed. She felt a twinge of curiosity. Was he married? Did he have kids? She blushed at the thought.

Fee was still watching intently when she realized that the woman next to the stranger—a stunning redhead—was eyeing her sharply. *Oh, good grief.* Had she been staring that blatantly? Oops. The woman appeared none too pleased about it either. She looked away from Felicia, leaned in close to the man at her side, and put her bright red lips close to his left ear. Fee wondered self-consciously if the woman was saying something about her. But the man did not look up. He appeared slightly irritated as he mumbled a response. The redhead's face broke into a catlike smile then, and she gave a quiet, delighted laugh as if she found him to be the most amusing companion in the world. As Fee watched, she placed her hand possessively on the man's shoulder. He frowned, but did not protest.

Fee looked away, allowing her eyes to trace the aerial path of a yellow jacket zipping past. *I hope they're happy,* she thought fiercely. *Somebody should be.*

"Lucy," the minister intoned. "Will you have this man to be your husband, to live together in the covenant of marriage? Will you love him, comfort him, honor and keep him, in sickness and in health, and, forsaking all others, be faithful to him as long as you both shall live?"

Felicia focused her gaze upon her sister, who was now looking up earnestly at her beloved.

"I will." Lucy spoke confidently, clearly.

Fee felt her eyes well up with tears as Campbell reached out with one hand and gently stroked the rosy cheek of his bride.

Another yellow jacket flew languidly past. Felicia hoped Dinah didn't see the thing. Her daughter had never been stung, and yet she had developed an irrational fear of such an event occurring. If she spotted the insect, she and her little white pinafore were liable to go flying themselves.

"Campbell, will you have this woman to be your wife, to live together in the covenant of marriage? Will you love her, comfort her, honor and keep her, in sickness and in health, and, forsaking all others, be faithful to her as long as you both shall live?"

Cam drew in a deep breath, then exhaled in a rush. "Will I ever!"

The garden filled with the roar of laughing guests. Felicia beamed. She trusted that Cam would do exactly as he promised. Though she wasn't quite as optimistic about marriage in general as she had once been, she felt absolutely certain that Cam would honor her sister with his life. The love the two shared was strong. Their faith, a bond that drew them closer together than Robert and Felicia ever had been.

If only every married couple could begin their life together with such an advantage. She wondered if the stranger had that kind of a marriage. She couldn't quite put her finger on the reason why, but Felicia felt instinctively distrustful of his red-headed companion. It saddened her to think that the man could possibly be struggling in his marriage, just as she had been in hers. But…she was just jumping to conclusions. She didn't know anything about him or his wife. The woman was probably a perfectly nice person.

Stop it, Fee, she told herself. *You're just feeling self-conscious because she looks like a supermodel…and these days you're feeling more like a supertanker.* That morning's Shrinking Bridesmaid Dress incident had, in fact, dealt a heavy blow to her already fragile ego. There was no reason to let it cloud her judgment, though. No doubt the gorgeous stranger, whoever he was, was perfectly happy—ecstatic even—with his life. He seemed to have every reason to be. The thought washed over her along with a wave of sadness.

You're being silly, Fee, she told herself angrily. *He's just a guy. You don't know him. You just wish you did because he's so cute and you're so lonely. But he's obviously with someone else. Stop being such an idiot.* She cast the man one more furtive glance. But despite her stern self-talk, Felicia could not shake the impression that she knew him. That dimple, that hair, those eyes…

At just that moment, "those eyes" met hers. At first the man seemed startled to see Fee looking at him, though she could not imagine why. Then his expression changed and he seemed both amused and pleased. It seemed that she should know him after all: His look of crystal-clear recognition was unmistakable. Felicia felt her cheeks grow hot. His smile deepening, the man arched one eyebrow in her direction.

Felicia returned the look with a timid smile.

The attractive stranger inched forward on the seat of his white folding chair, bestowed upon her a meaningful expression, and gave an awkward little wave as if he were shooing a bug away.

It felt satisfying, comforting, and exciting to be noticed and appreciated not for being Mom, but simply for being a woman. Perhaps the man wasn't married after all! He seemed to be interested in her. It felt wonderful to know that someone still was. At least for a moment. By now Fee was grinning outright and had to bite back an audible laugh. She could feel her facial muscles being stretched from her lips, across her cheeks, all the way up to her ears. It was the first time in years that she'd felt such pure delight.

Watch it, Fee, she reminded herself sternly, looking away as the yellow jacket hummed past her nose. The guy might not be married, but he was at the very least taken...not that this mattered or caused a problem for her. She wasn't looking for a new man in her life. She was simply flattered by the attention. Her feelings were perfectly natural and meant nothing of a truly romantic nature. It was just lovely to be admired by a celebrity or an old friend of Lucy's—if that was, in reality, who the man was.

At the same time, Fee thought a bit guiltily, whether or not her first impressions of the redhead were favorable, she was determined not to say or do anything that might cause the woman to feel badly. Fee had been snubbed by Robert at enough social events and had seen him flirt inappropriately with enough other women to make her sympathize with any wife whose husband drew unwanted attention from the opposite sex. Who could blame the woman for looking irritated? Fee made a mental note to be especially friendly to her if and when she ran into her at the reception.

A blur at the corner of her field of vision caused Felicia to turn sharply to the left. To her dismay, Dinah had at last caught sight of the yellow jacket that had been circling and was behaving as though it had targeted her with a very personal attack. Waving her bouquet like a dagger, Dinah attempted to bat the insect away from her small, white, terror-stricken face. When that attempt failed and instead resulted in drawing a second yellow jacket to her by spreading the flowers' fragrance, Dinah stuck out one arm straight in front of her, screwed up her face in fear, and held the sweet-smelling blossoms as far from her body as was physically possible.

Felicia glanced out at the audience to see if anyone had noticed. As far as she could tell, most of the guests remained unaware of what was taking place. The H. B. and her groom were now facing the minister and were completely unaware of their flower girl's theatrics. Only Jonas, in the front row, watched open-mouthed. And behind him, the gorgeous stranger clasped a large hand over his mouth in an apparent attempt to hold back laughter.

Besides Jonas, the man seemed to be the only one who had noticed the bee. He'd probably noticed it when it was circling her. In fact...Fee's face burned. The man probably hadn't been waving at her at all! He'd simply been warning her that the thing was nearby. He hadn't just been waving as if he was shooing a bug away; he *was* telling her to shoo a bug away!

By this time, Dinah still looked terror-stricken, but the yellow jacket had disappeared—at least for the moment.

"Lucy, I give you this ring as a symbol of my vow, and with all that I am, and all that I have, I honor you, in the name of the Father, and of the Son, and of the Holy Spirit." Tenderly, Cam slipped onto Lucy's finger the sparkling diamond-and-platinum token of his commitment to their relationship. Her eyes brimming with joyful tears, Lucy took her groom's hand between her own graceful fingers and presented him with the circle of polished silver that she, in turn, had carefully chosen.

"Campbell, I give you this ring..."

The officiant watched in silent approval until the exchange was complete. "Now that Campbell and Lucy have given themselves to each other by solemn vows, with the joining of hands and the giving and receiving of rings, I pronounce that they are husband and wife, in the name of the Father, and of the Son, and of the Holy Spirit.

"Those whom God has joined together let no one put asunder."

Felicia joined with the people in proclaiming an enthusiastic, "Amen!" As the recessional music began, she glanced toward the rows of chairs facing her, but the man's attention was already claimed by the redhead, who had laid one pale white finger upon his chin and physically manipulated his face so it was pointed in her direction. A moment later, it was Fee's turn to head down the aisle, and she obediently allowed the groomsman who offered her his arm to lead her down the linen path.

"Romantic, eh?" he breathed in her ear.

Felicia looked up to see that the groomsman was smiling at her with a bit too much familiarity. "Well…yes," she said, giving him a stiff smile.

"Almost makes me believe in *looove* again. How about you?"

His words caught Fee off guard, and she found herself speechless. Though the declaration itself might have been innocent enough, he had actually managed to utter it with a leer upon his face. And while she might not be romance's staunchest defender, she couldn't imagine any woman being impressed by a man whose opening words actually pitted him *against* love.

"I have nothing against love," Fee told him crisply. "It's the lack of it that seems to be such a problem in relationships these days."

"Good point." The man nodded appreciatively. "That's what I always say too." They had reached the end of the aisle, but his sweaty hand reached to grip her elbow. "You're a very wise woman…Felicia."

This last utterance took Fee by surprise, and she cocked her head at him, trying to figure out where she knew the man from.

"What?" The too-handsome stranger gave her a gleaming smile that could have sold a warehouseful of toothpaste. "Surprised that I know your name? I've made it my business to know as much as I can about you…Fee." That leer again. "I asked my cousin Cam about you. My name's Ted Harris. Maybe we can find a cozy spot where we can sit and talk…?"

Fee fought back the urge to gag. *Cam's cousin!* It was worse than she'd feared. *Kill the groom now, or kill him later?* Desperately, she glanced around for some form of rescue. Unfortunately, Lucy and Campbell had already been swallowed up in a sea of well-wishers. Dinah and Clifford, who were practically famous for their ability to interrupt, were—when such a distraction would actually prove helpful—nowhere to be seen. Though Daphne was standing just a few feet away, she had thrown herself into Elliott's arms and gave no indication that she would be tearing her eyes from his face anytime in the near future. Fee scowled. *Thanks a lot, Daphne, Elliott…*

Elliott…

Her heart leaped. He'd been sitting with his brother during the ceremony. Jonas—and, therefore, her baby—could not be far behind!

A moment later her hopes were realized as her dark-haired brother-in-law approached with a wrinkled nose and outstretched arms that held what soon proved to be a very stinky baby. Gratefully, Fee reached out to claim the odoriferous infant. Never before had she been so grateful to smell a soiled diaper.

"Of course," Fee said to Ted. She turned back to him, smiled sweetly, and held out the baby just inches from his face. "I was just going to change Gabe. Would you care to do the honors?"

The man looked about uncertainly. The hunter was now the hunted.

"Unless of course you wanted me to go on ahead, so you could get something to drink first?" Felicia generously offered him a way out.

The man looked relieved. "Actually, yes," he said, sounding like a prisoner who had just narrowly escaped being sent to death row. He reached out one hand and awkwardly patted Gabe on the head, his nose crinkled in distaste. "I'm quite parched, as a matter of fact." Nervously, he put one finger to his throat and loosened his tie. "Good of you to notice. Perhaps later…?"

"Of course. There are always diapers that need changing." Felicia gave him a noncommittal Mona Lisa smile, but Ted had already turned away.

Fee exhaled in relief. "Thanks, Jonas," she said to her brother-in-law, who had been standing there watching in amusement.

"No problem."

"Did Gabe behave for you?" she asked, lowering her head to nuzzle her child.

"The boy was a perfect angel. A foul-smelling angel, but an angel nonetheless. He takes after his Uncle Jonas—as far as being an angel, I mean…not the foul-smelling part."

"Jonas," Fee said sternly. "Gabe can't take after you. There are no blood ties."

"All right, then he learned angelic behavior from watching me."

"Did he now? And what about the other two…angels, Dinah and Clifford?" Though she adored her children, angelic behavior was not their forte. "What's their excuse?"

"What's our excuse for what, Mama?"

Felicia heard the rustle of silk brushing against her dress as Dinah skipped up and wrapped her arms around her waist, her little brother trailing behind her.

"Hullo, darling," Fee smiled down at her beloved daughter. "I say, what's your excuse for not running right up after the ceremony and giving your mother a big hug and a kiss? You, too, Clifford."

"Oh, Mama!" Dinah rolled her eyes, but willingly tipped her head upward and puckered her lips.

Fee handed Gabe off to Jonas, bent over, and pulled Dinah close.

"Did you see the bee, Mama? It almost got me!"

Fee pressed her hand against the soft, smooth hair at the back of her daughter's head. "You were wonderful, sweetheart. I was so proud of you."

"*I* was wonderful," Clifford announced loudly, giving Fee an impatient scowl.

"You," she readily agreed, throwing her other arm around him and ruffling his hair, "were a prince. Definitely the handsomest man in the room." *At least of the underage set…* Instinctively, she tried to catch a glimpse of the attractive stranger, but the more than five hundred guests had begun to throng all around the area directly surrounding them.

In Jonas's arms, Gabe started to fuss.

"Oops! Sorry, little trooper. Didn't mean to put you off. Let's go in and get you cleaned up." Felicia rose and reclaimed her youngest child. "Because you need it, Pepe le Pew. Come on, kids. I need to change Gabe."

"Oh, Mama," Dinah pouted, sounding quite put out. "Do we *have* to go with you? Gabe's smelly."

"No, you don't have to," Jonas offered. "Dinah, Clifford, stick with me."

"Oh, *goodie!*"

"Thanks, Jonas," Fee said gratefully as she slung the denim diaper bag over her silk-clad shoulder. She'd almost forgotten how nice it was to have help with the kids. She could get used to help like that. Too bad today's grace couldn't extend to the rest of the week, the rest of the month…

Too bad the wedding couldn't last forever, she thought sadly.

Gabe let out an impatient cry.

Felicia shook her head, as if to clear it. Then with one last, sheepish scan of the crowd, she retreated into the sanctuary of the hotel.

Five

Like Cinderella after the ball, she'd disappeared into the crowd, leaving him without so much as a contact lens—much less anything as helpful as a glass slipper—with which to find her.

Brody glanced about curiously. The bride and groom remained in the yard, in full view of the guests, as did almost the entire wedding party. But Felicia had evaporated before his very eyes. She was still quite lovely, but it wasn't just a physical attraction that compelled him to her. Brody worked with gorgeous women every day; it took more than a pretty face to catch his eye. Felicia's face, however, was not simply pretty; it was full of character—something he had never really noticed during high school. And the reporter in Brody imagined that behind the gentle laugh and worry lines was a story.

He was, in spite of himself, more than a little intrigued. When he'd noticed Felicia looking at him during the ceremony, he'd nearly jumped out of his skin. For one crazy moment, he had the distinct impression that she was looking not so much at him as through him. He'd worried then that she had correctly identified him as a fraud who had no business being at her sister's wedding and was plotting how to unmask him publicly as such. Certainly if Felicia had him pegged already, Lucy would have done so as well, he'd realized with an unpleasant little jolt. But Felicia's eyes had flickered over him, almost dancing, and he saw the faintest hint of delight in their depths. He had grinned then, in relief, and the smile Felicia had bestowed upon him in return had tugged strangely at his heart. It wasn't until she turned away, and until Carmen threw him a disparaging glance, that Brody realized how obvious his interest had been.

After that he'd alternately watched the bride and groom, then Fee, throughout the ceremony. When it was over, while Brody was collecting his things, for the briefest of moments, he had spied Felicia at the back of the garden, glaring at the groomsman who had led her down the aisle. Her husband perhaps? He consulted the program that had been given to him upon his arrival at the hotel. No, the second attendant was one Ted Harris…no apparent relation to Felicia Salinger Kelley. No wonder Felicia had practically frozen the man with her icy stare; the guy was acting inappropriately familiar with her, a married woman: grabbing her by the arm and waggling his eyebrows suggestively. Brody felt a sense of satisfaction rise within him. *Good for you, Fee.* He hoped that the woman he married—if he ever married at all—would send potential Casanovas packing with the same fervor. That husband of Fee's was a fortunate man. Brody wondered which one of the guests was this Robert Kelley fellow and if the guy had even the slightest inkling of what had just transpired.

"Shouldn't we go speak to the bride and get our photos?" Carmen suggested, laying one cool white hand on his arm. "After all, that is why we're here. Isn't it?"

"Of course." Brody turned back to Carmen and was surprised by the veiled animosity in her eyes. There was no mistaking the flicker of irritation he saw there. Though what Carmen had to be bothered about was a mystery to him.

Brody turned away, unconcerned. Far be it from him to try to guess what made women tick. Not that it mattered. Carmen's feelings really weren't any of his business, one way or another. She was right about one thing, though—they were there to get a story, and that's exactly what he was going to do.

Brody quickly relocated the bride, standing just twenty feet away, surrounded by friends and family…though, as far as he could tell, still no Fee. Running one hand along his jaw line, he sized up the situation as best he could. No doubt Lucy and Campbell would soon be whisked away to start a receiving line or to smile their way through the first of the day's interminable photo sessions. He and Carmen would have to speak to Lucy before that; if he let them escape before getting what he needed, he and Carmen would be there all afternoon.

Swallowing his irritation, Brody nodded briskly. "Come on," he said in the tone of a general addressing a private. "We're going in."

Brody turned away, feeling a slight tug on his sleeve as Carmen grabbed hold of his jacket as she followed him through the crowd. The gesture felt too intimate for their relationship. He wasn't her date, and he wasn't her daddy. Why couldn't Carmen find her own way through the assembly? There was no point in making an issue out of it, though, so Brody decided to let it ride.

Using his large frame to part the sea of wedding guests, he pressed forward without mercy. Apparently recognizing him as a force to be reckoned with, waiting partygoers grudgingly stepped aside and allowed him and Carmen access to the man and woman of the hour.

Get in, get what you need, then get out again… Brody knew the drill. First he'd talk to Lucy and Cam, get them to say something he could use, probably about the genuineness of their love, blah-blah-blah. After he was done interviewing the bride and groom, he'd mingle a little, gather some quotable material from the glitterati while Carmen got her photos, then it would be back to the office for another Saturday night spent writing copy for the upcoming issue.

As he stepped into the inner circle that surrounded Lucy and Cam, Brody's hard-nosed attitude softened a bit, and he found himself simply struck by the naked joy in the eyes of the man and woman who had just become husband and wife.

Though the massive crowd of well-wishers that pushed forward to greet them would have sent Brody screaming, Lucy and Cam seemed perfectly content to receive their guests— alternately bestowing kisses and enthusiastic, one-armed hugs upon their loved ones and casting shy, furtive glances at each other while keeping the fingers of their inner hands firmly interlocked.

Brody was still taking this in when a gnome-sized elderly woman in front of him stepped away from the bride and groom, and the young lovers seized the split second alone to exchange wonder-filled glances. Then Lucy turned a fraction of an inch, and her eyes met Brody's. Recognition gradually dawned upon her. "Brody Collins? As I live and breathe! Why, you look…" Words failed her.

"Different?" Brody offered self-consciously.

"I was going to say 'fantastic.' If I hadn't spoken to you recently and seen photos of you in the *Times*—if I hadn't been half keeping an eye out—I wouldn't have even recognized you. I can't believe my eyes!"

Brody stepped forward and clasped her free hand warmly. "And I can't believe mine. You are a beautiful bride, Lucy Salinger."

"Lucy Salinger Howard now! And stop with the flattery," she scolded him, but her eyes were dancing. "I know you wanted the story for your highfalutin magazine. You're just lucky I gave you the scoop. I didn't have to invite any of the press, you know. Not that the *National Interrogator* is shooting us from helicopters overhead. I'm not exactly Elizabeth Taylor!"

"Ah, but you underestimate your popularity, my dear." He turned to Cam and held out one hand. "Forgive me. Brody Collins: *California Dream* magazine."

"He's the one I told you about, hon," Lucy informed her new husband. "Fee's old boyfriend." At the word boyfriend, Cam loosened his grip on Lucy and took the hand Brody proffered. Brody tried to keep his expression from betraying any of the guilt he felt at lying to the man and woman on their wedding day.

"Any friend of Felicia's is a friend of ours," he said agreeably.

"At least, he *says* he's a friend of ours." Lucy eyed Brody warily. He balked under her interrogative gaze and felt himself break into a sweat. "You remembered your promise?"

"I did, indeed." Brody held up three fingers in the Boy Scout salute and let out the breath he'd been holding. "No photos during the ceremony, as Madam requested."

Lucy relaxed visibly at that.

"But if you recall," he went on, "I do need some images for the article, and I prefer to use our own photographer, with your permission." He angled one shoulder in the direction behind him, acknowledging his freelance associate for the first time since the conversation began. "Forgive me. Ms. Carmen Cantrell...Lucy and Campbell Howard. Lucy and Cam, this is Carmen."

Carmen paused almost imperceptibly before offering her hand, as if she was sizing the couple up, Brody thought incredulously, as if she saw them as a threat. But that was ridiculous. Why would she care anything about Lucy and Cam?

Carmen shot assignments nearly every day; rarely did she express any interest in her subjects, except on the rare occasion when she dropped names about the attractive, single, famous men she'd captured on film.

Lucy looked a bit puzzled, but greeted Carmen kindly. "It's a pleasure. Of course, as I told Brody on the phone, we have our own journalistic wedding photographer here today. We didn't want to do any posed shots. But Cam's sister, Alexandra, insisted, so in a few minutes we're going to humor her and step into one of the smaller garden areas for our own little private photo shoot. If you'd care to join us...?"

"Thank you." Carmen inclined her head imperiously.

"Absolutely. And please, in the meantime, make yourselves comfortable. Get yourselves a drink. Enjoy the gardens. It's a beautiful day...isn't it?" Lucy said, sounding vastly more Martha Stewart-y than Brody had remembered her to be. She beamed up at her husband.

"It is. But of course, it could be a hurricane, and I'd be happy," Campbell said in a low voice, "as long as I wound up married to you at the end of the day."

Carmen moved closer to Brody, reached an arm around his back, and gave his shoulder a healthy squeeze. He inched away uncomfortably.

"Oh, sweetie. Me, too." Lucy stepped up on tiptoe and planted a firm kiss on her husband's lips. When Cam released her a moment later, she turned back to Brody and Carmen and blinked at them as if she'd just remembered that she had guests. "Love is so wonderful," she said happily. "I highly recommend it." This last comment was directed solely at Brody, and she spoke as if the words were loaded with meaning.

"What, exactly, is so wonderful about it?" Brody asked, pen in hand, ignoring any personal message or benediction she might be attempting to bestow upon him. Married people seemed to always feel a need to pull their single friends into the state of matrimony with them. As a matchmaker, Lucy Salinger Howard was probably the worst offender yet.

The bride thought for a moment, then said quietly, "I really don't think there's any way to explain it. I'm still just so amazed at what we have, at what God's done in our lives. Before I met Cam, I was at a point in my life where I thought maybe I'd never get married. I couldn't imagine it working for me, even though I'd seen so many other people fall in love. But when it happened for me, I just knew. I thought I had loved guys before. But this time, I found out what it means to fall completely into love. To let it catch me. And then to rest there. Does that make sense?"

"Hmm?" Brody glanced up from the spiral notebook he'd hastily drawn out of his pocket. "Oh sure. Right. Let him catch you."

"Not *him*, you goof," she said, letting out a melodious peal of laughter. "It. Love. In a way, I think I'm really trying to say 'God,' especially since he's the one who brought us together. Though I suppose Cam and I did catch each other, more or less. Isn't that right, sweetie?" Lucy blinked shyly at the man beside her. "Love?"

Any moment now, the two might break into baby talk. "A-*hem*." Brody feigned great interest in the toe of one well-shined shoe. Enough was enough. He broke the tension with a few of the standard reporter-type questions—How did you meet? Was it love at first sight? What are your plans for the honeymoon? The love-struck couple answered to the best of their ability, although it was obvious that they were too distracted by each other to walk a straight line. It was absolutely sickening.

"Hey, you lovebirds!" A stately looking blond in blue silk slipped out of the crowd and into their midst. "The photographer wants to get started, if you can tear yourselves away from your adoring public."

Brody breathed a sigh of relief. *Saved by the blond…*

"Hi, Catherine," he said gratefully, remembering the eldest Salinger sister from her days at Washington High, where she had been two years ahead of him and Felicia. "It's good to see you again."

Catherine smiled politely, but it was clear by the blank look in her sapphire blue eyes that she hadn't even the vaguest notion who he was. "Hello, uh…" She paused, apparently searching her memory banks for a name and coming up empty. "Hello, there," she finished weakly.

"Brody Collins," he supplied for the second time in five minutes.

"Fee's old friend," Campbell told her knowingly.

Brody swallowed hard. Catherine blinked at him. "From high school?" he tried. Dead stare. Brody licked his lips. "Big hair? Thick glasses? Reporter for the *Bulletin*? The, uh…nerd?"

"Ohhhhhhh!" Catherine's blue eyes opened wide. "The—" She stopped herself. "Brody!"

"That's right," he said dryly. "The Brody."

"Wow. I think I kind of remember you. Barely. You've changed." She and Lucy exchanged glances.

"So I hear."

"Thick glasses? Do tell." Carmen laid one cool paw on his hand; Brody felt the muscles of his shoulders tighten. Why was this woman, whom he normally found to be amusing, irritating him so much today? Moving as if to scratch an itch on his chin, he silently extricated himself from her grip.

"Don't go there, Carmen," he said warningly, ignoring the pouty look she gave him. "You wouldn't have wanted to see me in high school. It wasn't pretty." It wasn't Carmen's opinion of him, though, that was so troubling. What was irritating was the way they were gaping at him—like fish out of water. It was clear that Lucy and Cat considered his transformation nothing short of miraculous. Somehow Brody managed not to glare at them.

"Carmen, this is Catherine. Catherine…Carmen. Look, I'd better get going," he said coolly. "Between the ceremony and our phone conversation, Lucy, I probably got all I needed for the article. I'll just mingle with the guests and get a couple more quotes, if you don't mind." He leveled her with his gaze. "I'd ask if I could kiss the bride, but I'd hate to send you away screaming in horror…"

Lucy laughed then, reached out both hands, and planted them firmly on his shoulders. "Don't be silly. We're not complaining about the old Brody Collins; just admiring the new, improved version." Leaning forward, she pressed her cheek against his. Brody felt his anger melting away.

When he drew back, he noticed Carmen's icy stare. She kept him trapped in the tractor beam of her eyes as she spoke. "Don't you have enough material for the article already? I'm sure you'd rather come watch the photo shoot." It wasn't a question, but was spoken as a statement of fact.

Brody looked at her in surprise. Since when did he have to baby-sit his photographers while they worked? It was almost as if she was afraid to let him out of her sight. Brody's eyes narrowed. Who was in charge here anyway? He didn't like the way Carmen was acting one bit. Nor did he like the strange looks Lucy and Company were throwing them.

"That's okay, Carmen. You don't want me looking over your shoulder, distracting you—"

"But you wouldn't be," Carmen interrupted.

"And I'm sure Lucy and Cam don't need us to turn this thing into a three-ring circus," Brody said, smoothly ignoring her protest. "It's hard enough for a couple to appear natural when they've got one photographer shooting them. They certainly don't need a crowd looking on. You go on, get the shots we need, and I'll be waiting for you when you're done." He turned back to their hosts, ready to dismiss himself. "Lucy...Cam?"

"Yes...?" Lucy looked at him expectantly.

Brody knew what she was waiting for—he was obligated to ask about Felicia. Not that he minded. He was still curious enough to strike up a conversation with her. He hoped she didn't—inadvertently or purposefully—blow his cover. He glanced around. "Do you know where I might find, uh, Fee and her husband? I've been looking for her since the ceremony ended." Though it was still early spring, he could already feel the effects of the Southern California sun. His palms were barely damp, and he could feel a bead forming on his temple. "How is she these days anyway?"

Cat raised her eyebrows. Lucy looked pointedly at him. "I'm glad you asked," she said in a low voice. "As a matter of fact—"

"Uh, sweetheart?" Cam patted his wife's arm. "Are you sure you want to—?"

"He's right," Catherine broke in. "We should probably let Fee tell him herself."

Brody looked at one, then the other. What on earth would Felicia have to tell him? Unless she—or perhaps all the Salinger sisters—actually knew and intended to confront him about his dishonesty?

"Of course, she doesn't have to talk to me," he backpedaled quickly, "if she'd rather not. Or if that would bother her husband, me being an...uh...'old boyfriend' and all."

The sisters exchanged speaking glances again.

"Good idea," Carmen said, grabbing Brody's sleeve. "Let's go."

"No, no," Lucy said, leaning forward and grabbing his other hand. "I'm sure Fee will want to see you. I'm sure that Robert," she snorted derisively, "won't care either way."

Brody eyed her curiously.

"Robert's…um, not here," Catherine said cryptically.

By this time, Brody was beginning to reconsider the wisdom of talking to Felicia at all. Obviously something was bothering Cat and Lucy. He wondered nervously what was going on. Hopefully, whatever it was, it had nothing to do with him. Besides, Felicia had already made herself scarce. If she didn't make an appearance before Carmen was done getting her photos, it would simply mean that their little tête-à-tête wasn't meant to be.

But…Brody knew in his heart he couldn't leave now. *Especially* after seeing Cat and Lucy's reactions to his harmless question. Every one of his reporter's instincts was awakened. To see the sisters interacting, one would think that they were trying to hide the fact the Felicia had been horribly burned and left with terrible scars all over her face.

Brody reflected on the recent memory of seeing Felicia standing before the assembly of guests, her face bathed in a glow of happiness for her sister. No, Fee certainly wasn't scarred. Something was different though. Something about her had changed. Her hair was shorter, but still dark and soft and swingy as he remembered. She'd filled out a bit over the years, as well, but that had made her simply look more womanly than the slight teenager she had been. There was something else, though, something that was a part of her "story." Something that eluded him.

"Jonas told me she went into the hotel," Catherine said, interrupting his thoughts. "You might wait by the main doors. I'm sure she'll be out as soon as she's done taking care of…" She paused. "Well, as soon as she's done, that's all."

"All right," Brody said, accepting her explanation at face value. It was clear that he wasn't going to get anything else out of her. "Thanks very much. And congratulations. It was good to meet you, Cam," he said, shaking the man's hand once more. "And to see you ladies again. Get great photos, Carmen," he said, nodding at his associate. "I'll meet you over by the ice sculpture when you're done."

"Yes, boss." Carmen glowered at him.

As he walked away, Brody made a mental note to ask some of his associates if such behavior was common for the fiery redhead. If so, he was definitely overpaying her.

By the time he was halfway across the verdant lawn, Brody had spied Felicia again, talking to a dark-haired young man who was holding a cooing baby. For a moment, he wondered if the guy was Fee's husband, but Cat had said that Robert wasn't there today.

The child was a particularly attractive one. Brody had seen enough infant models in his time at *Child's Play* to know a good-looking baby when he saw one. Fee seemed to be of the same opinion. As he stood watching for several minutes, she never took her eyes off the little one for more than a second. While the man held him, Felicia leaned forward, then back again, repeatedly blowing the child kisses, cooing, and playing peekaboo through her slim, tanned hands.

Looking up at Felicia adoringly, the baby made a few useless attempts to grab the pearls she wore about her neck, and he squealed happily whenever Felicia got close enough to smother his face with gentle kisses.

Brody's heart lurched in his chest. He didn't usually feel moved by such shows of affection, but…a man could really care for a woman like that. *He* certainly could have at one time. In fact, he had. Like Felicia, Lana had been wonderful with kids. And they in turn had adored her. It was unthinkable that she would go through life without becoming a mother—and Brody and she had both known it.

After he had proposed, they'd talked about having two or three children within the next six or seven years. But before they were to marry, Brody had learned about the disease he potentially carried in his blood. He'd assumed—or perhaps simply hoped—that Lana would be satisfied with adopting children. He had been willing to accept that as God's plan for his life. But Lana had tearfully told him that she needed to have her own children. Brody felt that he couldn't, shouldn't, blame her. But it didn't change the fact that he did. *If only she hadn't acted so hastily. If only we'd waited for the facts.* He'd repeatedly tortured himself with such thoughts over the years. *Maybe things would have turned out differently...*

He turned away just as one of the hotel's wait staff walked by bearing a tray filled with cups of punch. Brody easily flagged the man and snagged two. He didn't often allow himself to think about Lana...and all he'd lost. It was that infant who was getting to him, Brody decided with irritation. Felicia had triggered his reporter's instincts, and he was determined to speak with her. But now she was standing there, playing with that...that...*baby.* Babies depressed him. They had ever since that day five years ago when he'd first learned the news.

Brody shook his head. He'd vowed not to brood about it. Besides, this was neither the time nor the place. It was time to get this little greeting over with. Maybe Felicia recognized him during the ceremony; maybe she hadn't. Perhaps she realized that he was there under false pretenses; perhaps not. Either way, it was time to find out.

He stepped toward her, two crystal cups in his hands. Felicia had begun tickling the baby and, by the time Brody reached her, was laughing out loud herself—a light, bell-like sound that blended beautifully with the child's happy gurgles.

"Excuse me," Brody began, but despite his usual confidence, the words came out squeaky and high-pitched. Feeling his cheeks burn, he cleared his throat and tried again. "But could I interest the lady in a drink of punch?"

Fee finally drew her eyes away from the child, and as she turned to Brody, her jaw dropped. She started to speak, stopped to take a breath, then tried again. "I'm sorry," she said slowly. "Mr....um...I'm just sure that I know you, but I can't place from where!"

Brody tried to think of something clever to say, but he was distracted by the sight of Fee's gentle, smiling eyes and the way her lips curved gracefully upward at the sight of him. "Brody. Uh...Brody Collins," he said stupidly. *Good going, pal.* What happened to the Collins charm he'd spent his college years cultivating? The cool confidence that had made him a force to be reckoned with in the publishing world? For that matter, what had happened to his basic communication skills?

If she noticed his lack of aplomb, Felicia gave no sign of it. "Brody Collins? Oh, good grief! That's it! Of course. How silly of me! Brody, you look great," she said with feeling. But she didn't sound surprised at this, as her sisters had, for which he felt a great rush of gratitude. Felicia said it naturally and easily, as if she had found him to be attractive twelve years before. "I saw you out there today," she said unnecessarily.

"I know. I saw you notice me...and then you disappeared afterward." He laughed nervously. "I was afraid I'd scared you off."

"What? Oh! No, of course not. I just...I..." Her eyes darted in the direction of the man with the baby. "Forgive me. Elliott, this is an old friend from high school, Brody Collins. Brody, this is my almost-brother-in-law, Elliott Riley. His brother Jonas is married to Cat, and Elliott is sort of unofficially engaged to Daphne."

Almost-brother-in-law. So that was it. "Pleased to meet you." Brody reached out as if to shake hands, noticed that he still held both glasses of punch, then laughed self-consciously. "Punch?"

"No thanks." Elliott looked from Brody to Fee, then back again, as if considering something. "Actually, I was just leaving," he said. Brody knew it would be polite to ask the man to stay, but he made no move to stop him.

Neither did Fee, though for a moment she looked quite perplexed.

"Should I—?" she began, reaching out both arms, but Elliott interrupted her. "You and your friend have a nice talk. Gabe and I will go see what Jonas and the kids are up to." As he spoke, he began to retreat in the direction from which Brody had come. But before Elliott had gone even two steps, the baby in his arms—"Gabe," Brody gathered—had begun to whimper. Moments later, the whimper had progressed into a clearly audible cry. By the time the two were five feet away, the child had begun to emit a series of eardrum-piercing screams that drew stares from horrified onlookers more than twenty feet away.

"Thanks anyway, Elliott," Felicia shouted gratefully as she reached out to take the squalling infant, "but it looks like he's going to insist on having me."

As she lifted Gabe into her arms, the child silenced immediately. Brody took a long look as the situation became clear to him—Gabe was Felicia's baby. How could he have missed seeing it? He'd been so absorbed with his own thoughts, he'd hardly noticed how much the baby adored her.

Brody watched Felicia comfort her still-sniffling child. He cleared his throat and started to speak, just as Elliott shrugged and made his retreat. "Fee," Brody began, then stopped as the nickname fell awkwardly from his lips. "That is, Felicia—"

He looked down to see that he was still holding the two cups of fizzy, candy pink punch. He had no desire to drink it, and Fee clearly had her arms full. The only way she could sip from the cup was if Brody held it up to her lips. And though he was willing to do so, the action would certainly not be welcomed or appropriate. Brody turned aside for a moment and deposited the cups on a nearby table. Suddenly he felt the urge to come clean. He should tell Felicia about the fib he'd told her sister. If they were angry with him, so be it. He'd deal with the consequences like a grownup. But he couldn't stand to be so deceitful.

"Yes?" Obviously the seriousness of his tone had not escaped her. Fee's finely arched eyebrows furrowed together over her nose while baby Gabe reached out one sausagelike arm and wrapped a finger around her string of pearls.

"Look, there's something I should tell youuuu—oof!" Brody jerked his head downward to identify the small missile that had impacted his leg. He caught sight of a small tow-headed boy—six or seven years old, he guessed—who had brushed past him and latched his arms securely around Felicia's legs.

"Mama, can I have candy?" the missile demanded.

"Can *we* have candy?" A dark-haired girl who looked like a miniature Felicia emerged from the crowd and grabbed at Fee's free hand.

"Well, I..." Felicia looked from the children to Brody and gave him a rueful smile. "Sorry for the interruption, Brody. These are my children, Clifford and Dinah."

Brody swallowed hard. *Three.* She had three children.

Dinah looked at Brody suspiciously. "Mama? Can we?"

"Can you what, sweetheart?" Felicia looked confused.

The little girl folded her arms across her chest and let out a deep sigh. "*Candy.* Weren't you listening? We asked if we can have some candy. There are mints on the table with the cake."

"Sorry, love. I'm a bit distracted at the moment." Between seeing him, dealing with Gabe, and talking to the older children, Brody noticed, Felicia did seem a bit scattered. "I'm talking to an old friend from high school. Kids, this is Brody."

"Hi, Dinah," Brody said, sounding more cheerful than he felt. "You did a great job as flower girl today. I didn't realize you were Fee's daughter, though I should have; you look just like her. My mind must have been on other things."

"I was wonderful," Clifford announced, turning his bright blue eyes to Brody for confirmation. "Mama said so."

"Mama's right. You were *the* man," Brody confirmed. "Give me five." The picture of youthful joy, Clifford ran over and slapped Brody's outstretched palm.

"The candy?" Dinah insisted, giving Brody a disapproving look.

"Oh, all right, sweetheart. But just five butter mints each. There's going to be a buffet later, and then cake." Clifford's eyes lit up at his mother's words. "I don't want you to fill up on too much junk. Remember how sick you got that time your father let you have Red Vines, soda, and popcorn at the movie theater?" Brody winced as she uttered the word "father." "You were up half the night, throwing—"

"Mama!" Dinah looked embarrassed. She gave Brody another look of distrust then grabbed at her mother's hand again. "Come with us to get the mints."

"No, sweetie," Fee said gently but firmly. "Not right now. I'm talking with—"

"Please, Mama." It was clear that Dinah had no intention of giving in. "You've got to come. I *need* you," she said, pulling out the big guns.

Clifford stood staring at his feet, as if considering something.

"Dinah," Fee said heavily. "I said not right now. In a little bit." She threw Brody another apologetic glance. "I'm so sorry," she said. "Normally the kids are so well-behaved. I guess it's all the excitement—"

"Mama," Clifford said, tugging on her skirt, his decision made. "Can I have cake now?"

"No, Clifford. The cake is for later. Auntie Lucy and Uncle Cam have to cut it first. You can have five mints though. Dinah will help you."

"No, I won't," Dinah declared, planting her tiny hands on her almost nonexistent hips. "*You* help him."

"Dinah—"

"I...WANT...CAKE!" Apparently frustrated that he had not yet gotten his grimy little hands on the candy he'd been promised, Clifford tried another approach and began to screech out his demand. Felicia, Brody noticed, looked as if she was trying very hard not to cry. Every instinct within him urged Brody to take Gabe out of her arms to relieve her stress, even if just for a moment. But he hadn't held a baby since the old *Child's Play* days. And besides, he thought grimly, it wasn't his place.

"Mama, you have to come *now*."

"CAKE...CAKE...CAKE...CAKE!"

"All right, you two," Fee said, her tone deadly serious. "I'm going to count to three. One..."

"WANT CAKE!!!!!!" Clifford yelled.

"Two..."

"No, Mama. *Please just come*..." Dinah pleaded.

Felicia opened her mouth, her tongue on the back of her teeth to form the word "three," when suddenly Gabe pulled back one chubby arm and with perfect timing broke the tiny thread that held the string of pearls around her neck. Brody watched, stunned, as white pearls went flying through the air. His ears filled with a sound like hail striking stones as dozens of smooth, round beads fell onto the cement patio beneath them.

Realizing at last that they had perhaps pushed too far, Dinah and Clifford both froze. Fee, too, remained momentarily immobile. Only Gabe moved as he drew one tiny fist up to his mouth.

Instantly—instinctively—Brody broke into action. In a split second, he had pulled the baby's hand back, inserted one hooked finger past the child's lips, and conducted a thorough sweep of Gabe's mouth before pulling his own hand away.

Startled, the baby just stared at him at first. But as Brody stepped back, Gabe started to howl.

"What did you do *that* for?" Dinah asked, horrified. She looked at Brody as if he had just slapped her baby brother.

"He might have choked on a pearl," Brody explained, answering Felicia's own questioning look with an apologetic smile. Years ago, he'd written an article for *Child's Play* about choking hazards for babies. "I hope I didn't alarm you."

"No, of course not. I…" Felicia gave him a tremulous smile of her own. "Thank you. That was…wonderful. It didn't even occur to me that Gabe might…I mean…" Felicia looked down at the crying baby in her arms and shuddered, as if imagining the outcome that might have been. When she turned back to Brody her eyes were two small, watery gray seas. "What I'm trying to say is, I'm grateful. Really. Terribly grateful." She did not reach out to touch him in any way, but the intimate expression of gratitude in her eyes made Brody feel as though she had.

"Come on, Clifford," Dinah whispered loudly. "We'd better go find Uncle Jonas."

"You do that, Dinah," Felicia said wearily. "He's over there by Elliott. How'd you two ever slip away from him in the first place? Look there…he's looking all over for you. I'm going to watch and see that you go all the way over to him. Take your brother's hand now. I'll talk to you later about your behavior this afternoon."

"Yes ma'am." Dinah hung her head, obediently taking Clifford by the wrist and leading him away.

Felicia shifted Gabe's weight on her hip and awkwardly tried to lower herself to the ground to collect her pearls.

"No, no," Brody said, waving her back. "I'll get them." He knelt down and began collecting the creamy white beads. Where on earth was this Robert character anyway? he thought angrily. Three kids were a lot to handle under the best of circumstances. What on earth could be so important that it would induce the man to leave his wife alone to care for Dinah, Clifford, and Gabe while at the same time fulfilling her bridesmaid's duties? He remembered what Deke had said about the man being "a bit of a jerk," and he felt very sorry indeed. Within a minute or so, he felt relatively certain that he'd found all the pearls. As he stood, he caught Felicia wiping at one eye with the back of her hand.

"Are you okay?" he asked in concern, repressing the urge to wrap a comforting arm around the woman's shoulder.

"Sorry. It's silly, I know." She smiled timidly through her tears. "It just seems symbolic somehow, this necklace breaking. It used to mean a lot to me. But that was a long time ago."

"I...see," Brody said, even though he didn't. He watched as she took the handful of pearls from him and half bent, Gabe still on one hip, to slip the beads into a side pocket of the blue diaper bag that sat on the ground just five feet away. She looked exhausted.

"Is there someone I can get to help you?" Brody mumbled, backing away awkwardly. Where was Catherine? Where'd that Elliott fellow go? Felicia needed help, but he certainly wasn't the appropriate person to give it to her.

Felicia took a deep breath. "Not anymore," she said quietly, turning to face him.

Brody shook his head, not understanding. "Excuse me? I didn't quite catch that. It sounded as though you said, 'not anymore.'"

"I did." Fee pressed her lips softly to her baby's brow and closed her eyes. Her lips trembled slightly, then she said in a low, clear voice. "I'm a single mom. There isn't anyone else except my sisters and their husbands. My kids are all I have."

"You're...what?" Brody still wasn't sure he was hearing her right. "But Robert—"

"Robert's gone," Felicia said softly, meeting his eyes. There was no mistaking the anguish he saw there. "I never thought I'd hear myself say this, but...I'm divorced, Brody. My husband left me and the kids a year ago. My marriage is over."

Over... The word carried such finality. Brody knew how it felt to lose someone before getting married; he could only imagine how heart wrenching it would be to go through the agony of divorce. His heart went out to her—then nearly stopped when she dropped her next bombshell.

"He ran away with an actress...from that TV show *Itsy-Bitsy*. You know, the one about the swimsuit models? The title is supposed to refer to their bikinis, but I think it's a statement about the producers' minds!"

"Robert did what?" Brody's insides were swirling with such a rush of thoughts and feelings, he nearly missed what came next.

"He ran off with that starlet Tiffany Diamond. He'd treated her one afternoon at the hospital when she came in with a twisted ankle. I'm a single mom. And," Felicia said, speaking with the complete and utter conviction of one who had gone through gruesome torture and had no intention of going through such tribulation again, "that's the way it's gonna stay, because I promise you this: I will *never* fall in love again!"

Six

"*Robert's gone…. He ran away with an actress…that starlet Tiffany Diamond…*" Brody turned the words over and over in his mind, examining each one as if it were an exquisite and precious gem that had miraculously fallen into his possession.

Tiffany Diamond had run off with the doctor who'd tended her sprained ankle? So that was it! For the past six months the Hollywood gossip mill had been fairly humming with rumors about the actress's abrupt split from her boyfriend, Weevil, lead singer for the grunge band Sludge. Several tabloids had hinted that Tiffany had a secret new beau, but so far the reports had been nothing more than speculation.

It would be, once printed, the undisputed scoop of the year.

Like a dog lurking under the Thanksgiving dinner table, Brody practically salivated. He felt the unmistakable rush of adrenaline that had flooded his veins so often early in his reporting career. Forget the Rent-a-Yenta… Now *this* was a story! A depressing and somewhat tasteless story, to be sure. But the stories themselves had never much interested him during his term at *California Dream*. He was drawn instead to the challenge of being the first to break the news. Any news. And this news was news of the most marketable sort.

It couldn't have been more like a soap opera if it had been scripted that way. The actress and the emergency-room doctor… Brody wasn't a bit surprised. He'd met Tiff several times on the Hollywood circuit; she had a reputation as a blatant flirt who knew what she wanted and wasted no time in going after it. She'd been under consideration recently for a plum part on a new television hospital drama for twentysomethings, *Intensive Care*. Perhaps she had been caught up in the idea of dating a physician herself, hoping that she would glean some information or pick up some medical terminology that would improve her chances of landing the role. He imagined the bossy diva calling her suitor on a sleek cell phone, her tiny foot tapping impatiently. "Robert? You're five minutes late. You'd better get here *stat!*"

It wasn't uncommon for famous celebrities to hook up with individuals from the private sector. He'd seen stars pairing off like animals to the ark with their physical trainers, bodyguards, chauffeurs…even their children's nannies. At first he'd found it chilling the way many of these individuals took their marriage vows so lightly. How quick they were to abandon ship…and hope. After years of immersing himself in that culture, however, it hardly fazed Brody anymore. This realization surprised and saddened him.

"What kind of name is 'Tiffany Diamond' anyway?" Felicia was grumbling. She shifted Gabe from her right shoulder to her left. "It sounds like a lamp-size ring or something you'd buy at Saks Fifth Avenue."

"Actually," Brody said absently, scratching behind his left ear, "if it makes you feel any better, her given name was Inga Snavelly." He was so busy plotting out how he'd convince Felicia to give him exclusive rights to the story, he nearly missed the look of surprise she threw him. "I mean…," he hedged, trying to keep his expression blank, "that's what I hear. I read it somewhere." Technically, he'd read it in his own magazine after he'd written it, but that was beside the point.

Careful, Collins,…careful, he reminded himself. He would hardly win points with Felicia now by pointing out that he actually knew, much less socialized with, the woman she had every reason to consider "the enemy."

For that matter he wouldn't exactly endear himself to her by bringing to her attention the fact that he was the editor of *California Dream,* one of the magazines that had, sadly enough, helped further Tiffany Diamond's career. Better to ease into that revelation slowly, after he had convinced Felicia that he was on her side—which, he reflected, he actually was. Story or no story, he felt compassion toward any woman or man who had lost a love, particularly under circumstances as ugly as these.

Brody looked at Fee sideways. The revelation of Tiffany's given name had caused the corners of her lips to curve slightly upward, but the smile did not reach her eyes. Feeling a twinge of guilt, he realized that he'd been so caught up in his own windfall, he hadn't even noticed how difficult revealing this truth to him had been for her.

"Oh, Felicia…" He reached out to touch her, briefly laying a comforting hand on her shoulder. The feel of her soft, warm skin startled him and caused him to quickly draw his hand back. It had been a long time since he had touched a woman tenderly. "I'm so sorry," he said in a low voice. "This must be…" He tried to find the words. "…awful for you," he finished awkwardly, not knowing what he could say that would reassure her.

"Thank you. It is." She didn't try to sugarcoat it, Brody noticed. He appreciated such honesty. Giving a self-conscious little laugh, she reached up and wiped at her eyes again. "Always crying, that's me!" she said. "You must be ready to escape by now. I imagine you'd rather be talking to an adult who doesn't burst into tears every thirty seconds or so."

"I have no desire to speak to any such person," Brody said firmly. He wasn't about to go anywhere now. "I'm perfectly content here with you." What he wasn't so thrilled with was the noise of the crowd that was growing thicker around them. Felicia would never let her guard down in that mob; even if she did share further details, he was afraid they'd be drowned out by the loud voices of joyful celebrants. "I think we're positioned a bit too close to the food and drink. Would you like to go for a little walk and get some air?"

Felicia paused for a split second. "Actually, that would be nice," she said gratefully and started to reach for Gabe's things.

"I can get it," Brody said and a moment later had the cheerful denim diaper bag thrown over the shoulder of his Armani jacket.

"At the risk of sounding like a broken record, thanks. Again." Fee let him lead the way through a rough-hewn oak gate that led from the courtyard where the reception was being held into another portion of the meticulously landscaped grounds. On the far side of the pink-washed stucco garden wall, they found a smaller, more intimate garden that was also open for use by the hotel's patrons. It had not yet been discovered by most of the wedding guests, however, and was, as a result, infinitely less crowded. In this portion of the hotel grounds, too, the garden was in glorious bloom, and Felicia gratefully took long, deep drafts of the fragrant air. "Much better," she said and looked as though she meant it.

Brody led her to a small wrought-iron bench and jerked his chin at it. "How's this?"

"Perfect." She settled herself against the seat, Gabe tucked against her shoulder.

For several minutes, she and Brody sat side by side, listening only to the trickle of water flowing from a nearby fountain and an occasional matching gurgle from Gabe. As a general rule, Brody made a practice of filling awkward silences by barking out commands to his employees or by impressing acquaintances with his charm. At this moment, however, he felt neither charming nor in command. He felt on edge, anxious to press Felicia for information. But she was obviously skittish. It would be better if he were to wait until she was ready to open up of her own accord.

After a couple of minutes of relative quiet, Gabe began to whine loudly. Fee reached into the bag at her feet, rummaged through it, and pulled out a cracker, which she handed to her baby. With a drooly smile, the child accepted the treat and wrapped his lips around its creamy white corners.

"He *always* wants to put something in his mouth. But then I guess you already noticed that," Fee said wryly.

"He seems like a good baby," Brody observed, not inclined to hold the necklace incident against the bright-eyed infant.

"Oh, he is." Fee smiled at Gabe fondly. "Sometimes I still can't believe I have him. Robert left not long after Gabe was conceived. It makes me ill to think that he might never have been born at all." She paled. "As it was, I almost lost him. He was born prematurely and there were complications. He's fine now, but at the time he spent several days on a ventilator. I couldn't even hold him."

"I've seen those contraptions." Brody remembered doing a feature for *Child's Play* on the complications of premature birth. "They look sort of like a terrarium, except there's a naked baby inside instead of an iguana. Very *Wild Kingdom*."

"I'm afraid I don't see any resemblance between my child and a lizard," Fee said delicately. Her eyebrows were arched in disapproval, but her lips twitched as if she might be holding back a smirk.

"Well, of course not," Brody said generously. "I'm sure you had other things on your mind at the time, what with giving birth and all. Women tend to get really caught up in all that. All they can think about is themselves. It's 'my contractions this' and 'my labor pains' that. Everything is me, me, me. I don't mind telling you, it's rather annoying for the rest of us," he said seriously. Felicia actually laughed outright then, a sound that gave Brody a great deal of satisfaction.

He eyed the baby, fully intending not to find him particularly appealing. Gabe gazed back at him with wise old eyes, as if he instinctively knew this and was giving Brody a brief window of opportunity during which to change his mind. Brody cracked a smile and poked a piece of gummed-up cracker that had fallen onto the child's pudgy chin back into Gabe's mouth. "Gabe, huh?" he said politely, hoping the conversation would spin naturally in the direction of Felicia's children and, ultimately, her former husband, without his having to force it.

"It means 'hero of God.'" Fee informed him. "I hadn't really settled on a boy's name. Of course, it's hard to tell by an ultrasound, but the doctor had thought I was probably having a girl. But when Gabe was born, the name *Gabriel* just seemed to fit him perfectly. Talk about 'A Boy Named Sue…'" She laughed. "Gabe was almost a boy named Anna."

"That's the girl's name you had picked out?"

Fee nodded. "I was going to name my baby after my mother," she said wistfully. "In fact, I'd wanted that to be Dinah's name, but Robert didn't like it. And if Robert didn't like something…" Her voice trailed off.

"What's your mother like?" Brody asked, hoping to turn the tide of conversation to more pleasant subjects. He wanted— needed—to hear the whole story about Robert and Tiffany, but Felicia looked like she was going to burst into tears at any moment. If she did, she'd probably run off to the bathroom to compose herself, and he might never have the chance to speak to her again.

Felicia looked at him sorrowfully, and it struck Brody then that hers was one of the saddest, and most complicated, faces he had ever seen. This was the missing piece that had eluded him during the wedding ceremony; this was what had changed about her since high school. No longer was Felicia the perky, boy-crazed cheerleader he had initially admired, then later ignored out of a sense of self-protection. More than a decade had passed, and in that time there had grown within her a well of sadness that gave Felicia-the-woman a depth that had been missing, or at the very least hidden, in Felicia-the-girl.

"I never really got to know my mother," she said slowly, plucking at the threads of Gabe's receiving blanket. "Not really. She died when I was eight. It was my sisters who got me through. We didn't have a mom to teach us how to wear makeup and how to act with boys...all that. But we sort of helped each other." She shrugged. "They were always really important to me. I guess that's why I wanted to give Dinah a sister. But Gabe..." Her eyes sparkled. "He's perfect. Dinah and Clifford both love having a little brother. I don't have a single complaint. Not one. Not about Gabe anyway."

Brody set his mouth in a firm line. It wasn't too late for her. Fee had plenty of time left to have another baby, if she wanted to, and he was certain from her expression that she did. He couldn't blame her. Seeing her with Gabe made him more than half want a child of his own. He shook the thought away angrily. *Forget it, Collins. You know it's not going to happen.* Though genetic testing for the gene that carries Huntington's disease was now readily available, Brody had never been able to muster the courage to be tested. To have it confirmed that he was, in fact, a carrier for the disease would be devastating. To learn that he was not—and that his future with Lana was lost for nothing—would be even more tragic. Even the news that Abby was HD-free did not sway him. Brody was not prepared to get his hopes up. He'd decided long ago that it was better not to know.

Felicia turned her pained gray eyes upon his. "I'm sorry to dump all this on you. It's been a long time since I've had a fresh ear to bend; my sisters have heard my sob story a million times by now." She sat up straight and hoisted Gabe up farther on her shoulder. "I'm tough though. I'll make it. I've come to accept the facts of my life," she said, "even if I don't like them. Robert's getting remarried soon…"

Brody looked at her sharply but held his tongue.

"He's moving on with his life. And I'll just have to do the same."

"Fee…" He could think of nothing comforting to say. He knew he should ask about Robert's remarriage, but it seemed too callous.

"You must think I'm such a loser," she said, brushing back a lock of dark hair that had come untucked from behind her ear.

Brody blinked at her. "Why on earth would you say something like that?"

"Well, I mean, come on. It's one thing to fail at a job or drop out of a class or something like that. It's quite another to lose the love of the man who was supposed to spend the rest of his life with you. You must think I'm a pathetic person to have driven my husband away."

"I don't think that at all. I don't think you've driven anyone anywhere."

"Well," she said glumly, "that makes one of us."

"You don't really mean that." Brody stared at her. He was just beginning to see how her husband's desertion had impacted this woman's self-esteem. "Every year there are millions of women who are abandoned by their husbands—and, for that matter, men who are abandoned by their wives." *Not to mention fiancées who leave their boyfriends.* "You can't honestly think that that's necessarily the fault of the one who's been left?"

"Not rationally, no. Of course I realize divorce is a complicated thing. Everyone keeps telling me it's rarely one thing that causes a husband and wife to split. But I can't help but think that maybe if I hadn't been so...so..."

"So what?"

"Oh, I don't know!" Felicia sighed. "Maybe that's the problem. If I only knew what I'd done wrong, maybe I could let go of this whole mess. It wasn't for lack of trying, I'll tell you that. For years I thought Robert would stay if I could just be all the things he said he wanted: a well-dressed, presentable, socially competent wife to take to hospital functions; an efficient home manager; a good mother to his kids."

"That Robert sounds like quite the romantic," Brody said dryly.

"Yes, well... He probably *was* more interested in control than romance," Fee admitted. "Those other things were the ones that he said mattered to him. But ultimately, they weren't enough to make him—or me—happy. Sometimes I wonder if he didn't just get bored with me," she said quietly. "Once he'd turned me into what he wanted—for the most part anyway—I wasn't a challenge for him anymore. There wasn't any mystery. I can't really blame him for not loving me anymore. I've hardly felt loving toward myself." She shifted Gabe from her left shoulder to her right. "Maybe because I don't know who I am."

"Or maybe because you don't believe you're worth loving," Brody suggested. "You've always seemed to want guys to like you," he observed. "But have you ever stopped to think if any of them were the sort of guys who deserved you?"

"Ouch." Felicia blinked at him. "Come on. Don't hold back, Brody. Tell me what you really think of me. We've been re-acquainted again for…what? Fifteen minutes now? Certainly you know me well enough to form a stronger opinion than that."

"Your point—and sarcasm—are duly noted." He gave her a lopsided grin. "I didn't mean to offend you."

"Oh, you didn't." She sighed. "Not really. My sisters have said pretty much the same thing. It didn't make much sense to me back in high school. I assumed that every guy had good intentions, and I couldn't imagine anyone deliberately hurting me. Nowadays, it's the other way around; I can't imagine a man not hurting me. Even more fantastic is the idea of one actually taking care of me in any way. I've more or less given up on that idea."

"Maybe you should start by taking care of yourself," Brody suggested. "You're obviously an incredible mother. But someone's got to take care of Felicia, too."

"I'm fine. God's taking care of me," Felicia said, patting Gabe softly on the back. She sounded only partially convinced.

"Of course he is." The comment struck him as both appealing and somewhat naive, yet on a deeper level, he knew he still believed it. "But you need to do your part too. Tell me, when was the last time you took an afternoon to do something special for yourself?"

Fee stared at him as if he'd asked her when was the last time she'd discovered a new constellation with her telescope. "An afternoon to myself? You've got to be joking. Perhaps you haven't noticed: I have three children."

"Okay…an hour or two. Your other kids are in school, aren't they? And you can't tell me this one doesn't nap."

"Mumm-mumm!" Gabe answered on his own behalf.

"Of course he naps. All babies nap. But that's the only time I have to clean up the house, pay the bills, do my exercises…"

"Felicia," Brody said sternly. Years ago, during his years at *Child's Play*, he'd written several articles about the risk of mothers burning out. "There will always be bills to pay, dishes to clean, fat cells to do battle with—"

"Who said anything about fat cells?" she said defensively.

Brody ignored her. "Those things will always be there. That's the nature of life. But does even one of the tasks you mentioned feed your soul?" As if Brody ever took the time to feed his own soul!

"Well, no. But—"

"Well, no, but nothing."

"All right, all right," Fee said wearily. "I get the point. But you have no idea how hard it is for me now, without adding anything to my list. Raising three children is more than a full-time job, even for a woman with a husband to help out. With Robert gone, there's hardly enough of me to go around." Felicia shifted Gabe from one shoulder to the other. "For as long as I can remember, I've tried to be the perfect wife. Now Lucy says I *need* a wife."

"Excuse me?"

"You know, somebody to help me do the housework, take care of the kids… Not a wife, exactly, but someone who will do all those thankless jobs a wife and mother is almost always responsible for. Sort of a nanny-slash-housekeeper-slash-cook-slash-gardener-slash-"

"Stop already. I get the slash-picture. On behalf of men everywhere, I stand shamed."

"This is not," Felicia told him sternly, "about shame. It's about survival. I'm beginning to think Lucy's right. I'm going to have to hire someone to come and help out, if for no other reason than preserving what's left of my sanity. I've thought about taking a part-time job. A little extra money sure would be nice. But it's not really about the money. I'll admit, I'm starved for a little adult interaction. It wasn't so hard when Robert was at home. But now, it's not unheard of for me to go a day or more without speaking to anyone over the age of ten. I'll definitely need help at home, though, if I take on a job. That makes it a less profitable proposition, though, so I couldn't pay anyone much. We've got a guesthouse out back that a childcare worker could stay in for free, as part of their pay. Still, I don't suppose anyone would do it for so little money." She sounded despondent.

"You never know…," Brody hedged. If he could use his *Child's Play* connections to find someone who could help Felicia, she might be more inclined to give him the rights to her story. His friend Adam probably had access to a database filled with the names of local cooks and nannies.

"Don't you tease me!" She warned, eyeing him suspiciously. "Everyone's been telling me it's almost impossible to find good help. I've been so discouraged about it, I haven't even tried yet."

"In my professional opinion," Brody said, thinking about all the insights he'd gleaned over the years while running *Child's Play*, "there are plenty of qualified childcare workers out there. You just need to know where to look."

"Your professional opinion, huh?" Felicia looked at him doubtfully, as if wondering what sort of background he could have that would make him an expert on the subject. For a moment Brody considered explaining, but decided to delay just a few minutes longer.

"That's right. In fact, I may have just the person in mind." He didn't. But it wouldn't take long to find someone qualified once he put his mind to it. By the look in Felicia's wide gray eyes, he could tell that he had her.

"Don't *even* kid about something like that!" she breathed. "Only a fairy godmother could perform such a miracle."

"A fairy godmother," Brody told her firmly, folding his arms across his broad chest, "I am not."

"No," Felicia agreed, patting Gabe between his tiny shoulder blades. "You're more like Prince Charming." As soon as the words were out of her mouth, her cheeks turned a bright crimson. "Of course, Prince Charmings are a bit overrated. I don't have any use for one myself. Uh...no offense intended."

"None taken," Brody assured her, his lips twitching in amusement. "If anyone asked me, however, I'd have to say you seem to be doing pretty well in that department."

"Huh? What do you mean?" Fee stared at him blankly.

"That guy who walked you down the aisle. He was certainly, uh, attentive. You can't tell me that you didn't notice?"

"Notice?" Fee blew a raspberry. Gabe lifted his head off her shoulder and looked at his mother intently, as if he was studying how to do the procedure properly. "I've been trying to forget ever since. I don't know *why* Cam had that guy as his groomsman, unless it was a family obligation thing. I had no idea being single made a woman such a target. I hadn't even met the guy before this wedding; I have three children, for crying out loud! And he was determined to... Well, I have no idea what he was determined to do, but I'm certainly glad I never found out. The nerve!" She squeezed her baby tight. "And he didn't even like kids! Can you believe it?"

"It must be reassuring, though, to know that men are still interested in pursuing you?"

"They can pursue me till their feet bleed," she said with a vengeance. "It won't change a thing. I'm not interested."

"But surely you don't intend to stay single forever?"

"I've had enough of men for a lifetime. Even if I wanted to," she said, looking at him a bit sadly, "I'm sure all the good ones are taken by now. No, Brody. It was nice of you to say that, but I'll never remarry. I don't even want to get involved again. I'm in no shape to be in a relationship. I pity the poor guy who'd even try to pursue me."

Brody regarded her with a feeling of compassion. *So do I...* He couldn't really blame her. He had the same attitude toward relationships himself. Though he couldn't help but wonder if his own argument sounded just as weak in other peoples' ears as Felicia's sounded in his.

Twenty feet away, the carved gate swept open a crack, and the sound of laughing partygoers grew louder in Brody's ears. A second later, a familiar face peered through the doorway.

"Ah...there you are!" Carmen breathed. Within seconds, she had crossed the space that separated her and Brody. "Naughty boy, disappearing on me like that!" She threw a conspiratorial look at Felicia. "Men," she said with a high-pitched little giggle. "Don't you just love them?"

Fee's lips twitched slightly. "Well, as a matter of fact...," she began dryly.

"Something tells me this is a conversation that I'd prefer not be held in my presence," Brody interrupted.

Fee laughed.

Carmen's eyes narrowed. Brody could tell she hated not being in on the joke. "Come on," she said and grabbed him by the hand. "They're getting ready to make toasts. After that we can be on our way."

We? Brody lifted his eyebrows. Clearly, riding with Carmen had been a mistake. "I'll be there in a moment." He kept his hand planted firmly on his knee, refusing to be led away.

"But...the toasts are going to begin any minute," Carmen said plaintively.

"Well, you don't want to miss that. *Do* you?"

Felicia looked nervously from one to the other. "It's all right, Brody. I really should get back too. I'd like to make a toast. I haven't even spoken to Lucy since the ceremony."

"Of course," he said, meeting her eyes. "But I'd like to speak with you for just one more moment, if you don't mind."

Fee looked helplessly at Carmen, who appeared quite pained. "Well…"

"Go on, Carmen," Brody ordered his photographer. "I'll be there in a minute. Make sure you don't miss anything."

"Oh, all *right*." Anchoring one hand around the strap of the camera she'd slung over her shoulder, Carmen flounced back to the gate and, without so much as a polite "see you in a while," was gone.

"Wow." Fee let out a long whistle. "Brody," she said, looking after Carmen, "I really don't think it's a good idea to—" She patted Gabe soothingly on the back as she stood.

"I know, I know," he interrupted, rising to stand beside her. "You need to get back to your sister. I don't want to keep you from the party. I just wanted to say one more thing, concerning what we were talking about before." He racked his brain for something he could say that would cause her to trust him. But all he could think of was, "Fee, you know, you deserve to be happy."

She nodded miserably and clutched her child even tighter. "And what about you, Brody?"

"What do you mean?" He eyed her warily. "What about me?"

"Are *you* happy?"

Brody had no intention of letting her turn this interview around to him, but the inquiry caught him off guard. *Was* he happy? He was busy, certainly. Financially secure, prestigious, and successful, to boot. Since he'd taken the helm of *California Dream*, all that had seemed to be enough.

More or less.

"We weren't talking about me," he hedged.

"I know."

"So why did you ask?"

"I don't know. I'm just…concerned, I guess. You and your wife seem so…" She bit her lip and started to walk away. "I'm sorry. It's none of my business."

My wife? He gaped at her, fisheyed. *What is this woman, crazy?*

"I didn't mean to make her feel jealous," Felicia threw over her shoulder. "It was dumb of me…and you, too. I should have known better. I mean, it was good of you to be concerned about me, to listen to me ramble on about my problems and all. But you really shouldn't go off with another woman like that, even if it is just an old schoolmate. It's bound to make her feel bad. You should consider how she feels. And how your kids feel, if you have any." Her words sounded two-thirds self-righteous, one-third guilty.

Kids? Brody was still trying to figure out where and when he had obtained himself a wife. "You mean *Carmen?*" He jogged after her. When he'd come full circle around front to face her, Felicia did not stop, and he had to keep walking backward to continue speaking to her face to face. He tried not to laugh at the mere idea of what Felicia had suggested. If he ever did get married—and he was certain that he wouldn't—Brody was sure he'd pick someone honest and loving and gentle and sweet. Carmen was the least wifely woman he had ever met.

"Do you have any other wives?" Fee asked dryly.

"I," Brody told her firmly, "do not have any wives, thank you very much."

That stopped her. "You don't?" Felicia ceased walking, but she appeared poised to start up again at any moment.

"Look," he directed, jabbing out his left hand for her to inspect. "No ring."

"Humph," she said, her eyes narrowing to silver slits. "That doesn't mean anything."

"No tan line either, where the ring would have been."

"So? Lots of married men don't even wear a wedding ring."

Brody let out an exasperated sigh. "Would you like a notarized affidavit? Or perhaps my mother's phone number? I assure you, she would be more than happy to launch into a lengthy soliloquy about my state of singleness. Watch out though. She might try to talk *you* into going out with me." Felicia's cheeks turned the color of cranberries. "It's nothing personal," he assured her quickly, noticing her discomfort. "She's just desperate for me to find a wife."

Felicia's face quickly turned a dull gray-white. "Gee. Thanks a lot." As she stomped off, Gabe peeked over the slope of her shoulder. Brody could have sworn the boy was laughing at him.

Oh, for crying out loud. "Fee—" For the second time in as many minutes, Brody found himself trailing after her like a deserted child. He wasn't used to being on the defensive, and he didn't like the feel of it one bit.

Fee slipped easily through the carved gate and almost disappeared into the dense crowd.

"Wait a minute." Brody managed to catch her by the arm. "Now be fair," he said angrily. "I wasn't trying to insult you. I was just trying to defend myself against your accusation, which, by the way, I did not appreciate one bit. I'll admit, however, that I didn't stop to think what I was saying. I can see that I was very rude, and I'm sorry."

Felicia's eyes pooled with tears, but she did not pull away.

"Now," he said carefully, "if you'll let me explain?"

She nodded once, slowly.

"All right then." Brody released her arm and breathed easier. "For the record, I am not married. Carmen is my…" He searched for the right word. He could hardly say "photographer" or "associate" until after he had explained the real reason why he was at the wedding. "…an acquaintance," he finished. "I am not a cheating louse, and contrary to what you believe, I'd like to state also for the record that not all men are jerks." Felicia made a face as if she had just touched her tongue to something bitter, but she did not say anything. "Neither do I have children," Brody continued, "as you suggested."

"But the way you were with Gabe and the pearls…" Felicia protested.

"Believe me," he assured her. "I do not have children. I just happen to know a lot about them."

"Why?" Felicia shifted Gabe so that he was facing forward. The child waved one arm aimlessly. Brody ignored him.

"Because it's my business to know," he said. *Or at least it used to be.* He kept his tone noncommittal, trying not to give away too much too soon. "For five years, I made my living off of kids. The care and handling of children was pretty much my world—or at least my means of support. That's not what I'm doing these days; I have another, uh, project I'm working on at the moment." After easing into an explanation of his work at *Child's Play*, Brody decided, then he could segue into telling Fee about his current role at *Dream*.

"Excuse me, sir?" a stiff voice intoned from behind his shoulder.

"Hmm. What?" Brody turned to see a man of about twenty-two years of age dressed in formal attire, holding out a tray stacked with champagne flutes.

"For the toasts," the young man suggested. "It's sparkling cider."

"Thank you." Brody quickly snagged two and handed one to Fee as a peace offering. "At the moment though," he said to her, picking up where he left off, "I'm at a slightly different place in my life. It's a long story, but I'd like to expl—"

Just then, Gabe threw his entire body forward like a kamikaze stunt man, causing Fee to jerk her right hand forward—the hand holding her glass of cider—and try to catch him.

"Aaaiiiiii!" Gabe squealed with joy.

"Aaaaaaiiiiiiiii!" Brody cried as the contents of Fee's champagne flute spilled onto his five-hundred-dollar sleeve.

"Ooohhhhhh," Fee breathed, making a face. "Brody, I am sooo sorry!"

"Don't worry about it," he said, sounding as magnanimous as possible for a man dripping with sticky cider. "It's not the first time it's happened today." *And the way things are going, it probably won't be the last.* Felicia passed off her nearly empty glass to a passing waitress, grabbed a stack of pink paper napkins from her, and began patting helplessly at his jacket. She stopped after a moment and looked closer at a hardened blob that he had apparently missed when cleaning off his sleeve.

"Is that…applesauce?" She blinked at him.

Applesauce, the lunch choice of urban professionals everywhere! Brody suppressed a groan. "Kids," he quipped with a shrug and a self-conscious laugh, wishing he really could pass the blame that easily. Abby was the youngest "kid" he was intimately acquainted with, but there was no reason Fee had to know that.

Felicia gave him an odd look, as if she were trying to figure something out about him. But before she could speak, their attention was caught by the sound of silver clanging against crystal. Brody turned to see Campbell stepping up to a microphone in front of the head table, which was draped in linen and positioned on a platform at the far end of the garden.

"'Scuse me, everybody!" the groom called, his voice blaring from two immense, jet black speakers. On the word "everybody," a high-pitched feedback squeal pierced the air, causing half the crowd to cover their ears with one or both hands, and virtually every person present to pinch his or her face in pain. "Sorry about that!" Cam grinned, taking his volume level down a notch, while nearby, the sound man began furiously adjusting knobs.

"Thanks for coming, everybody," Campbell said, reaching out to squeeze the fingers of his bride, who stood behind him—a graceful white shadow. "In just a moment, we're going to make a few toasts, so grab a glass from one of the wait staff, and we'll get started in about five minutes!"

The crowd, which had grown silent during Cam's announcement, began to buzz again as people moved to get their drinks.

"I'd better get up there," Felicia said to Brody. But she stood there looking at him as if she did not really want to go. "It's been good talking with you." She spoke with finality, as if they were saying their last good-byes.

"Fee…," Brody began, then stopped. He knew he had to ask her for the rights to her story. Now. But he couldn't bring himself to do it…not yet.

"Yes?" She looked at him eagerly, as if she was hoping for something.

"I…" He thought for a moment. "What are you going to do now?" The question slipped out without his even realizing he was thinking it. "With your life, I mean."

What's the matter with you, Collins? he cursed himself. *Get in, get what you need, then get out again. He was messing up the drill. Big time.*

Gabe continued to wriggle in Fee's arms. His eyes had narrowed to angry slits, and he looked as if he was gearing up to test the power of his tiny lungs.

"Well…," Fee said slowly, as if she was trying to figure out exactly what he was asking. "I guess I'll do what Lucy suggested and try to find someone to help out around the house part-time. If you really do know anyone who's available," she said, throwing him a quick look of appeal, "let me know." She glanced down again, looking embarrassed. "And in the meantime, I'll be looking for work. I majored in English during college, before I got pregnant with Dinah and had to drop out," she said. "I was really good at it. And I…" She blushed.

"You what?" Brody gently prodded.

She shook her head emphatically. "You'll laugh," she said, sounding like a petulant child.

"I will not laugh."

"You will too. But…" She took a deep breath. Brody got the distinct impression that she wanted to tell someone so badly, she was willing to risk whatever reaction she might receive. "Well…I-have-a-friend-who-publishes-this-newsletter-about-family-issues," Felicia poured out in a rush. "She's let me write a few articles for her in the last year, and I really liked it. I'm pulling together my clippings now and submitting them to some magazines and actual newspapers. I'm hoping that I'll get a little bit of freelance work, or maybe even a part-time job as a proofreader or something. I know I don't have my degree," she said, blushing again, "but maybe I can get something, even if it's doing filing. I don't mind. I know I need to start somewhere."

Brody frowned. The publishing business was highly competitive. With neither experience nor a degree behind her, Fee's chances of finding work in the field were not great.

"And there's one other thing," she rushed on, not noticing his look of discouragement. "It's a long shot, but—I can't believe I'm even admitting this to you—Robert has a second or third cousin who works at *Style House* magazine in New York."

Brody knew exactly where *Style House* was located; the magazine was one of his fiercest competitors.

"I've never met the woman," Felicia told him, "but I've heard about her from Robert's mother. I'm hoping I can still pull some strings; maybe she can help me out after I get actual paying work for one of the local papers. Robert's mom will put in a good word for me; she still adores me, even though Robert and I have split up. He hasn't told anyone in his family about this whole Tiffany thing, can you believe it? His mother would be horrified, and he doesn't want to face the music."

Brody's mind was racing. Robert's family might not know about Tiffany yet, but it was only a matter of time, especially if the man did, in fact, plan to marry the starlet. And when the family did find out, it was almost certain that this second-cousin person was going to get the scoop.

Unless Brody got it first. But, he wondered helplessly, what in the world would induce Felicia to give him her story, when she could use it as a bargaining chip to help snag a job in New York?

"I don't really want to move out of state," Felicia was telling him. "My sisters are here, and the kids are all settled. But I suppose if the right offer came, I might consider moving—"

"Mumm-mumm," Gabe announced, grabbing at Felicia's nose. Gently she batted the slobbery fingers away.

"You know," Brody said smoothly, "it occurs to me that you're in a much better position than you seem to realize."

"How so?"

Felicia could not have been more innocent, Brody observed. He could tell by the blank expression on her face that she hadn't the slightest idea what he was about to suggest.

"Well," he said, fine-tuning his argument in his mind even as he spoke, "if you play your cards right, you can get back at Robert *and* get enough money so that you could pay a nanny or housekeeper or whatever is required."

"I'm sorry," Felicia told him, a shadow of wariness coming into her eyes, "but I don't understand. Get back at—?"

"Robert," Brody finished for her. "Exactly. All you have to do is sell your story to one of the major magazines. One of the most reputable magazines, of course," he amended. "If you give an exclusive, you'll get a pretty decent sum. Especially if you do it now, before anyone else has even gotten a whiff of the story…"

His voice trailed off as Felicia speared him with the sharpest look he had ever seen. "What?" Brody asked.

"Are you kidding?" Felicia took two steps backward, as if standing any nearer to him might subject her to some sort of contamination. "I would *never* do that!" Brody could not decide whether she looked more insulted or wounded. She clutched Gabe tighter, giving the impression that she thought he might actually reach out and swallow her child whole. "Think about my kids—what that would do to them!"

As if to punctuate his mother's words, Gabe let out another of his eardrum-piercing screeches.

"Look, I didn't mean to—" Brody held out one hand to soothe her, but the way Felicia pulled back, it may as well have been a snake.

"And if you think that I'm the sort of woman who would…would…*capitalize* monetarily on the destruction of her family, then you are sadly mistaken!"

"Whoa, now. Time out." Brody waved both arms in front of his face in surrender. I'm sorry. I didn't mean it that way."

"Well, what way *did* you mean it?"

"It was a very unfortunate choice of words on my part," he said, trying to buy time while he regrouped. Gabe wailed again, this time a long-drawn-out battle cry that sounded as though it held the promise of many more to follow. Brody spoke a little louder so Fee could hear him over the din. "Can we just forget it and start all over again?" If he could just make Felicia see that such a plan truly was in her best interests… *Not to mention your own,* an inner voice accused.

"Well. All right." Felicia patted her squalling infant. Gabe was completely into his tantrum now and didn't appear to be inclined to settle down anytime soon. Fee hung her head and sighed heavily, as if she were ready to take flight herself.

Brody glared at the baby impatiently. He'd never get through to Fee if the child didn't stop screaming.

"Brody," she said, sounding tired. "I really do need to go."

"I know. Just a second." He reached out and lifted Gabe out of her arms before she could even object. In the area immediately surrounding them, decked-out partygoers gave them little sidelong glances of disapproval. Brody tucked the child under his chin and began gently massaging between Gabe's shoulder blades while rocking back and forth on his own heels.

"That's not necessary," Felicia told him, but she appeared relieved to have a moment's rest, even though Gabe hadn't actually stopped crying.

After a minute or so of administering his massage, Brody looked into Gabe's scrunched-up face.

"I think he needs to burp," he said. The child was clearly in pain. Brody switched from massaging to firmly patting, as he pushed the baby up and slightly over the back of his shoulder.

"But he already burped after he ate," Fee told him. "It was a pretty manly one too. This kid doesn't do anything halfway." But when Brody kept on patting, she didn't stop him. And a moment later, to Brody's relief, Gabe let out a long-drawn-out belch that would have made an eighth-grade boy proud.

"Nice," Fee said with genuine admiration. "You're good at this."

"Experience," Brody told her. He couldn't count the number of times when, while overseeing photo shoots for his former magazine, he had been called upon to comfort one or more squalling infant models. "Look, I'm sorry about what I said before," he told her over Gabe's powder-scented head. "I really do want to help you."

"You do?" she asked dubiously.

"I *do*," he said with as much conviction as he could muster. "I think I can help you, if you'll…let me assist you in my professional capacity."

"What?" A slow, sweet smile unfolded before him like a bud opening up under time-release photography. "Are you serious? You'd do that?"

Brody blinked at her. She sounded as though he'd just handed her the moon. "Well, yes. Let me just explain what I mean by that—"

But Felicia was no longer listening. "I can't believe it!" She threw both hands to her mouth and looked over them at him with eyes the size and color of quarters. "God did it!" Her cry came, muffled, through her hands.

"He what?" Brody continued to thump Gabe on the back since Felicia still hadn't reclaimed him.

"God did it! See, I told you. I've been doubting him—I hate to admit it—but look at how this all came together: He is taking care of me! He sent me help, and I didn't even have to go looking for it!" Brody was still trying to decode her cryptic statements when she added, "I know you said you weren't taking care of any kids right now because you're working on another project. But if you really could help out—even for a while, at least, until I could find someone more permanent—you would absolutely save my life! Even just a few hours a week!" She reached out and threw both arms around him, pressing one warm cheek briefly against his. "It's really true?" she asked breathlessly, pulling away. "You're not taking care of any other kids right now?"

"Well, uh…no. I'm not taking care of anybody but myself. But I don't see what—"

Felicia grinned. It was the greatest show of positive emotion he had seen out of her yet. "Unbelievable!" she cried. "A childcare worker with experience—drug free, I presume? And no criminal past? Somebody pinch me! No…don't. If I'm asleep, I don't want to know!" She snatched up his free hand, the one not holding Gabe. "Brody Collins," she said with feeling, "you are my dream come true!" Her eyes were like little silver stars.

"I'm…" As Brody struggled for words, snatches of their conversation came together like the pieces of a puzzle. His instinctive sweep of Gabe's mouth, his offer of a professional opinion about childcare, his explanation that he'd made his living off the care and handling of children, his comment about the applesauce on his sleeve… All these had been grossly misinterpreted.

Felicia thought he was a childcare professional.

Worse, she apparently now considered him *her* childcare professional!

"But I'm not—" he began again.

"Not what, Brody?" The light in her eyes flickered.

Way to go, Collins, he chided himself. *What are you gonna do now? Tell her you're not really a childcare worker at all? That you were speaking in code because you didn't want her to know the truth: that you came here today under false pretenses and that you've befriended her because you want something from her? Something she has no intention of giving you or anyone else? Oh, and by the way, you're not going to help her out after all, not the way she means? Not the way she needs someone to?* Great. There was no way she was going to give him the story now. And to his surprise, he actually felt even worse about the fact that he was going to have to let her down. She had been so relieved to know that he was going to help her out a few hours a week. But he couldn't do that...

Could he?

"Brody Collins," her words echoed in his head. *"You are my dream come true!"*

"A few hours a week, you say?" He scratched his chin thoughtfully. *Why not? You've got the time. You've been thinking that you wanted to take on an outside project, even do something a bit more altruistic like Abby's been nagging you to do. What could be more altruistic than helping a single mom with the burden of taking care of her house and kids?*

Brody knew there was nothing altruistic about his real motive. He wanted the scoop.

But then Felicia wanted some things too. She wanted help around the house. She wanted some extra money. She wanted a career in the publishing business. With enough time, Brody knew, he'd be able to find her the domestic help and the career contacts she needed. He'd also be able to get her a hefty sum of money for her story, which he could give her as soon as he could convince her to sell it.

Perhaps they could both get what they wanted after all.

Felicia eyed him expectantly.

Brody made his decision right there on the spot. He would do it! For the sake of the magazine. For the sake of the scoop. And for Felicia's sake as well.

Besides, the errant thought came to him, *it's not the most unpleasant assignment you've ever taken. That Felicia Salinger is pretty cute...*

He scowled. "What time do you want me?"

Felicia looked at him shyly. "How about if we meet tomorrow afternoon so we can go over the details? I can come to you if you want."

Brody shook his head. No good. If he was going to pass himself off as a childcare worker, he couldn't let Felicia see his expensive, Neo-Empty condominium. "Uh…I don't think that would be possible. How about if I come to your place? Later in the day works best for me. Does six o'clock sound about right?"

"Yes." Felicia paused for a moment, as if reconsidering. "You're sure this is all right?" she asked timidly. She looked afraid to hear the answer. "For a minute there, you didn't sound so sure."

"Oh, I'm sure," Brody heard himself saying. He didn't want her backing out of the deal now. This was his only chance to get more time in which to convince her of the wisdom of his plan. "In fact, I'll make you and the kids dinner," he said, sweetening the pot. It wasn't until after he generously made the offer that he remembered, almost as an afterthought, that he couldn't cook.

"Dinner, huh? Wow. All right," she said in wonderment, turning her gentle gray eyes upon him. "Our address is in the book. We'll see you at six then."

But as she turned away, he thought he heard her say under her breath, "I just hope you know what you're getting into!"

Brody swallowed hard.

He hoped so too.

Seven

"You what?" Abby gawked at Brody over the gooey, cheese-drenched slice of Veggie Lover's pizza she had been lifting toward her wide mouth, and now had poised midair in front of her face. She sat above him on his couch of russet leather, wearing knee-length khaki shorts over long johns and a heather gray sweatshirt with the word "State" emblazoned across its chest, looking every bit the college student she once was and—in his humble opinion—still should have been. Brody was dismayed that she had dropped out of school even for a semester or two; yet at the same time, he admired her determination to choose a career path that was in sync with her values and goals. He just wished she would hurry up and decide already, so he could quit worrying about her.

"You heard me." He grabbed a piece of anchovy-and-sausage from his own side of the cardboard takeout box. It wasn't his favorite pairing of toppings, but Abby found the combination revolting, and he thoroughly enjoyed offending her.

"Yeah, I heard you. I'm just not so sure I heard you correctly. You? A nanny? Oh, excuse me...I mean, a 'childcare professional.'" Abby snickered, then chuckled. Within seconds, she was laughing so hard, Brody was afraid Diet Coke might come spraying out of her nose.

"It is not *that* funny," he said darkly.

"It is to me!" Abby hooted.

"Yeah, well...what can I say? Apparently she sees me as the diaper-changing, apron-wearing type." Brody crammed the pizza violently into his mouth.

"Ha! She should be so lucky."

"Meaning...?"

"Meaning nannies—male or female—are kind, sensitive, and nurturing, while you're...you're..."

"Oh, I can't wait to hear this," Brody mumbled, then pressed more loudly, "And I'm...?"

"Well, you're just not," Abby concluded with a shrug.

"Your confidence is underwhelming."

"Sorry. Did I hurt your feelings, Bro?" She grinned. "Mr. I'm-in-Control, Take-No-Prisoners Brody Collins? Oh no. Wait. I forgot. You're the new, sensitive, contemporary urban male." She waved five sticky, sauce-covered fingers mockingly in the air.

"That's about enough out of you." Brody shifted uncomfortably from his position on the oatmeal-colored Berber carpet. He'd never admit it to her, but his sister's verbal arrows were striking a bit too close to the mark. Maybe he wasn't exactly famous for his gentler traits. But that didn't mean he didn't have a soft side. And it certainly didn't mean that he couldn't have been a fine husband and father if he had chosen to be.

It wasn't as though marriage and parenthood had never been an option. He and Lana had been well into the process of planning their wedding—or, to be more accurate, Lana had been well into the process, and Brody had generally agreed with everything she decided—when his father had first seen a doctor concerning his problems with balance five years ago. Wes Collins was sixty years old at the time and had been in good health for as long as Brody could remember. The last thing he, his sister, or his mother expected was that the father and husband they so loved would be diagnosed with a disabling disease, the same disease that had taken folk music hero Woody Guthrie's life.

Up to that point, Brody's life had gone as close to plan as was humanly possible. At twenty-five years old, he was already a success in the publishing business. He'd launched his own magazine, *Child's Play*, in college as his senior project on the advice of a teacher who had suggested the market was wide open for such an offering.

The gamble had more than paid off. What he'd merely hoped would be a break-even project had turned into a successful business venture. Within its first year, *Child's Play* had gained a respectable readership and had received both critical and popular acclaim. In the three years that followed, Brody's expertise and the magazine's circulation had both grown. Then he met Lana—a gentle, sweet-tempered legal assistant who had shared his love for both literature and children. In fact, he hoped to have several children himself one day. What he didn't know about children and families, he figured, he could learn through reporting. And all the knowledge and insight he gained while working on the magazine could ultimately be applied to his own family. Brody had been ready to take the leap to the next phase of his life, and he had proposed exactly six months to the day of his and Lana's first date.

A couple of months later, Brody's mother had called from Phoenix, where she and his father had retired the year before.

"Oh, you know your dad. He's always been a bit klutzy," she said, pooh-poohing Brody's concerns. "But he seems to be a bit worse lately. Last week he banged his head on the doorway, and now his doctor wants him to go in for some tests," she'd told him. "It's nothing to worry about."

And Brody had believed her. But within the week, she had called back with the diagnosis.

"Huntington's disease?" Brody had stared at the phone in his hand. "What's that? I've never even heard of it." In the next few weeks, however, he'd learned enough about the condition to know that it would change his life forever.

Huntington's disease, he discovered, was a hereditary degenerative brain disease most often diagnosed during midlife, as it had been in his father's case. Though his dad had in fact always been a bit klutzy, as his mother put it, this was something entirely different and completely unrelated. Cells in the caudate nucleus of his father's brain were beginning to die. That was in turn leading to Wes's problems with balance. What would follow would be deterioration of intellectual ability, emotional control, and speech, as well as involuntary movements known as chorea. In the majority of cases, Brody learned, Huntington's disease was ultimately fatal.

He was still recovering from the shock of this news when his mother dropped the next bombshell. Huntington's disease, she said, was caused by a single dominant gene. Every child of an affected parent had a fifty percent chance of inheriting the gene that causes HD. Wes Collins's doctor had told her—mistakenly, it later turned out—that there was no way to test Brody or Abby for the condition. They would simply have to wait until they reached midlife themselves to see if they developed the disease.

And if they did, there was a fifty percent chance that they would pass the gene on to their own kids.

It was then that Brody decided he would never have children. It wasn't that he couldn't. It was simply that, the more he learned about the disease, the more he saw his father deteriorate, the more he realized he was unwilling to subject any child of his to that kind of suffering.

He'd explained his decision carefully to Lana, and he'd thought she understood. But she could not live with the impact his decision would have upon her own life, and after tearfully informing Brody that she desperately wanted to bear children of her own, she'd broken off the engagement. Six months later, through mutual friends, Brody learned that she had eloped with a securities broker from Sacramento.

As it turned out, there was a slight possibility that their breakup was unnecessary. In the years that followed, Brody learned that a genetic marker for the disease *had* been identified and predictive testing had been made available to the public. But by that time it hardly seemed to matter—now that Lana was married to someone else.

Five years later, despite the pain Lana's leaving had caused him, Brody still felt convinced that he had made the right decision. It wasn't always easy, living his life in such a detached manner. But he wasn't about to hurt a woman again the way he'd hurt Lana. And he certainly wasn't about to let another woman do the same thing to him.

"So when do you start your new 'job,' Nanny Boy?" Abby grinned around her mouthful of pizza.

"Ugh." Brody threw her a look of disgust. "Is it too much to ask you to swallow your food before you address me?"

With exaggerated precision, Abby ground her mouthful of pizza between her molars, swallowed, and opened her teeth wide to prove that every last morsel was gone. It never ceased to amaze Brody how big her mouth really was. "There. Happy?"

"Not really. I didn't want to see the inside of your mouth any more than I wanted to see you digesting your dinner."

"I wasn't digesting; I was just chewing."

"Semantics," Brody grumbled. "It's all a part of the digestive process."

"And you," Abby said, pointing a finger sharply at him, "are avoiding the question."

Brody ripped a paper towel off the fat roll he'd placed on the coffee table and wiped his mouth. "If you must know, I'm going over to the house tomorrow night to see the place, set up a schedule, and make her and the kids dinner." He said it casually, as if it were the sort of thing he did every day.

"You're going to *what?*" Abby settled back against the couch, folding her arms across her chest and beaming in horrified delight. "Make them dinner? But you can't cook! You can't even boil water!"

"I can too," he lied. "Anyway, how hard could it be? I'll stop by the bookstore and pick up a copy of *Cooking for Morons.*"

"Well now, at least that would be appropriate."

"Abby—" He flashed her a look of warning.

"Oh, come on now! This is too much! You really ought to be selling tickets to this little event. I know I'd buy one."

"Of course you would. You have nothing better to do."

"I resent that," she sniffed.

"Resent it all you want, but don't even try to deny it. If it wasn't true, you wouldn't be here with me." Brody thought about that a moment. "Wait a sec," he said, throwing his sister a dirty look. "I think I just disparaged *myself.*"

"Don't look at me. You're the one who did it," Abby said innocently, grabbing one of the crusts he'd discarded into the box and cramming a corner into her mouth. The resemblance to Gabe with his cracker, Brody thought with disgust, was frightening.

"I do have one teensy little question," Abby said, reaching for the nearly empty two-liter bottle of diet pop.

"Shoot if you must."

"What about these sisters of hers? The ones you saw at the wedding? Surely they've told her by now who you really are. If they have, you'd better wear a bulletproof vest over to her house tomorrow."

Thankfully, Brody had thought of this himself before leaving the wedding that afternoon. "Not a problem. I talked to them. They promised not to say anything about me working at the magazine."

Abby raised one thin, blond eyebrow. "Right. They're going to keep your secret from *their* sister?" She rolled her big blue eyes. "Obviously you don't know anything about women."

"Save it, squirt. I've got it covered," Brody said authoritatively. He folded his long, stiff legs into an awkward, quasi-lotus position. "After I left Felicia, I managed to flag down Lucy and Cat again. I told them about my background at *Child's Play* and explained that I had told Felicia I wanted to help her out."

Abby snorted derisively at this. "Yeah, right. Sure you want to help her."

"I told them I thought she wouldn't let me do it if she found out I had another real job," Brody said, ignoring her. "Lucy got this wicked little matchmaker gleam in her eye. I'm sure she thinks I told Fee I wanted to help out because I like her. She got Cat to agree not to say anything, as long as I promised to tell Fee the truth and come clean within twenty-four hours—after I'd given her a night off from the kids." Brody mulled this over for a moment. "I'm pretty sure I've got some leeway though. Apparently Cat and Jonas are leaving Monday anyway for some sort of business trip to New York. And Lucy and her husband will be on their honeymoon for a while. It's a good thing too. Lucy seems so excited by the prospect of someone taking an interest in Fee, I'm sure if she were in town she'd be unable to keep her mouth shut."

"So it's 'Fee' now, huh?" Abby peered at him with a bit more interest. "So do you?"

Brody peered back at her. "Do I what?"

"Goof," Abby said fondly. "Do you like her? This Fee person? You know, *like* her?"

He felt the back of his neck grow hot. "What kind of question is that?" Brody jumped to his feet and slapped down the pizza box lid.

"Hey!" Abby protested, dropping one stocking-covered foot to the floor. "I'm not done with that!"

"You are now." He grabbed at the greasy, wadded-up, snowball-size napkins surrounding them and managed to cram nearly all into one fist before heading into the kitchen with them and the remnants of their dinner.

"Ooh," Abby said, following him. "Touchy subject, I see."

"It's not a touchy subject," he snapped. "I just don't think my love life—or lack of it—is any of your business."

"Why not?" she said easily, hopping up to plant her small bottom on his Corian countertop. "You think my love life— or lack of it—is yours."

"That," Brody informed her, "is because I'm older and wiser."

"And crabbier," she noted. "Come on. Tell me. What's she like?"

"Abby—"

"Come on," she pleaded, batting her eyelashes at him. "Be a sport. I have no friends of my own. Let me live vicariously through you. What's she like?"

Brody chuckled then, just as she'd known he would. "There's not much to tell," he said, though he knew it wasn't the truth. Felicia Salinger was, in fact, a beautiful and complicated woman. He had no idea how to explain her in a way that would do her justice.

"Is she attractive?"

"Yes." He nodded. "Very."

"Very, huh?"

He frowned. "Look, let's just forget about—"

"Come on. What else?"

Brody leaned back against the smooth white cabinets and thought a moment. "Well, she's very sweet. Very kind. A fantastic mother, that's for sure. She's the sort of woman who was really meant to have kids, you know?" His mouth felt dry, and he swallowed. "She's the kind of woman a guy would bring home to his mom." Brody felt certain that his own mother would adore Fee. They seemed to be the same breed of women—sweet, gentle, deeply spiritual. He'd grown up secure in the knowledge of his parents' faith, and from what Fee had said about God taking care of her, he could tell that Felicia's trust in God was of the same quiet, unshakable sort.

"And she is quite attractive. I don't think she knows that. It's not a loud, in-your-face type of beauty. It's subtler than that and has a lot more to do with who she is than what she wears or what kind of goop she puts on her face." Brody stared at the row of track lighting over his countertop, as if hypnotized by its glare. "And she's very honest. Very real. There's nothing bogus or phony about Fee. Not a single thing. Actually, I'd have to say she's quite an amazing woman."

"Oh, Brody." Abby shook her head. "Bro-dy, Bro-dy, *Brooo-dy*. My poor brother."

"What?" He dragged his eyes away from the light that held them.

"You *do* like her!" She stared at him as if he were a science experiment gone horribly wrong. "This is terrible!"

"I do not like her!" he protested, then added a bit less forcefully, "I mean, I like her. I just don't…that is…oh, forget it. Anyway, what if I did? What would be so terrible about that?"

"You big oaf! Don't you see?" Abby plopped down from her position on the countertop and planted her two small hands on his shoulders. "You've lied to Felicia from the very beginning, and this is a woman who you practically define by her honesty and truthfulness? There's no way she's going to forgive you for this! And there's certainly no way she's going to give you her crummy old story." She spoke the last sentence as if it were distasteful to her.

Though he hated to admit it, Brody suspected she was right. He'd been doubting his ability to pull off this scheme ever since he'd gotten himself into this mess that afternoon. "So what do you advise? Seeing as how I 'don't know anything about women,' as you so eloquently put it."

Abby lifted her hands off the top of his shoulders and grasped him firmly by the forearms. She stood on her tiptoes in order to look him more directly in the eye. "Come clean," she said, enunciating clearly. "It's your only hope. I mean it."

Brody gave her an exaggerated sneer. "That's it? That's the best advice you've got?"

"That's it." Abby planted her feet back solidly on the floor. "Poor baby," she said, regarding him with compassion. "Eating crow twice in one weekend. That's gotta be hard. But, yes. You're going to have to come clean. That is, if you want this woman to ever speak to you again. And I have the distinct impression that you do want that, but not for the reasons you think you do." Brody didn't even acknowledge this statement. Abby was always going on about subjects she didn't know the first thing about. "She's going to find out eventually," his sister warned him. "And I can assure you, things are going to go a lot better for you if you're the one to tell her the truth."

"I know, you're right." Brody glared at his feet as if they were the ones who had gotten him into this mess.

"She deserves to know," Abby said in a firm voice.

"I know," he repeated dully, then raised his defeated eyes to face the victory in hers. "How does it feel to be right...again?"

Abby shrugged, spun on one heel, and threw him one last smirk over her shoulder. "I don't know. It happens so often these days," she said with an air of one who knew herself to be vastly superior. "I hardly even notice anymore."

Chewing nervously on a hangnail, Felicia surveyed the massive minefield of plastic trucks, dog-eared library books, and abandoned teething rings that was her living room. She'd been overjoyed that Brody was willing and available to come to her house that very weekend to hash out the details of their arrangement—until she despairingly realized he would be getting his first look at the disaster zone she called home.

She'd had every intention of cleaning the mess up Saturday night after the wedding. But Lucy and Cam's reception had dragged on all through the afternoon and into the night. Even after the bride and groom had made their getaway sometime after seven-thirty, Fee and her sisters had danced to the lively tunes offered up by the hired three-piece polka band: Cat with Jonas, Daphne with Elliott, and Felicia with Clifford, since Dinah had stubbornly refused to hold her little brother's hand. With her ten-year-old daughter tending to Gabe, Fee had taught Clifford the basics of the waltz, alternately bending over at the waist to meet him at his seven-year-old level and lifting him into her arms to spin him crazily around the dance floor while he cried, "One-two-three, one-two-three, ONE-TWO-THREE! WHEEEEEEEEEEEEE!"

Just before she'd left with Campbell, Lucy had pulled Felicia to one side and arched her eyebrows knowingly.

"What?" She'd seen that look on Lucy's face a thousand times before, but she still pretended that she didn't understand its meaning.

"How about that Brody Collins, huh?" Lucy winked broadly. "I hear he's helping you out with the kids."

"Yes," Fee said primly. "But it's not what you're implying, my romantic little friend. I'm paying him to do it."

"Oh. I see." Lucy pursed her lips and made a face as if she had a mouth full of marbles. "I'm sure that's all it is. So how much are you paying him to do this so-called job?"

"I..." Fee blinked. "Actually," she said, realizing it for the first time, "we never really specified that part. I guess we'll talk about it tomorrow night when he comes over to work out the details."

"Huh. So he's apparently not doing it for the money." Lucy nodded sagely. "Interesting."

"Lucy, stop that!" Felicia glared at her. It was bad enough that she considered Brody the most delectable man she'd ever seen. She certainly didn't need her sister filling her head with crazy ideas! She'd sworn off men for good reason.

And even if she hadn't...

Fee shook her head. No, she couldn't go down that road. There were a million reasons why she shouldn't allow herself to get hung up on any man, and a million more why she shouldn't even think twice about this one in particular. Men were trouble. They'd been stomping on her heart ever since she'd been old enough to understand that they were good for more than just bringing home birthday presents and opening stuck jar lids.

Besides, if her pathetic high-school dating experiences hadn't been enough to convince her of her natural inability to have a good relationship, her disastrous marriage should have finally made it unmistakably clear. From her early teenage years—perhaps because she had wanted and needed so much more attention that her overworked, overburdened father had been able to give—Felicia had simply wanted someone to love. Marriage wasn't rocket science; she figured anyone could do it. In fact, it was the one thing she had thought she would never fail at.

And she'd determined that she never would. After marrying at eighteen years old, she'd thrown herself completely into the role of wife, two years later happily adding on the role of mother. She'd even felt superior to, and sorry for, the people she knew who hadn't managed to stay married. Over the years, she'd become a charter member of several "pro-family" organizations and had dragged Robert to a number of weekend marriage conferences, which he had willingly—if not exactly enthusiastically—participated in. She'd thought that by the force of her will, if nothing else, she would be able to hold their relationship together. Since childhood, Felicia had never been organized or driven like Catherine, nor had she been particularly creative like Daphne and Lucy. Her idea of a successful life had simply been having a man to love and a comfortable home filled with happy children.

Now the man she'd loved was gone for good. And since Robert had left, the kids had certainly not been entirely happy. But, Felicia consoled herself, at least she still had them. And even if she didn't have anything else in this world, they were enough to make her life completely worthwhile. Thank God for that.

Fee glanced at her watch. Five-forty. She desperately wished she'd managed to straighten up the family pigpen after church.

But first there had been the kids to feed. Then Gabe had stubbornly refused to take a nap. The only thing she'd cleaned at all was the kitchen, and that had been just a quick once-over, necessitated by the fact that Brody had promised to make them dinner. She shuddered to think of what he would think of the rainbow-colored leftovers in the fridge or the stuck-on gunk in her oven. She was just glad she'd gotten a shower that morning. Some days that was a miracle in and of itself. She hated to even speculate on what Brody would think of her if he caught a glimpse of her on one of the days when she didn't manage such a feat.

Knock it off, Fee, she told herself sternly. *The guy is coming to help out with the kids, not to be your boyfriend. If he's looking for someone to have a romance with, no doubt his acquaintance from the wedding is more than qualified—and, by the looks of things, more than willing.* Who could compete with *that?* Not her. Although if Brody Collins was the prize, she might actually consider trying…

"Auuuuuuuuuugh!" Her pent-up frustration found its voice, escaping in one long, aggravated cry. Since yesterday afternoon, her mind had gone back to Brody hundreds of times. This had to stop. If he was going to work for her, she was going to have to put any thoughts of romance aside for good. It wouldn't be prudent to allow such an intimate relationship to unfold under the guise of a professional association, even if Brody wanted it to—which, she reflected unhappily, she was certain he did not.

Felicia's heart sank as the unwanted thought took form. She'd been avoiding the truth, but that was, in fact, the real issue: She was certain that Brody wasn't the least bit interested in her, not in the way that she secretly wanted him to be. And she couldn't afford to ever again throw her heart at a man who would do anything but cherish it. She was lucky enough to have Brody in her life in a professional capacity. She'd have to be careful not to do anything that might drive him away, she reminded herself. He was certainly a rare find.

As she made her way around the open, airy living room, collecting socks and hats and other stray items of clothing, Felicia wondered what special project Brody was working on that kept him from taking on a full-time childcare assignment. He had been elusive about what he'd been spending his time doing and had seemed to feel a bit awkward when she'd asked him about where he lived. *He must be between jobs,* she decided, *and feeling self-conscious about it. Perhaps he was even without a permanent place to live!* She *had* mentioned that living in the guesthouse would serve as part of the payment for the job, otherwise she couldn't afford to hire someone. Maybe that was why he'd accepted.

Felicia considered this possibility. He'd been dressed well enough. But that didn't mean a thing. *Phooey, I'm just jumping to conclusions*, she thought, walking down the hall to dump her armload into the laundry basket she'd placed between the children's rooms. If only Lucy hadn't already left on her honeymoon! She hadn't even thought to ask her sister what Brody was doing at the wedding, didn't even know how he'd become associated with Lucy and Cam. If Lucy was still in town, Felicia reflected, she could call her and find out if she knew where Brody was staying. As it was, she'd have to wait until her sister came back to town the following Saturday.

Of course, he hadn't said anything about his actually living in the guesthouse. And yet a part of her wanted his protective presence nearby. She remembered how he'd worked his magic on Gabe at the wedding. But then having him so close would definitely *not* be good for her resolve to keep her distance from men.

She was still wrestling with this dilemma when the doorbell sounded less than ten minutes later.

"Ack!" she squeaked, kicking open her bedroom door with one white canvas sneaker and flinging an armload of her own belongings into the room's slovenly depths. "He's early!" she said to no one in particular. "What kind of guy shows up early?" After a hasty glance at the mirror that revealed that her earth-toned lipstick was still in place, she smoothed back her sleek, dark hair, straightened her flax-colored, lamb's wool cardigan, and rushed eagerly to the front door.

"Hullo!" she said breathlessly, swinging it open it to find an uncomfortable-looking Brody Collins standing on her doorstep.

"Hi," he said, sounding as stiff as he appeared. "May I come in?"

"Please do." The stiffness was contagious. She stepped aside to allow him entry, trying to draw a bead on his mood. "Can I get you something to drink?"

"No, no. I'm fine."

"Take your coat?"

"What? Oh. Right. Thanks." Brody slipped out of his light overcoat, revealing a cotton hound's-tooth shirt and brown corduroys. Felicia quickly deposited the jacket in the hallway closet before following him into the living room. When she got there, he was looking around with an unreadable expression on his broad face. She cringed, imagining that he was judging her messy house.

"'Don't hate me because I'm messy,'" she quipped.

"Huh?"

"You know…that old commercial: 'Don't hate me because I'm beautiful…'"

"Of course I don't hate you for that," he said absentmindedly, missing the joke entirely. "That's silly." Felicia didn't correct him, she was so busy wondering if his comment meant that he did, in fact, find her beautiful.

"Did you have any trouble finding the place?" Fee felt idiotic. She could think of nothing else to say.

"Hmm?" Brody acted as if he wasn't even listening to her. "What?" He finally met her eyes. "Oh. Uh…sorry. I was just thinking about something. Look, Fee. I have to admit something to you, something you probably won't like very much. But I have to tell you the truth anyway. No matter what it makes you think of me."

Whatever it was, Fee could tell, it wasn't good. On some primitive, instinctive level, she knew that he was backing out, moving away from her. Suddenly, she found herself compelled to do something, anything, to prevent it.

"Of course," she said, pasting a wooden smile on her face. "But first, I want the kids to come out and say hi to you."

"They really don't have to," Brody said, frowning. "This will only take a minute." But Fee had already taken several steps down the hallway.

"Dinah! Clifford!" she called. "Come out and say hello to our guest!" She threw Brody an apologetic smile. "I insist. Even though it sometimes feels like I'm fighting a losing battle, I am determined to instill manners in them, and that includes greeting guests. I'm afraid you'll have to forgive Gabe's rudeness though. He's still asleep, but he should be up soon. He just went down a couple of hours ago for his two o'clock nap."

Brody frowned again. "It's six."

Fee rolled her eyes in answer. "Tell me something I don't know. Now you see why I need help so badly." She thought she saw him looking around nervously again. "I hope you'll forgive the mess," she said, embarrassed. "I was busy all afternoon, and of course yesterday was the wedding. It isn't always such a sty around here," she told him. *Just usually, these days.*

Brody's gaze landed on her laptop computer on the desk in the corner. "Been doing some writing?"

"I did a little bit on Friday," she admitted. "My friend Amy's trying to get me a shot at doing a piece for a local bridal paper. It doesn't pay much—only about fifty bucks a pop. But I figure, it's a start. How about you?" she asked, suddenly remembering his stints on the paper and the yearbook. "You were always into journalism, as I recall. Have you written anything I should know about?"

Brody paled and glanced at her sharply, as if she'd thrown something at him. He licked his dry lips. "Well...," he said slowly. "I'd intended to write some children's books. But that was a long time ago. I don't think that's going to happen now. I've got other things to worry about these days. Other priorities." He looked incredibly guilty, Fee decided. Like a man who wasn't telling the whole truth.

It hit her then. Of course! That was it! This was the project Brody had alluded to at the wedding reception. He wasn't taking care of any children right now because he was trying to work on a book! From the sour look on his face, she guessed that the "project" wasn't going too well. Maybe she'd been right after all: Maybe Brody had accepted the job just so he'd have a place to stay. It made sense, if he didn't even have a job. Fee screwed up her eyes and studied him. He looked decidedly less put-together today than he had at the wedding. His eyes were red rimmed, and he looked as if he hadn't had much sleep. He was probably flopping on a friend's couch somewhere. She set her lips in a firm line. "Actually," she said, the words falling from her lips almost before she had even had the chance to think them through. "I probably need to put my own writing projects aside for a while and focus on the one thing I really need to do: Get the guesthouse ready for you to move in. I assumed you'd stay there since I mentioned it was part of the pay."

"Guesthouse?" Brody sounded almost surprised to hear about it. If Fee didn't know better, she'd have thought he was only being polite.

"You remember. I mentioned it yesterday—as part of the pay for working here. It's a great little place," Fee said, trying to make it sound as appealing as possible. "I've never bothered to rent it out; it's too small for anyone to want to live in long-term. But for someone to stay in, oh, say, temporarily…?" She looked at him casually. He didn't give any indication that he'd even noticed the bait dangling in front of his nose. "It would make me feel better about paying you so little. And it would be nice to have someone else around the property—especially a man—now that Robert's gone. For safety issues, of course. There have been some burglaries in the neighborhood.

"You'd be doing me a favor really. But, please. Don't feel obligated in any way. I could find some other way to pay you… You're already helping me out so much."

Brody scowled.

Feeling suddenly desperate to keep him nearby, Felicia took a step toward him so that she was just inches from his face. "I just hope," she whispered ominously, "that nothing dreadful hap—"

At just that moment, the front door—which Felicia had not even heard open—slammed shut with a loud *bang*.

"hap-AHHHH!" Fee cried. Startled, she tripped over her own foot and fell forward into Brody's arms.

"AHHHH!" he echoed, instinctively pulling her into the protection of his embrace.

"Mama, puh-*leeze*," Dinah said, her voice dripping with disapproval. "What are you doing?" Fee turned to see her daughter standing in the doorway, flanked by Clifford, giving Brody an icy stare.

"Uh...sorry," Fee laughed nervously. Reluctantly, she pulled herself from Brody's arms while he stared at her as if he could not for the life of him figure out how she'd gotten there. "Oops! I tripped. Dinah, you scared me."

"Who is that man?" the child asked accusingly.

"Why, it's Brody Collins, remember?" Fee told her. "You met him at the wedding yesterday. I told you he'd be coming by tonight." She glanced over at the front door. "I thought you two were in your rooms." The kids were getting harder and harder to keep track of.

"We went outside to get another beetle for my collection," Clifford told her, his blue eyes bright. "I needed another black one."

"Well..." Fee shuddered to think of why Clifford would need another black beetle. She didn't even want to guess how many of his creatures were loose in the house at that exact moment. "All right. Come say hi to Mr. Collins, and then I want you two to go get cleaned up before dinner."

At the word "dinner," Brody hunched his shoulders like a hunted animal.

"Is there anything wrong?" Fee asked curiously.

"Um...I forgot my cookbook," he said in a low voice.

"Well, that's all right." She could not imagine why this had made him so distressed. "I've got plenty of them for you to choose from, and the pantry's pretty full of anything you'd need. I'm sure you'll find something in there to make."

"I don't want to eat anything that he makes," Dinah announced, stamping one foot on the living room floor. "I want hamburgers! And French fries!"

"Dinah!" Fee averted her eyes from Brody. She was so embarrassed, she couldn't bear to meet his gaze. "That's no way to talk to a guest! You apologize right now."

Her face like a tiny storm cloud, Dinah looked directly at Brody and said in a small, angry voice, "I'm sorry." She looked over at Felicia and whispered loudly, "But I still want hamburgers. From Burger World!"

Fee opened her mouth to lay down the law, but stopped when Brody reached out and grabbed her hand. "Actually," he said, "that might not be such a bad idea."

"Mama," Clifford interrupted, his lower lip protruding from his perfectly round face. "When is Daddy coming? He said he and Tiffany were gonna come an' see me this week."

Felicia felt her heart expand and contract within her chest, like a fist opening and closing. This was why her kids were being so hard to control. They missed their father. And she couldn't blame them.

She stepped over to Clifford and stroked his soft yellow hair. "I know, sweetie," she said kindly. "Daddy's been on a trip. But he promised that he'd call as soon as they got back. I think he'll be coming over to see you in the next day or so. Wouldn't you like that?"

She turned to see Brody staring at her with a fierce expression on his face.

"A favor, huh? Living in the guesthouse?" he said.

Fee nodded mutely.

He considered this for a moment, then said, "All right then. You've got yourself a deal. If you agree to let me help out at no charge, I'll move in."

"Move in?" Dinah glared.

"MOVE IN!" Clifford crowed, even though Fee was certain he didn't even know what exactly that meant.

"Move in? Really?" Fee felt a blush of pleasure rise to her cheeks. "That would be great!"

"Room and board at your guesthouse in exchange for childcare and some help around this place." Brody nodded to himself, as if he found this arrangement to be particularly satisfactory.

"All right then," Fee agreed happily. "It's a deal." They shook on it, Brody's strong fingers wrapping firmly around her long, slim ones.

"What about dinner?" Dinah said, tugging on the leg of her mother's jeans.

"Just a second, Dinah," Fee said, putting off her decision a moment. It had just occurred to her that when Brody arrived, he'd had something to tell her. She turned to him. She'd gotten him to promise that he'd stay. Now, before he moved in at least, she ought to find out what he had wanted to share with her. "Didn't you say you had something to tell me?"

"Well, uh, yes." Brody paused for a moment, then leaned toward her and whispered, "Actually, I was going to say, I'm afraid I misled you about something."

"Misled me?" Fee felt a tremor of apprehension run through her.

Brody looked directly into her eyes for a moment, then he turned away. "That's right. You see, uh, I'm really not that great of a cook. It's not what you would call my area of expertise."

Fee laughed, a wave of relief washing over her. "Well, I think we can work around that," she said cheerfully. "Dinah! Clifford!" she called over her shoulder. "Grab your coats. I think we'll go get those burgers of yours tonight after all." Giving Brody one last grin, she turned and made her way down the hall to get Gabe.

Brody was going to stay. He was going to help them out for free! She'd be willing to eat TV dinners every night if that's what it took to keep him.

Because *keeping* Brody, she realized with an air of absolute certainty, was something she was wanting more and more all the time.

Eight

The dank smell of moist cardboard filled Brody's nostrils as he pressed his chin against the half-empty packing box cradled in his arms. The carton was one of several that had been left abandoned in the open storage area at his condominium, and he'd gratefully snagged three of them the night before. He had considered himself lucky to get them; the local packing supply office had already been closed for hours. But as the weathered boxes now sagged under the weight of his meager possessions, he could see why nobody had bothered to claim the sorry containers.

A carload of his most easily transportable belongings waited for him fifty feet down the drive in the classic Ford Falcon he'd parked on the street under Felicia's elm tree. Knowing that the Lexus would quickly reveal the true state of his financial affairs, Brody had suggested the night before that they take Felicia's minivan to Burger World, and had used his command of the English language to artfully imply—but never outright state—that he'd caught a cab to her place. He'd later flagged a taxi outside the fast-food restaurant, paid the driver one block from Felicia's place, and sneaked back to his Lexus parked near her driveway once he was reasonably sure that Fee was in the rear portion of the house, tucking the children into their beds.

Early this morning he'd driven to the storage unit where he kept the Falcon he'd bought on a whim several months before. It was nearly identical to—though with only an unimpressive dent in the right front fender and an even more infinitesimal one in the passenger side door, in infinitely better shape than—the first car he'd bought at age fifteen. This model was also a '61, jet black with tons of chrome, its paint slightly oxidized on the hood, top, and trunk. When he bought it, Brody had determined to restore the car to its original, immaculate condition, if and when he ever had any free time. Such discretionary time had, of course, never materialized, and the vehicle had remained immobile since he'd parked it following the tune-up it received one week after its purchase. But early this morning, he'd picked it up and had it detailed before driving it back to his condominium and filling it with two threadbare suitcases he'd been planning to bequeath to Abby, plus the mildewed boxes.

It wasn't hard for him to choose what to take to Fee's. Brody wasn't much of a pack rat, anyway, and wasn't tempted to take a whole lot with him, especially for what promised to be a very brief stay. He did, however, need to make it appear as though he was going to hang around, at least for a while. He was hard-pressed to find many mementos that would help him to make such an impression. But he had grabbed from his hallway wall his one framed family photo: a five-by-seven print of him and Abby with their parents, sailing off the coast of Newport Beach during the summer of '91. Shortly after the photo was taken, Wes had taken ill. Keeping that framed image in plain view was one of the few lapses into sentimentality that Brody allowed himself.

Into the same box, he had slipped a stack of thick, heavy volumes on child rearing he'd used for research while working at *Child's Play*. In a second carton, he'd packed a simple point-and-shoot camera, to have on hand in case Robert and Tiffany made an unannounced visit, along with his laptop computer and modem, which he intended to use to stay on top of things while his work for Fee kept him physically out of the *California Dream* office. He hated to think about how disorganized and undisciplined his staff was likely to become in his absence, especially with Abby in a position of limited influence. However, his boss, Mr. Fortunata, had approved of the plan when Brody called the night before to apprise him of the situation and had encouraged him to do whatever it took to get the scoop.

Brody wasn't entirely thrilled about the prospect of conducting his business from, much less spending all his nights at, Felicia's one-room guesthouse. This was without a doubt the most ridiculous plan he'd ever hatched. It sounded more like something Abby would pull than anything he would have considered himself likely to try. But…he had always made it his business to be the first to get the story, and that's what he was going to do. Besides, the situation wouldn't last long. As soon as humanly possible, he planned to put an end to this ridiculous farce.

With any luck, he'd get the scoop with Felicia's cooperation, although that was no longer technically a necessity. If he was staying on the premises himself, chances were he would be able to get the story on his own. Eventually, Robert and Tiffany would show up; Felicia had promised the children as much the night before. And when they did, Brody—and, hopefully, one of his professional photographers—would be there, waiting for them.

He had a hard time imagining himself actually doing such a thing without Felicia's approval. He hoped that would not be necessary. Brody tried to think positively. He told himself he simply needed more time. Before long, he'd be able to persuade Fee that selling her story to a publication that would report it with integrity was more than just an option; it was her responsibility to herself and to her children.

The argument sounded so convincing, Brody thought, he almost—but not quite—believed it himself.

Shifting the modest weight of the box to his right hipbone, he dug into the pocket of his rumpled khakis—the most casual pants he owned, since he rarely had occasion to wear jeans and hadn't gotten around to replacing the pair that had worn out a month ago—and wrapped his fingers around the key Felicia had given him the night before. The metal slipped into the door as easily as a knife into butter and he turned it, feeling a solid *click* as the lock gave way under his hand.

Brody stepped inside deliberately, feeling like an intruder despite the tacit permission Felicia had given him along with the key. He was not as a rule claustrophobic, but as he entered the room he felt with a shiver that it would not be nearly large enough for him, though it was at least a good fifteen by fourteen feet wide.

He deposited the box onto the dark-stained hardwood floor and headed back to the car quickly, before he could change his mind. Two more trips brought two more cartons, and a third, the pair of matching suitcases, one of which was empty. If she was watching from one of the windows, he wanted to at least make a decent show of moving in.

Grabbing the zipper on his largest case, Brody yanked it in a squashed U-shape until the bag gaped open all the way around. He stared into its mouth for several minutes, as if the contents were unfamiliar to him. The most time-consuming part of the packing process had been selecting the least expensive and most well-worn items of clothing from his wardrobe. But he had managed to come up with a reasonably good selection of Dockers and loafers, long-sleeved cotton shirts and

lightweight sweaters, boxer shorts and clean white socks—
certainly enough to get him through what he hoped would
be a mercifully temporary assignment.

It took him less than five minutes to unpack his clothes
and another ten to set up his makeshift office at the tiny
walnut-stained desk in the far left corner. With those most
pressing tasks accomplished, he found there was little else
to do but take stock of his surroundings.

Beneath his feet, the smooth hardwood floors were layered
with a thin film of dust, but Brody had seen a straw broom
in the corner of the closet, so that would be easy enough to
put to rights. The Southwestern-style stucco walls were painted
a deep burnt orange that he would never have picked himself but that he had to admit worked wonders at giving the
garden shed–size building a cozy feeling of homeyness.

The center two-thirds of the floor were covered with a
heavy-weave Native American carpet in muted tobacco browns,
rich reds, and blacks. From the front door facing in, the closet
was positioned to Brody's immediate right behind a foldout
door with shutters. It was small and cramped, but large enough
for hanging up one suitcase full of clothes. Now emptied, the
luggage was stacked one on top of the other, the two of them
barely fitting into the closet's narrow width.

To the side of the closet was a second door, which led
into a bathroom barely larger than the closet. Beyond that
doorway, in the far right corner of the central room, was a
low, queen-size trundle bed, piled high with plush chocolate-
and-coral-colored throw pillows. Brody guessed that it func-
tioned as both mattress and couch.

A long, narrow, cherry-stained bookcase stretched along
the back wall between bed and desk, giving the room a stu-
dious air. Crossing the room to inspect the contents, Brody
found to his surprise that it was filled with titles by literary

greats, including such authors as C. S. Lewis and Flannery O'Connor—two of his favorites. Swallowing his astonishment, he turned his attention to a well-worn Bible at the far right. Brody pulled it out and flipped through its pages, which were filled with notes written in a delicate, feminine hand that he figured must be Fee's. On each page, several passages were underlined, many of which were familiar to him from the days when he'd attended a local high-school church youth group.

It was during this stage of his life that Brody had made the decision to become a Christian. However, after praying for his father's healing, and after losing Lana, Brody had stopped trusting that God was actively involved in his life, though he still wished—sometimes desperately—that this was the case.

The pages, thin like onionskin, slipped past his rough fingers until the book landed open. "Cast all your anxiety on him because he cares for you," Brody read an underlined passage from the book of 1 Peter. Next to the Scripture verse was a date from the last year, not long after Robert had left Fee, he guessed. In her times of trouble, she had trusted in God. Why hadn't he? The thought nagged him.

Brody put the Bible down, uncomfortably, and continued his exploration of the room. On the bookshelf's second tier, he noticed two framed photographs. The first was a grainy black-and-white snapshot of Fee's two elder children, taken, he guessed, maybe a year or two earlier; the kids appeared to have been around five and eight. They were standing on a vast stretch of sand: Dinah flirting coyly with the camera, a small metal sand pail in one fist and plastic shovel in the other. Just in front of her and to her right, Clifford was grinning and waving what appeared to be a cookie-size sand dollar.

Brody gave this first photo a cursory glance. But it was the second, a formal studio portrait, that caught and held his gaze, primarily because of its subject matter. Taken several years before the beach shot, the full-color image included what would have been at the time Dinah and Clifford's entire nuclear family, including, to Brody's considerable interest, Fee's mysterious ex-husband. Eyes narrowed, Brody bent at the waist to get a closer look, to ensure that he'd recognize the man when he saw him in person.

Robert Kelley looked more or less as he had pictured him: half a decade older than Fee, with thick blond, pompadoured hair; sharp, dark gray, nearly black, eyes; and a long, pointy nose jutting out of an even longer, too-tanned face. Where the photograph cut off at the bottom, Brody thought, though he could not be sure, that he saw the very beginnings of a potbelly.

"You," he spat out at the man in the photo, his voice dripping with disdain, "have early midlife crisis written all over you." Brody poked a finger fiercely against the glass over the man's puffed-out chest. "What were you thinking anyway?" he grumbled. The man stared back at him with vacant eyes. "Tiffany Diamond? Over the mother of your children? *Felicia*? You have got to be out of your mind!" Brody snorted. He knew he never would have made such an idiotic decision. Perhaps it was simply because he knew Tiffany, and those of her ilk, so well.

Fee's sunny countenance beamed up at him from the image in his hand, as if thanking him for the unspoken compliment. A look of quiet contentment on her face, she sat with one arm draped gracefully around a dark-haired toddler in a butter yellow dress, the other cradling a baby who looked a lot like Gabe. Robert stood behind the trio and slightly off to the left, his eyes not tracking exactly with the camera, as if his attention was caught by something not seen by the rest of the family.

A feeling of protective anger rose within Brody. Remembering the combined look of exhaustion, sadness, and wariness that was now Felicia's default expression, he had the unmistakable urge to go back in time and thump some sense into Robert Kelley's thick skull.

Yet at the same time he felt completely convinced that Robert did not deserve such a chance, even if Brody could have given it to him. Nor did he deserve the incredible wife and children he seemingly hadn't cared that he'd had. Feeling more keyed up than he had in some time, Brody resolutely decided that should God ever see fit to bring him a wife despite his Huntington's-carrier status, he would make every effort to cherish her. More than that, he would move heaven and earth to make certain that she knew she was adored.

His scowl deepened. Felicia deserved that kind of love. And her children deserved the sort of father who would give it to her—and to them. His heart swelled with hope that she would one day find such a man. It seemed reasonably possible, even likely to happen. She was still young, lovely, and captivating in a quiet, almost mysterious way. He could only imagine what it would be like to be the object of her love…

Brody stared at Felicia's smiling, unblinking image, realizing that for the last several minutes he had been imagining exactly that.

Felicia and…me? It was too ridiculous even to consider.

Gingerly, Brody placed the photo back on the shelf and looked at it as if it were a cobra that had just struck at him. There was no denying that, on some level, he felt drawn to her. He'd felt that way as a sophomore in high school; it had only been a sour grapes mentality that caused him to think of her less favorably in the years that followed, when she'd swooned after guys who treated her poorly while completely overlooking him.

That was more than a decade ago though. Yet for some unexplainable reason, he'd felt immediately and irresistibly drawn to her again at Lucy's wedding. And if he was completely honest with himself, he had to admit that he hadn't stopped thinking about her since.

Brody sat down on the edge of the bed, feeling as though he might be ill. This wasn't what he'd had in mind at all. What had happened to his plan? The only "relationship" he'd had in mind was a little candlelight dinner with Carmen one of these evenings…perhaps a harmless moonlight stroll. Something that had all the earmarks of romance, with none of the trappings. Extricating himself from Carmen's clutches, should she have tried to actually sink her claws permanently into him, would have been relatively easy and painless. A relationship with Felicia was something else entirely—something that, if he got into, he wasn't sure he'd want to get out of again at all. For the briefest of moments, Brody allowed himself to consider the possibility.

Perhaps it wasn't the craziest idea he'd ever had after all. Felicia was, as far as he could tell, exactly the sort of woman he had always imagined himself settling down and building a life with. Before his father had taken ill and he had forced himself to give up such dreams. And Felicia even had three children already; she might not be put off by learning that Brody was potentially a carrier of the gene that caused Huntington's disease and, if proven to be so, would not be willing to father any children.

Brody's heart sank then as he remembered the comments Felicia had made when she'd told him about naming Gabe. He was certain that she'd wanted to have another girl; she'd clearly been disappointed not to have been able to give Dinah a baby sister. Felicia wasn't too old to have more children; she had many fruitful childbearing years ahead of her. If she wanted another little girl, there was no reason in the world why she shouldn't have one.

Unless, of course, she was actually—by some miracle—to fall in love with him.

A faint glimmer of hope flickered within him. Perhaps he *didn't* carry the gene for Huntington's disease. He could always be tested...

Brody set his mouth in a firm, hard line. He could not afford to entertain such dreams. It wasn't worth the risk to him or to Felicia. Besides, Fee had had enough trouble with men in her lifetime. She didn't need him to bring her any more pain. She deserved a man who was loving and nurturing—traits that Abby had so tactlessly pointed out that he lacked. She merited somebody who could commit to her without hesitancy, fear, or question; somebody who would be honest with her from the very onset of their relationship.

In other words, Brody realized, flopping backward onto the couch in pained defeat...

Somebody he was not.

Felicia had been aware of Brody's presence on her property almost before she had actually laid eyes upon him. Knowledge of his nearness may have come from instinct, but could also have been explained by some small sound he'd made in the driveway as he passed under the window where she worked—a sound not consciously registered in her mind but one that she'd been listening for with her heart. Whatever the catalyst, it was enough to cause her to lift her head from her dish washing and peer out over the window box filled with laughing red geraniums—her hands full of slicked-up silverware and slimy orange antibacterial soap—to see if she could catch a glimpse of her handsome new boarder-employee.

To her great satisfaction, she could, and she spent the next several minutes peering past her homemade chambray curtains, silently tracking his steps back and forth between the guesthouse and some late-model vehicle she could not identify. The night before when he'd taken a taxi home, she'd been fairly certain that Brody did not own a car at all; but this morning, he'd arrived in one, looking for all the world as if it was his. Felicia had dismissed the mystery as not being worth the energy it would take to unravel. Whether he'd begged, borrowed, or stolen the car was none of her affair. Besides, she was beginning to realize that there was much about Brody that she did not understand. The puzzle she was most interested in solving was that of his love life, though it didn't seem likely that he would soon open up to her about that of his own accord. And she had no intention of introducing the subject. Felicia continued to watch Brody going in and out of his door. When at last he did not emerge after several minutes, she sighed and stepped away from her comfortable perch at the kitchen window to resume her task— the murky, lukewarm dishwater only slightly cooled since she'd abandoned it several minutes before.

She was still deep in her thoughts about Brody when the phone rang shortly after noon. Fee wiped the dingy suds off on her pebble gray T-shirt before lifting the cordless receiver to her ear.

"Hello? Oh, Robert. It's you." She hadn't been expecting a call from anyone in particular, but somehow hearing her ex-husband's voice felt like somewhat of a letdown. Fee inched over to the window to check on Brody's progress. He was still nowhere to be seen.

"What? Sorry, I didn't hear you. I was just…hmm? Speak up, Robert, can you? Where are you anyway? You sound like you're a thousand miles away." Fee's eyes widened; she gripped the telephone more tightly. "You *are* a thousand miles away? In *Mexico*? Robert, I thought you were at a medical conference in Sacramento over the weekend." She listened carefully. He had her full attention now. "You were. But now you're not. You took off early because...ex*cuse* me?"

Fee heard a soft banging noise at her front door, but could not bring herself to move a single inch to respond.

"Yes, of course I knew you were going to do it. I just—" She bit her lip, blinking back the water that had sprung to her eyes. "No, I'm fine. No...that's not it at all. I'm just...um, surprised...and a little shocked. I thought you would have wanted the kids to be there. Isn't that what you said? Have you thought about how this is going to impact them?" The tears flowed now, hot and angry. "I am not jealous, Robert! I wish you'd stop saying that. I'm just telling you, going about it this way is going to hurt the kids." The banging came again, louder this time. Fury had caused Fee to regain her ability to move, and she took long, violent strides toward the front entry. "Why don't you call them back this afternoon and tell them yourself?" Her gentle gray eyes were now two sharp, steel-colored points.

"Fine," she snapped into the phone. "I'll tell them. I guess they'll see you when they see you then. Won't they? Yes, I'll tell them. Yes, I said I would." A second later, she beeped off and reached the front door just as a new round of banging erupted.

"What *IS* it?" she fairly shouted, flinging the door open with all her might. Then, "Oh! Brody!" she exclaimed as the door crashed full force into the wall behind her. Her cheeks and ears turned the exact shade of her geraniums.

Brody stood in front of her, eyes wide, his right fist frozen midair.

"So sorry," he muttered. "Wrong house. I was looking for a demure, gentle little woman named Fee? And you must be Xena, Warrior Princess?"

At any other moment, Felicia would have laughed. But this time, it was all just too much for her. "Oh, Brody!" she cried again, and the tears began to stream down her cheeks.

He paused for only a second, then—with a determined look on his face—took her gently by the hand and led her to a nearby couch. As soon as he had deposited her on its blue-and-white striped cushions, he pushed her bangs back, softly stroked her cheek, then pulled away and quickly disappeared down the hallway.

Fee watched him go, feeling oddly bereft. But within seconds he reappeared, carrying an entire roll of toilet paper. He knelt beside her, ripped off eight or nine squares, wrapped them around his hand, then reached up and began to blot at her eyes.

By this time she had managed to compose herself slightly. "Glad I got the quilted kind," she quipped. But Brody was no longer laughing either.

"It's okay, Fee," he said in a low voice. "You don't have to joke about it. Whatever is wrong, it's all right with me. You don't have to tell me if you don't want to. But I'm here to listen if you do."

Felicia felt her lower lip tremble. Robert had said things like that when they'd first started dating. But she soon learned that he'd never really meant it. It was one thing for a man to pretend to be sensitive in order to win a woman's affections. It was another thing for him to be there for her, providing a shoulder for her to cry on when life got hard. Robert had never been particularly fond of getting mascara stains on his shirt collars.

She cleared her throat and gave Brody a shaky smile. "It's all right," she whispered. "I just had a bit of a shock, that's all."

Brody met her eyes, but did not say anything. She shifted nervously on the sofa cushion. "It's just that Robert's gotten remarried," she confessed and took a long, deep breath to steady herself.

"You already knew that was going to happen, didn't you?"

"Yes, but I just got a call from him. He's in Mexico with Tiffany—I don't know where. It seems that they've eloped."

Brody sat back on his heels and stared straight ahead. He looked like Wile E. Coyote after he'd been struck on the head with an Acme anvil. Felicia felt a twinge of vindication, but this only made her sadder. Even Brody appeared to think it was the most horrible thing he'd ever heard.

"Fee," he said, finding his voice at last. "I'm so sorry." His mouth was pinched tight; his words sounded bitter. "I didn't realize you still loved him."

"Love him?" Felicia shook her head weakly. She suspected any love she'd still felt for Robert had faded away around the time that he'd moved into Tiffany Diamond's Bel Air estate. "No, I don't love Robert anymore. I still loved him when he walked out, I think. And I wouldn't have ended my marriage for the world. But he's been gone for a long time now." It had only been a year, but it felt as if a lifetime had passed. "And," she said wryly, "there's nothing like knowing that your former spouse has begun keeping house with someone else to douse any last little flames that might be trying to keep burning." She shook her head again, more emphatically this time, to punctuate her point. "Love Robert? No way. Not anymore."

Brody lifted her hand and caught it close to his cheek. Felicia blinked at him with watery eyes, trying to keep her breathing even. "Then why are you crying?" he asked softly.

"I…don't know," she admitted awkwardly. It didn't make sense to her either. She'd thought that she had put all this behind her months ago. "Mostly, I think, because this is going to be so hard on the kids. They weren't thrilled when

Robert told them he was getting remarried, especially since he's barely seen them since he started dating Tiffany.

"He fought the courts for the right to have the kids every weekend. But now that he has the time, he doesn't even bother to take advantage of it." Looking stunned by this revelation, Brody lowered her hand back down to her knee and covered it with his own. "Clifford has taken it all pretty well," Felicia told him, half her attention focused on his hand, "but Dinah really sees Tiffany's presence in her father's life as an intrusion. She's needed something to look forward to that would make her feel she's still an important part of her father's life. The idea of being in another wedding, and being her father's flower girl, had sort of pacified her a bit. Both she and Clifford had been looking forward to it. Isn't it funny," she said with a touch of irony, "how kids love weddings? Even a wedding in which one of their parents is marrying somebody else?"

Brody looked at her as though he didn't think it was the slightest bit humorous. "Some kids do," he allowed. "But not all of them."

Fee pulled back as if she'd been slapped. "You don't need to make it sound like that," she mumbled.

"Like what?"

"As if it's a test. You're implying that loyal kids or smart ones wouldn't get caught up in the festivities like Dinah and Clifford did." Brody's implied judgment stung far worse than had any of Robert's outright accusations.

The eyes across from hers registered a glint of understanding. "Whoa. Sorry, Fee. I didn't mean it that way! I guess I was just letting my own feelings toward Robert creep in, saying how I thought I'd feel in the same situation if I were a kid."

Felicia ventured a quick glance at him but said nothing.

"And based on the way I feel right now," Brody told her confidently, "I have a pretty good idea of how that would be." He leaned in and caught her gaze as securely as if he'd snagged it with a net. "Do you know what those feelings are, Fee?"

"No," she whispered. His face was very close to hers now. She could feel his warm breath on her cheek. She could not have moved away if her life had depended up on it.

"Fury," he told her, his eyes snapping. "Disgust. Disbelief. Nausea. Outrage. Offense. Shock. Repugnance. Loathing. Abhorrence…"

"Whew!" Felicia gave a long, low whistle.

"Not to mention," Brody said, not missing a beat, "empathy. Compassion. Heartache."

To her dismay, Felicia realized that she was starting to tear up again. "Heartache? But why on earth…?"

"Because," Brody said fiercely, drawing her into his arms and gently easing her head down onto his broad shoulder, "what's happened to you—and to your family—is terribly sad." He began to stroke her hair softly.

Fee gratefully submitted herself to his embrace. "I know you're right," she said quietly, settling into the curve of his shoulder. "But…why does it matter to you?"

Brody's hand stopped moving along her hair for a moment, then he pulled her even closer. "Because," he said in a low voice that was almost a growl. "You matter to me. Okay?" He spat the words out as if they were some sort of challenge.

"Um…okay," Fee managed to respond, but the tone of his voice made her feel more confusion than reassurance. For a moment, she was afraid he might tip her chin upward and sweep her lips with a kiss. She shivered. Her heart and mind were in turmoil; she wasn't sure how she wanted to, or how she even should, respond. After a second or two, though, it seemed clear that he had no intention of pursuing a greater degree of intimacy, for his arms remained wound firmly around her shoulders, his lips a good twelve inches from her face at all times. She should have felt relief, Felicia realized. But instead, she felt even more desolate.

After a while of sitting together like that, Brody finally stirred and rose clumsily to his feet. As he drew away, Felicia thought his eyes appeared suspiciously red. Then he turned back to her. "Come on," he said, and gave her a bright smile that made her decide she'd imagined the whole thing. "I'm buying you an ice cream."

"But—" Fee glanced at her watch. "It's past noon, and I haven't even had lunch yet."

"This," Brody said sternly, "is not about nutrition. This is about spoiling you. It's about time someone did."

Felicia considered this for a moment. "Well—" she hedged. "All right," she said, deciding to splurge. "But just this once," she said, waving a stern finger in front of Brody's aristocratic nose.

"Of course." He sounded insulted that she'd think he would have it any other way. "You think I'm proposing that we do this every day? You think I'm made of money?" His face froze; something about his own question startled him.

Poor guy, Felicia thought. *He's still embarrassed about the fact that he's so broke.* "Actually," she suggested innocently, "I really ought to pay. As a 'Welcome to your new home' gift."

Brody looked at her coolly. "I think," he said, sounding a bit put out, "that I can afford a couple of scoops of rocky-road ice cream."

Fee grinned. "Ahhh," she said playfully, relenting, "but will you splurge on the sugar cone? And what about sprinkles? How 'bout that, Mr. Big Spender?"

He hung his head in mock defeat. "Women," he said heavily. He raised his eyes heavenward, as if petitioning for sympathy. "They want a guy to give them the world."

But as he bathed her in the warmth of one last smile before she headed off to collect Gabe, Felicia could not shake the odd feeling that if she really did need the world, Brody Collins would do everything within his power to give it to her.

Nine

"Morning, sleepyhead." Felicia stood in the open doorway
to her son's lair and rapped gently on the polished wood
with the knuckles of her right hand. "I could have sworn I
was already up here a couple of times. Didn't you hear me
calling you?" It amazed her that the children could sleep
through so much. Fee believed that if an air-raid siren sounded
directly over their beds, the kids could remain thoroughly
comatose.

"Mmmrrph." A Clifford-size lump stirred beneath the mass
of blankets and comforter on the carved walnut twin bed,
then was still.

"You've got to get up, bud," she said, kindly but firmly.
"You're going to be late for school."

"'m not going to school," the lump informed her in muffled
tones.

"Oh, you're not, huh?" Fee went to Clifford's bedside and
perched herself on the edge of his mattress. "How come?"

"Because." The comforter rustled violently, as if something
was trying to thrash its way out. After a moment, a small head
appeared and two sapphire eyes peered out at her from under
a fringe of yellow bangs. "Somebody has to stay here an' keep
an eye on him," the child said in a loud whisper.

"Him?"

Clifford nodded seriously. "Yup. *Him.*" He hissed the word.

Felicia matched her son's tone and volume level. "Why are we whispering?"

"Because he'll hear us!" The whisper grew a notch louder.

"Who will?"

Clifford glared at her with exasperation. *"Him."*

"Who, him?"

"*Him*, him," Clifford insisted impatiently. "That man downstairs! Dinah says he's gonna wait until we're all gone, an' then he's gonna come up here an' steal all our toys. Dinah says maybe he's just only pretending to like us so he can get all our stuff. Like Santa Claus, except he takes toys from little kids instead of giving 'em to 'em."

"Dinah says that, huh?"

Clifford only nodded again.

Felicia bit back the words that immediately came to her lips. She wanted to tell Clifford that his sister was wrong and that Dinah knew it. That she had no business telling him such things, that she was only trying to cause trouble. But Fee also wanted to handle the situation carefully. Dinah was obviously disturbed by Brody's presence in the household. Just as she'd seen Tiffany as an intruder in her father's life, Dinah perceived Brody as some sort of threat. And though Fee didn't want to raise a tiny tyrant whose whims and desires controlled the family, she knew it was important to respect her child's inner struggle.

"I realize that Dinah is concerned about Brody," Felicia said, choosing her words carefully. "But he's really just here to help us. You know I have to be gone sometimes because I'm going to go back to work."

"Ye-es." Clifford didn't look too thrilled by the prospect.

"Well, I'm going to try to be here with you and Dinah as much as I can. Hopefully you'll hardly know that I'm ever even gone, because most of the time it'll be when you're at school. But I won't have as much time to play with you and read to you if I don't get somebody to help me do the dishes and make dinner and watch Gabe during the day. Does all that make sense?"

Clifford vigorously bounced his small head up and down.

Fee let out a long breath. Five years ago, if someone had told her she'd be having this conversation with her children, she never would have believed it. "All right then. I think you'll like Brody if you give him a chance," she said. "He's worked with kids for years. Auntie Cat and Auntie Lucy and I went to high school with him. Your Grandpa Salinger even golfed with his dad at the club, I think." Felicia thought she remembered, too, that Brody had participated in the Christian Young Life club that met at their high school. "He's a good guy, Clifford, honestly. I can tell."

Clifford sat with his small chin resting on his fist, considering.

"Okay, bud?" she asked, rumpling his fine hair.

"Well…" The boy looked at her doubtfully. "But what about my toys?"

Talk about a one-track mind. Fee tried not to laugh. "Clifford," she said very seriously. "I can definitely promise you that Brody is not going to steal your toys." The child looked at Fee as if he wasn't sure he believed her.

"Cross my heart," she said, and did so.

Clifford's face brightened. He looked as if she'd just lifted the weight of the world from his narrow shoulders. "Okay," he said.

"Okay," she echoed. "You'll come down to breakfast now?" Brody had arrived at the front door ten minutes earlier bearing a medium-size grocery sack. He'd said a quick hello, given her an approving glance, then made a beeline for the kitchen.

Already she could smell a sweet, appetizing aroma wafting up the stairwell. And he'd said he couldn't cook well!

"Yeah," Clifford said. He clambered out of bed and headed for the stairs.

Fee made her way down the hallway toward Dinah's bedroom, but her daughter had obviously heard her coming and was squirreled away in the bathroom by the time she got there.

Felicia tried not to let it bother her. Dinah would talk to her about her feelings when she was ready and not a minute before. In the meantime Fee would simply do her best to make sure her behavior did not completely disrupt family life.

Felicia retreated to her bedroom to put the finishing touches on her makeup. She'd already spent nearly twice as much time on her personal grooming as usual that morning—telling herself it was because she'd wanted to make a good first impression when picking up job applications but knowing in her heart it had more than a little to do with the fact that she would be seeing Brody.

Her leaf green cardigan was tucked into charcoal wool pants that flattered her small waist, and ebony city boots added a fraction of height to her five-foot-seven-inch frame. Felicia appraised her hands in the mirror. Months after her divorce was finalized, they still looked bare, but she no longer felt naked without her wedding ring.

After putting on another layer of apricot lip gloss, she decided she was ready. To her surprise, Felicia actually felt good about her appearance. The look of appreciation Brody gave her in the dining room several minutes later made it clear that he did too.

"Morning, Fee," he said without any particular inflection to his voice. But the way his eyes rested on her, then quickly darted away, betrayed his thoughts. Felicia felt a tiny thrill of excitement pass through her. "Go ahead and sit at the table," he instructed before disappearing back into the kitchen. "I'll have your breakfast in just a minute."

Felicia obeyed, taking her place next to Clifford, who was already seated. A grim-faced Dinah entered just as Brody was reemerging from the kitchen, carrying a platter piled high with toast-colored waffles and a small pitcher of steaming syrup.

"This looks and smells wonderful, Brody!" Fee said encouragingly, remembering what he'd said about his cooking skills. Dressed in a blue ribbed sweater over a white Henley and khakis, she noted, he looked wonderful too.

She took the tray from his waiting hands and peered at the food curiously; each piece was the exact same size. There was something familiar about their appearance. She stabbed one with a fork and dropped it onto the plate Brody had set out for her daughter.

"Hey!" Dinah accused, giving the item a look of disdain. "These are Waffle-O's!"

"So?" Brody looked at her coolly.

"So?" Dinah glared at him. "They come out of the toaster. You didn't even make them!"

Brody moved around the table and lowered his face until it was an inch from Dinah's plate. The child watched him, her face still pinched and angry, her eyes baffled.

"Is it cooked?" Brody asked after a moment. "Is it edible?"

"Ye-es," Dinah said. "But—"

"Then I made them," Brody announced. "They are officially *made.*" His tone brooked no argument.

Dinah watched, mouth agape, as he strode purposefully away. Felicia pressed her hand to her lips to hide her smile. And she'd been worried about Brody? She'd thought her strong-willed daughter would stomp all over the poor man. But he'd made it clear from the start that he was not going to let a ten-year-old child intimidate him. Her admiration for him grew.

The Waffle-O sat in front of Dinah for several minutes, untouched. The syrup had already been passed around the table, and Clifford was on his second helping before Dinah even picked up her fork. But eventually, Felicia saw out of the corner of her eye, the child began to eat.

Fee let the action pass without comment.

Brody did not join them in their meal, but rather hovered like an eager waiter. Several minutes later, when Gabe's unmistakable screech sounded from the nursery monitor Fee had placed in one corner, she started to rise. Brody hesitated for only a second before waving her back into her seat.

"I'll get him," he said. Felicia thought he looked a little ill.

"Are you sure?" she asked. She began to reconsider her decision to begin the job search that day. If Brody wasn't feeling up to the task…

"Of course I'm sure," he said in a clear voice. "Am I, or am I not, your childcare provider?"

Upon a second glance, he looked perfectly fine. Felicia decided she'd been imagining his discomfort. "Yes sir!" she said, saluting.

Brody took off down the hall, and a few minutes later came back with a grumpy-looking Gabe nestled in his arms. Noticing the baby squinting, Brody reached for the dimmer switch and decreased the overhead light by one third. Then, gently placing one large thumb just below Gabe's mouth, Brody began to move the baby's lips, much like a ventriloquist moving a dummy's. *"What's the matter with you people?"* Brody made him say, using a squeaky little high-pitched voice that Felicia wouldn't have thought the virile, deep-voiced man capable of making. *"What's a guy gotta do to get some attention around here? I'm Grumpy Baby! Where's my breakfast?"*

"Grumpy Baby's breakfast," Fee answered, swallowing a chuckle, "is in the fridge. I prepared several bottles last night. His baby food's in the cupboard over the microwave." Though it was wonderful to have Brody's help, she couldn't resist getting up to give her baby a squeeze. As Gabe leaned toward her and wrapped his tiny arms around her neck, she suddenly found that she had no more desire to leave. "Are you sure you can handle all this?" she asked Brody dubiously. Robert had never been much of a hands-on dad; she had a hard time imagining a man tackling all the tasks she faced at home each day.

"What's not to handle?" Brody asked confidently, thumping Gabe on the back.

"Well..." Trying to look more self-assured than she felt, Fee handed the baby back to him, went around the table to give Dinah a kiss, then came back around and planted a second one on Clifford's cheek. Finding herself back where she started, she gave Gabe one more smooch and recognized with a rush of embarrassment how tempted she felt to climb up on tiptoe and kiss Brody, too.

"The carpool will be here for the kids in fifteen minutes," she said to him instead. "You're sure you can get those two ready?"

"Of course."

"All right...if you say so," she said, but in the same tone as she might have uttered, "It's your funeral." She gathered up her purse and keys. As soon as she'd opened the front door, Gabe started to scream at the top of his lungs. Felicia stopped, uncertain of what to do. "What's the matter, sweetie?" she said, and started toward him.

"Don't worry about it," Brody told her. "It's just separation anxiety. He wants you to feel guilty so you'll stay home. It's normal at this stage of development. He'll be fine once you're gone and he sees that screaming won't do him any good."

"Really?" He sounded like he knew what he was talking about, at least.

"Really. Just give him a hug and a kiss, tell him you'll miss him, and assure him that you'll be back soon."

"Okay," Fee said uneasily and did as she was told. Gabe's shrill screeching didn't abate in the slightest. "I guess I'll see you later then?" she called to Brody over the din.

"Yup. What time will you be home?"

"Oh, I'd like to make a full day of it, if I can. Since I'm going to be downtown anyway. That's all right, isn't it?"

Brody lowered his chin in assent, his expression unreadable. "Do you have a cell phone, so I can call you if I need to?"

"Not yet," Fee said with regret. "I was going to pick one up today. I'll call you around noon, though, and see how things are going. I'll be downtown around then. I'm heading over to the newspaper offices first. Then I've got a whole stack of want ads I wanted to respond to. If I stay on schedule, I'll probably stop by *Child's Play* before noon. I'll try to use a phone there."

"You're stopping by *where?*" Brody's look of shock triggered the defensiveness Felicia had so often felt when Robert had expressed a lack of faith in her abilities.

"What? They're advertising in the paper for a part-time proofreader and restaurant reviewer. You don't think I have as good a chance as anyone else?" Fee jutted out her chin stubbornly.

"Of course you do." Brody's voice was smooth, his tone conciliatory. "Go on now. Gabe's getting all wound up." Her baby was, in fact, actually growing louder—another feat she wouldn't have believed possible. "Better to do it quick. Like ripping a Band-Aid off a wound."

"That's a disgusting analogy," Fee complained, but opened the door and stepped out onto the porch. "I'll see you tonight then?"

She looked back at Brody standing in the doorway, her child cradled against his chest. "You better believe it," he said and lifted one hand in an endearing little half wave that made her want to run back into his arms herself. "I'll be waiting."

"Separation anxiety," Brody muttered, holding out the squalling infant at arm's length. "To hear you, you'd think your head was being separated from your neck."

"I think," Dinah said, appearing out of nowhere, "Gabe needs to be changed."

Brody hated to admit it, but from the odor emanating from Gabe's lower end, it seemed that the child was right. "I knew that," he said defensively.

The little girl gave him a long, hard look. "I'll bet," she said after she had studied him for a while, "you don't even know how to change a diaper."

"I'll bet," Brody said, meeting the challenge in her eyes, "I do."

Dinah followed him into Gabe's room to make sure he proved it.

Brody moved around the room, collecting the items he'd need, one by one ticking them off the mental list he'd made that morning while studying one of his old childcare manuals: diaper wipes, a change of clothes, ointment in case of diaper rash. He glanced around, feeling that he was forgetting something.

"You don't have a diaper," Dinah observed.

"I'm *getting* to that," Brody told her, hoping the color of his face didn't betray his embarrassment. He walked across the room, pulled a new disposable out of its plastic container, and carried it back to the changing table with the baby.

"Come here, short stuff," he said to Dinah.

"Who, me?"

"Yeah, you." Brody laid Gabe down on the table. "You're going to be the live entertainment." He wasn't exactly an expert on babies, but he knew enough to try to keep a wriggling Gabe distracted during the process. "Here," he said, handing her a small, blue terry-cloth bear from Gabe's crib. "Wave this over his head, just out of his reach." While Dinah obeyed, he washed his hands with a baby wipe, then unsnapped the child's sleeper, pulled its flaps out of the way, and unfastened the diaper. "I always thought these things should come with dipsticks," he commented. "Like car engines. So that you'd know when—" Brody and Dinah wrinkled up their noses and leaned backward simultaneously to escape the smell. "Whoa, there!" He'd had no idea a child could fill his shorts so completely.

"Gross," Dinah pronounced.

"You said it." Brody gave the baby a mock-stern look. "For crying out loud, Gabe. I know the diaper package says 'up to twenty-four pounds,' but do you have to take that as a personal challenge?"

Dinah giggled, then clapped one small hand over her mouth.

"Well, you know what they say," Brody told her. "Behind every little bundle of joy is a little bundle of doo-doo." Within a matter of seconds, the undesirable task was completed. After he'd cleaned up and wrestled Gabe into a fresh shirt and miniature coveralls, Brody turned to Dinah. "How about you?" he asked. "Are you ready for school?"

"I just have to brush my hair and put on my shoes," she said.

"Do you need help?"

She looked at him shyly, and for a moment Brody thought she might say yes. Then a shadow came into her eyes, and she spun on one heel and went out the door. "I can do it myself!" Brody heard her call. Then there was silence.

It occurred to him then that he hadn't seen his other charge in a while. *"Clifford?"* he called. A moment later, from the top of the stairs, he tried again, more loudly. "Clifford?"

"In here," he heard a timid voice coming from the living room.

When he got there, Brody found Clifford sitting on a stool-size Lego box, looking a bit too innocent.

"What have you been doing?" he asked warily.

"Nothing." Clifford scooted his bottom around on the Lego box, his grin stretching from one ear to the next.

"O-o-o-kay." Brody sat down on the couch with the baby, who was now exploring Brody's lips and teeth with his chubby hands. "Ow, Gabe. That hurts." To his dismay, the child moved on to his nose. "Careful," he warned before Gabe had gotten too far. "Just so you know, those holes aren't finger holes, and I am not a bowling ball."

Clifford scowled. "Do you want to see something?" he asked impatiently, clearly frustrated that he had failed to claim Brody's full attention.

"Sure," he agreed.

The boy jumped up and dug his fingers under the tin box's tight seal. The lid flew off in his hands. After a second a small, furry gray animal poked its head out of the box and weaved drunkenly from right to left. Then before Brody could even open his mouth, the creature jumped out of its prison and scurried out of the living room.

"That was a cat," Brody said stupidly.

"Tigger," Clifford nodded. He appeared quite delighted with himself.

Brody felt anger rising up within him. "Do you realize," he said, keeping his fury in check, "that you could have hurt that kitty very badly? That you might even have killed it?"

Clifford just stared at him. He no longer seemed delighted.

But Brody could not tell whether or not he understood the gravity of what he'd done.

Brody started to rise, then stopped. He didn't know how to deal with the situation. He suspected that Clifford deserved some form of discipline. But he and Felicia hadn't even discussed the issue yet, and he didn't want to go against her wishes.

"Clifford," he said slowly. "What you did was not a good thing. If the kitty could understand you, I'd want you to tell it you're sorry. You scared it a lot. You might have hurt it very much. You don't want to hurt the kitty, do you?"

Wide-eyed, Clifford shook his head *no*.

"Okay then. We'll talk about this tonight when your mother gets home. Go get your shoes on. Your ride will be here any minute."

Gratefully, the child bolted, just as a horn sounded in the driveway.

After checking to make sure the car was the same make and model Felicia had told him to watch for, Brody opened the door and asked the children who had piled up behind him, "Is that your ride?"

"Yep," Dinah confirmed. "That's Kenneth's mom."

"All right. Hi, Kenneth's mom." He waved. "I'll see you guys this afternoon."

"Okay," Clifford said, his moment of shame already forgotten. Dinah murmured something unintelligible, and the two were off.

Brody watched the children climb into the car, then closed the door behind him and leaned heavily against it. It was only eight o'clock in the morning, and he already felt as though he'd run a marathon.

"Come on, man. You can do this," he muttered to himself. "Are you a nanny? Or a mouse?"

"Mumm-mumm," Gabe suggested.

"I do not recall," Brody growled, "asking *you*."

The remainder of the morning slipped away almost unnoticed. Between feeding Gabe—an hour-long process to the uninitiated—changing him *again*, then finally scarfing down a bit of food himself—a plate of cold Waffle-O's—Brody discovered, to his horror, that it was already half past ten when he found time enough to pick up the phone and call Abby.

"Brody Collins's office," her perky young voice came to him through the phone lines.

Giving in to a childish impulse, Brody lowered his voice to a deeper timbre and intoned, "Hello. May I speak to Mr. Collins, please?" Might as well find out how his sister was handling his absence.

"I'm sorry," she said. "Mr. Collins is not in at the moment."

"Do you know when he'll be back?"

"All I know," she said with a sigh, "is that he's up to some harebrained scheme that I will admit to knowing nothing about. I don't expect him back until he comes to his senses, which is likely to be never—"

Brody sucked in his breath.

"—or until the law catches up with him, which is much more probable. *And do you actually think I don't know this is you, Brody?*"

"Well, it was worth a shot." He blew out his breath, relieved.

"Speaking of *shots*, I'd like to take one at you right about now."

"I'm sure you would," he said smoothly, imagining her circling around him, fists waving, as she had as a child, "but there's no time for that now. I just wanted to touch base. And I need your help. I have an appointment with Nicholas Fortunata at one o'clock—"

"Ooh. The head honcho, huh?"

"That's *Mr.* Head Honcho to you. And yes, I am meeting with the owner of the magazine. But I may be a few minutes late, and if so, I'll need you to stall him. Felicia's planning to check in with me here around noon. After I talk to her, I'll come in, meet with Nicholas, and head back before Fee even knows I've been gone. Dinah and Clifford are going to their friend Kenneth's house after school. No one should be home until after four."

"Great plan."

"Thanks."

"There's just one thing."

"What's that?"

"What about the baby?"

"The what? Oh, him." Brody glared at Gabe, who was now playing tranquilly in his playpen. "Um…well, obviously I'll have to bring him with me. I think Fee left the baby seat over by the door." He did a quick check; she had.

"And who's going to watch him while you're with Nicholas?"

"My secretary, of course," Brody said, sounding unconcerned.

"Humph. I don't recall that being in the job description."

"Oh, come on, Abby. You love kids."

"It's not the baby I'm concerned about. Not *that* baby, anyway."

"Which baby then?"

"The big one, of course," Abby complained. "*You.* If I do this, if you get your way, you're just going to expect that to happen all the time. I've spent too much time training you otherwise to let all that work go to waste now."

"There's fifty bucks in it for you."

"Tell the little dearie that Aunt Abby will see him at about one o'clock." She didn't even miss a beat. "And try not to be too late."

Brody clicked off the line, then immediately dialed his closest friend and working associate.

"*Child's Play*," the receptionist answered the line. Brody didn't recognize the voice. *Must be a temp.*

"Adam Bly, please."

"I'm sorry, sir. Mr. Bly is unavailable at the moment."

"Is he in the office?"

"I'm sorry, sir," the woman repeated. "Could I take a message?"

"If Adam is in the office," he ground out through clenched teeth, "please put him on the line."

"Um…may I tell him who's calling?"

"Tell him," Brody told her sternly, "it's his boss."

"His… Oh! Mr. Collins? I'm so sorry. Just a moment."

The interlude of on-hold elevator music was brief.

"Hey there, buddy," Adam answered a moment later. "What on earth did you say to my receptionist? She looks so frazzled, I thought for a minute there I was gonna have to call 9-1-1."

"I just told her I had to speak to you," Brody said brusquely. "It's important."

"Okay." Adam's voice lost its teasing lilt. "Shoot."

"Look, a woman's coming in there today to fill out an application for the proofreader and restaurant-reviewer position. Which, by the way, I didn't even know you were advertising for…"

"I didn't think you wanted to be bothered with all the details of running this place."

Brody leaned back against the couch and tapped his foot against the coffee table. He hated getting caught up by his own words. "Yeah, I know. Forget it. I just wanted to let you know this woman was coming in and to ask you to meet her in person, if at all possible."

"I don't know, Brody. When's she coming? I've got a meeting at twelve-thirty."

"I'm not sure. Look, if you can't do it, fine. I just wanted you to pay extra close attention to her application. She doesn't have a lot of experience, but she's a friend of mine, and I'd like to see her get the job if she has the skills, which I suspect she does. That's not an order. I just want you to give her a fair shot. I'm hoping you'll try to see beyond her lack of experience."

"Sure. No problem. Anything else?"

"Just that I'd prefer you didn't mention my name if you happen to speak to her. It's important that she not know that I'm involved in any way."

"If you say so. I don't suppose you're going to tell me why?"

"Not at the moment. But I assure you, when I'm at liberty to explain, you'll be the first one I call."

"Yeah, yeah. Whatever. So what else is up? What's new with you?"

At that exact moment, Gabe let out the shrillest scream Brody had heard from him yet.

Adam hesitated. "Boy, we really *haven't* talked in a while, have we?"

"Very funny," Brody grumbled. "We'll talk about it later. I've gotta go."

"Okay," Adam said agreeably. Brody could practically hear his grin through the phone. "Bye…Dad."

"Ha-ha, Mr. Funny Man. Just for that," Brody told him, "you're grounded." He could still hear the thirty-year-old Adam, just two months his junior, laughing when he hung up the phone.

After spending the next forty-five minutes determining that Gabe was neither hungry nor wet, sleepy nor thirsty, Brody was forced to concede that the child simply wanted to be held. "Okay, kid," he murmured against the baby's soft dark shock of hair. "It's a mystery to me why you'd want to be cuddled by a big monster like me, but if that's what makes you happy…"

For the next half-hour, he paced the length of the nursery, sometimes humming, sometimes bouncing up and down on his heels…anything to soothe the restless child in his arms. When he started, his muscles began to ache; soon they began to burn. "How in heaven's name does your mother do this?" he asked Gabe, who looked as surprised as Brody. Brody prided himself on the fact that he worked out and was in pretty good shape, but carrying Gabe around all day was requiring the use of muscles he didn't even know he had. How did someone as fragile looking as Fee do it?

"You know," he told the child, who had calmed down quite a bit and was now staring up at his face in wonder as if he was gazing at the moon. "You really ought to cut your mom some slack. She was up with you half the night." He knew this himself because he'd been up half the night as well, watching Fee's lovely silhouette from his open window as she paced back and forth with Gabe, just as he was doing now.

He'd wanted to go to her then, to help ease her burden. To press a gentle kiss against her forehead and tell her to go get some sleep. Of course he'd done no such thing. But he hadn't been able to drift off either, until the light had gone off in the nursery for the last time, and he'd guessed that Fee had finally been able to retire for the night.

Brody was still pacing and still daydreaming about Felicia when the phone rang just before twelve o'clock.

"Hullo there! How's my sweetie?" Fee's melodious voice sang into his ear.

Brody's heart lurched. For a moment, he thought she was talking about him.

"Um…Gabe's fine," he stammered.

"And how are you?"

"Fine, fine," he assured her. "I was made for motherhood."

"Well, I don't know about that," she laughed. "But *father-hood…*"

Brody stiffened. *If she only knew.*

"I was thinking of taking Gabe out for a drive," he said. He didn't know why he felt so guilty. It wasn't a lie exactly. He never said where he was driving him.

"That's great," Fee assured him. "Gabe loves to go for rides in the car. I won't keep you. I just wanted to check in. I'm calling you from the *Child's Play* office, as I said I would. I'm going to run up and get an application, then grab some lunch and hit the other side of town. I should be home by five at the latest."

"You go on up and get your application," Brody urged her, remembering that Adam would be heading into a meeting soon. "We'll see you when you get home." The words sounded strange in his own ears—he never thought he'd hear himself saying them to a woman.

"Okay then," Fee said after wishing him a great afternoon. Brody could not help but reflect as he hung up the phone, even if things went as well as he could possibly hope, the rest of his day would not be nearly as "great" as it would be if he were able to spend it with Felicia at his side.

As it turned out, Brody's afternoon was one of the most miserable he'd spent in ages. During his meeting with his publisher, Nicholas had pressed him for a date when he would have the Tiffany Diamond story wrapped up. Brody had answered as evasively as he dared; he had no idea exactly when Robert and Tiffany would show up again, and he couldn't even promise that Tiffany would be there when the children's father decided to make another appearance. Worst of all, Brody was having second thoughts about even pursuing the story. Printing it with Felicia's permission was one thing, but betraying her trust in order to get the scoop was another.

Nicholas had been less than sympathetic. Brody had been able to escape only after reminding his boss that he'd already delivered the Rent-a-Yenta wedding story and by promising to have something for him on Tiffany Diamond within two weeks—preferably, Fortunata had told him, by the following Monday. Just six days away.

By the time Brody got home with Gabe, the child was nearly hysterical, having missed his all-important two o'clock nap. After much coaxing, Brody was able to soothe the baby into a fitful sleep. He hadn't even had a chance to catch his own breath after that when Dinah and Clifford came flying through the back door, loudly demanding snacks. He'd tossed them each a crisp, green Granny Smith apple then shooed them out of the kitchen door toward the living room so that he could begin getting dinner ready.

His *Cooking for Morons* book had assured him that preparation of its "Luscious Lasagna" recipe would take approximately ninety minutes including baking time, but Brody was chopping vegetables, soaking and laying out lasagna strips, and pouring out tomato sauce for well over an hour before he was even ready to put the dish into the oven. It was at that point that he read about the importance of preheating, which of course he had not done. This set him back another five minutes. In the end, the entire meal preparation took just under two hours. Yet when dinner was finally ready at ten minutes to six, Felicia still had not arrived.

When she walked in the door at last, at a quarter past the hour, he was elbow deep in a new task: feeding—or at least trying to feed—Gabe his supper. The child was not cooperating, however. He was much more interested in flinging his food than he was in consuming it. By the eighth spoonful of mashed carrots, there was far more in Brody's hair than had come anywhere near the baby's mouth. Pausing to wipe away an errant blob that had landed on the bridge of his nose, Brody felt the unmistakable sensation that he was being watched. He turned to see Fee leaning in the doorway, delightedly eyeing him and Gabe, looking for all the world as though she might have been watching her favorite television program.

With all the dignity he could muster, Brody rose to greet her and folded his arms across his formerly white apron, blobs of tomato sauce and carrots spotting its enormous illustration of two bright red lips and the cheerful directive, "Kiss the Cook."

"Hi!" Fee smiled, dumping her handbag, newspaper, and keys onto the counter that Brody had just cleaned. His eyes flickered, registering her transgression, but he remained silent. "Where are the other kids?"

"In the living room, playing a game," he informed her coolly.

"Great. Good for them." Fee gave him a curious look. "Is there something wrong?"

"Wrong? *Wrong?* What could be wrong?" Now that he finally had someone on whom to vent his frustration, the words fairly flew past Brody's lips. "Just because you said you'd be home before five o'clock and you're home well after six? What about that should that bother me? Unless, of course, it's because I worked on dinner for you and the kids all afternoon, and now it's completely *ruined* because you couldn't simply pick up a phone to call and tell somebody you'd be late!"

Felicia looked at him, stricken, for several horrible seconds. Then she snickered.

Brody felt his cheeks burn. "Did all that really come out of my mouth?"

"I'm afraid so." Felicia started to giggle. Brody dropped his arms to his sides and gave her a wounded little glare. "I'm so sorry, Brody," she laughed and reached out to squeeze his hand. "I'm not making fun of you; honestly, I'm not. I just never thought I'd be on the receiving end of that little tirade. It was, uh…educational, to say the least."

Brody tried not to crack a smile, but even he couldn't help but see the humor in the situation. Besides, Felicia's happiness was so contagious, there was no way on earth he could keep himself from grinning back at her. The two of them were still joking about his little hissy fit five minutes later when Dinah and Clifford came running into the kitchen.

"Mama, you're back!" Dinah said and gleefully leaped at her to claim a kiss.

Clifford wrapped his arms around Fee's knees and impatiently tugged at her skirt until she pulled him up and held him close. Silently, Brody wished that he could do the same.

While Felicia told him and the kids all about the highlights of her day—including an opportune meeting with the editor of *Child's Play*, who she reported with excitement had asked her to come back the next morning for an official interview—Brody set the table with his blackened lasagna and burnt string beans. He thoroughly expected both Dinah and Clifford to turn up their noses at the revolting meal. But though this time they had every right to do so, unexplainably both children accepted what he offered them without complaint.

Looking as grateful as if Brody had killed a bear with his bare hands in order to provide for them, Felicia wolfed down every noodle and mopped up every drop of sauce with a crust of bread, then even asked for seconds. He smiled as he watched her eat. Sitting across from her at the head of the table, Brody knew that he should not allow himself to become too comfortable. He was an outsider. This family wasn't something he should want, regardless of how pretty a picture the scene before him made to his lonely eyes.

But as he watched the woman and children around him and immersed himself in their laughter, Brody thought to himself that this did not feel like a foreign place. It felt accepting and familiar and comfortable. It felt as though he belonged.

It felt, he realized with a little jolt that shook him to his soul, exactly like home.

Ten

Sitting in front of her three-paneled, teakwood vanity, Felicia prepared for her interview carefully and deliberately while counting her blessings. She still could not believe that this could actually be happening to her. She'd been job hunting for exactly one day, and already she had landed an interview at the organization where she most wanted to work.

It was as if she had a guardian angel on her side.

She still recalled the look of smug satisfaction on Brody's face when she'd given him the news at dinner the night before. Fee wasn't an expert on what his expressions meant, but if she had to guess, she would have to say that he wasn't surprised in the slightest. Despite her lack of experience and education, Brody hadn't seemed to doubt for a moment that she was capable of snagging an interview. He sounded every bit as confident when he'd assured her he thought she was a natural for the job. Brody Collins actually believed in her.

It was enough to make her want to believe in herself.

Fee's lips curved slightly upward under her lip wand as she brushed on a layer of Burgundy Breeze. Her gray flannel suit jacket and matching knee-length skirt—purchased on a recent shopping trip with her power exec sister Cat—gave her just the professional edge she'd hoped for. Felicia was just slipping her black calfskin pumps over sheer stockings when she noticed a small shadow in the doorway.

"Dinah? Come here, honey." She held out one arm, and Dinah ran to her without hesitating. "Is something wrong?" she asked as tiny hands clutched at her waist.

The child tilted her chin upward and met Fee's questioning gaze with wide, sad eyes. "Are you going to leave us with Brody again?"

"Yes. For a while, at least. What's the matter, sweetie? Don't you like Brody?"

Dinah raised her shoulders a fraction of an inch. "He's okay, I guess," she said without much feeling. Fee wasn't fooled. She'd seen the way her daughter had watched Brody's every move the night before. Fee hadn't observed such interest—if not outright devotion—on her child's face since Robert had left. "But—"

"But what, honey?"

Dinah began to play with her mother's fingers. She was no longer meeting Fee's eyes. "Now that he lives here," she said, the slightest hint of accusation in her tone, "are you gonna marry him?"

"Dinah!" The question so startled her, Felicia nearly fell off her stool. "Whoever said anything about me marrying anybody?"

"Nobody." Another shrug. "I just figured that since you said that Daddy went off to marry Tiffany, you probably would want to marry somebody too." Her lower lip jutted out like a shelf to catch the tears that were about ready to spill from her eyes.

"Honey." Fee wrapped her arms around Dinah and pulled her completely up into her lap, unconcerned about the possibility of wrinkling her carefully pressed suit. She squeezed her child fiercely. "I know this is hard for you. You probably wish Mama and Daddy could get back together, don't you?"

"Mm-hm." The sound came, muffled, from the general area of her lapel, where Dinah's head rested.

"Dinah, you're old enough to know how really hard this has been. Even more than Clifford, you remember a lot of the good times we had with your daddy, don't you?"

Dinah burrowed even closer. Felicia drew one hand along the silky softness of her hair.

"Sweetie, I don't blame you for being upset. God wants mammas and daddies to stay together. A lot of mammas and daddies want that too. But sometimes one of them decides to leave. And there really isn't anything the other one can do to stop it. I couldn't stop your daddy from going away, and I couldn't stop him from marrying somebody else. But the fact that he doesn't live here anymore doesn't mean that he doesn't love you! He loves you and your brothers very much." Felicia was sure that on some level, this was true. Even if Robert wasn't very good about expressing his feelings, the kids all needed to be reassured that his love for them was real.

"Someday, I may find somebody who loves me very much too," she said. She did, in fact, want a man. Strangely, she wanted one particular man. But as far as she could tell, Brody did not want her. Whenever she met his eyes for too long, she noticed, he looked uncomfortable and hurried away. Whenever she tried to turn the conversation to more personal subjects, he quickly turned it back upon her or simply left the room. Fee didn't need any more obvious clues than that to convince her that Brody had no intention of letting her get close to him. But perhaps she would find someone to love someday. "Somebody who wants to live with us," she told her daughter, "and help take care of us, and have fun with us. Somebody who wants to live with us always, and I don't mean in the guesthouse. Do you understand?"

Dinah pulled back and looked at her. "I'm not sure."

"I guess what I'm saying is, yes. I may want to get married someday, sweetie." For a year, she'd been denying that she wanted anything to do with men. But the reality was, she did want to find love again. She wanted her children to have a father who would be there for them every day, and not just when the fancy struck him. She wanted a husband who would cherish her. If Brody's presence had done nothing else, it had awakened her to that irrefutable fact. But this time, she promised herself, things would be different. If she allowed herself to fall in love again, it would be with a man who loved and appreciated her for who she was, and not one who was simply out to use her.

"I promise, I won't pick anyone who you and your brothers don't come to love first. And I promise I'll tell you what's going on as it's happening, and not just after I make my decision. And that brings me to my last point: You asked about Brody." Felicia drew in a deep breath. "Brody and I are just friends," she said, trying to keep her daughter from seeing the sadness this fact caused her. "He hasn't said anything that would make me think he would ever want to marry me or even to ask me out on a date. But," she admitted, "he is exactly the sort of man I hope I will find someday. So I hope you like him. Because I know I do."

"I think he likes you, too," Dinah said seriously.

"Really?" Fee gave her a patronizing smile. Her child probably thought that everybody loved her mother.

"Yeah." The little girl nodded. "He's always looking at you and stuff."

"He's *what*?" Fee looked at her, startled.

"Uh-huh. Last night I saw him watching you when you went into the kitchen to get more juice. He watched you eat, too. He had this big goofy look on his face. An' he watched you finish feeding Gabe, when he *said* he was going into the kitchen to wash dishes."

What looks goofy to a ten-year-old, Fee reminded herself sternly, *could be perfectly normal to an adult.* She could not allow herself to become dewy-eyed and sentimental about Brody based on the observations of her child.

"Well, I would appreciate it if you wouldn't say anything to him about that," she said sternly. "Brody just works here. We wouldn't want to make him feel uncomfortable, now would we? We wouldn't want him to have any reason to leave."

"No," Dinah agreed. Her face lit up like a hundred-watt bulb. "He said he'd make us fish sticks tonight!"

Felicia despised fish sticks but knew her children loved them. Anyway, after the previous night's near disaster, she figured Brody deserved a break. "Isn't that nice?" she said and managed not to make a face.

Dinah climbed out of her lap and, without even pausing to give her mother a kiss, scurried from the room, her anxiety assuaged, leaving Felicia alone to think about fish sticks, goofy looks, resurrected dreams...and the irresistible stranger living in her guesthouse who was responsible for them all.

Brody hadn't intended to get caught at Adam Bly's office. The last thing he needed was for Felicia to discover him in a place where her nanny had no business being. In fact he hadn't even intended to stop by Adam's office at all. He couldn't even recall consciously making the decision to go there.

Before leaving that morning, Felicia had given Brody a fairly detailed itinerary for her day. He knew that she planned on running several errands and picking up four or five more applications—"just in case"—before going to *Child's Play* for her interview at eleven.

This meant that he had a very short window of opportunity in which he could stop by his office at *California Dream,* and having been out since Monday, he intended to make the most of it. Within forty-five minutes after Fee and the two older kids were out the door, Brody had already managed to feed, clothe, and change Gabriel—an impressive feat even to him, though he wasn't entirely certain how much of the breakfast had actually gone into the child. The biggest snag in his schedule was Gabe's stubborn refusal to burp after taking his bottle. Thankfully, he finally did let out a man-size belch just as Brody was preparing to carry him out the front door. Unfortunately, there was more to the burp than just noise, and Brody wound up having to change Gabe's clothes and his own before making a hasty exit fifteen minutes later than he had hoped.

He'd loaded Gabe into the Falcon and double-checked the safety restraints in record time, then headed off toward the building where, until this last weekend, he had worked seven days a week. Somewhere along the way, however, Brody's subconscious mind made the decision to steer the vehicle toward Adam's office, though he was not actually cognizant of this choice until he was less than five blocks away.

"Some kind of navigator you are," he accused the tiny passenger in the seat behind him as he realized what he'd done. His eyes flickered to the rearview mirror, in which he could see Gabe happily reaching for his own toes. "*One* of us should have been paying attention to where he was going." That person certainly wasn't him. He'd been so caught up in his thoughts about Felicia and her job interview, he'd been operating on autopilot ever since they left the house. "Where's your map anyway?"

"Mumm-mumm," Gabe told him.

"Mumm-mumm," Brody answered dryly, "is no excuse."

He consulted his watch, a stainless steel cheapie he'd picked up at the mall to take the place of his Rolex. Ten-fifteen. A full three-quarters of an hour before Fee was due to arrive at *Child's Play*. Why not just check in with Adam, since he was already there? It would only take fifteen minutes. And his plans for the morning were already shot—not that it really mattered. He hadn't actually promised Abby that he would stop into the office today. No doubt any pressing business at *California Dream* that required his presence could wait another twenty-four hours. He'd say a quick hello to the editor of his own magazine, see what Adam was thinking about hiring Fee for the position, then scoot back home, touch base with Abby by telephone, and have lunch ready before Felicia returned.

"All right, sport," he said to Gabe, feeling complete confidence in his strategy, "we're gonna stop and see your Uncle Adam. You'll like Uncle Adam. He's got a big, round face, like you do, and just about as much hair—though yours is coming, and his, sadly enough, is going…fast. Come to think of it, he eats about as often, and as neatly, as you do. You two are practically soul mates." He steered the Falcon through the parking structure, turning not up but down to the bottom level, made available only to privileged employees, and maneuvered his car into a parking spot marked in white painted letters *Reserved*.

Five minutes later, diaper bag over one shoulder and baby on the other, Brody strode through the outer reception area and into Adam Bly's private office.

"Well, I'll be a monkey's uncle." Adam folded both arms behind his slightly balding head and tipped back in his chair until Brody thought he might actually fall. Somehow, the man managed to balance there and regarded him with a look of intense concentration in his hazel eyes before his wide, round face finally broke into a pleased grin.

"Gabe resents that remark," Brody told him sternly. "He doesn't like being called a monkey."

"I see. And to whom does this little nonprimate belong? Or should I be afraid to ask?"

"He belongs to a friend," Brody said evasively.

"Uh-huh. A friend." Adam folded his hands neatly together and regarded Brody over them. "And would this…er…*friend* happen to be a certain beautiful woman with dark, chin-length hair, soulful gray eyes, and a burning desire to work in the publishing business?"

Brody glared at him. "I don't remember that being on anyone's résumé."

"Ah, but you admit the child is hers?"

"Of course." He settled himself in the chair across from Adam. "She's looking for work. I'm helping out for a little while, since I have a fair amount of experience with kids…"

Adam let out a hearty guffaw. "Oh, *experience*. Is that what you call it?"

"What? You don't think your job—what used to be my job—has taught you anything about children?"

"My poor, deluded friend," Adam said sadly. "Anything I know about kids, I learned from my own. Incidentally, I have two of them: ages two and six. Interestingly enough, one of them is named after you. He's a cute little fellow. Looks nothing like his namesake—"

"I know who Collin is named after," Brody cut in impatiently. "And I'm perfectly aware of what he looks like."

"Sorry." Adam grounded his chair and threw Brody a wounded look. "It's just that it's been so long since we've seen you around the house, Jeannie and I weren't really sure if you remembered us anymore."

"Yeah, yeah. Cry me a river. How are Jeannie and the kids anyway?"

"Jeannie," Adam said with great satisfaction, "is a saint."

"I'm happy for you."

"The children, unfortunately, take after me."

"You have my deepest sympathies."

"Thank you." Adam glanced at a framed picture near his right elbow: a striking honey blond with short curly hair; a little girl in pigtails with her mother's coloring and her father's round face; a mischievous looking toddler in a Winnie-the-Pooh T-shirt and navy cotton shorts—all standing in front of the entrance to Disneyland, hamming it up for the camera. "Jeannie's a real sport about it, though, I've got to hand it to her. She handles those adorable urchins like a real pro, which she is. I'm telling you, Brody, there is nothing like a good woman to do a man's heart good. But maybe I'm telling you something you already know?" he suggested hopefully.

"L.A. already has enough matchmakers," Brody stated, hoping to nip that conversation in the bud. "It doesn't need another one. Especially if that matchmaker is you. Anyway, I didn't come here to talk about my love life. I came here to talk about Felicia—"

"Sorry. I was kinda hoping they were one and the same."

"—and the proofreader/reviewer position," Brody finished, ignoring him. "I don't want to tell you your business, Adam, and I have no intention of telling you who you should hire. I just wanted to see what your impression was so far, and if you had any idea of what direction you want to go in hiring."

"Well…" Adam's face took on a more serious expression. "I did like what I saw yesterday," Brody's friend told him, folding his arms across the desk. "She's sharp; I'll give you that. I've had several résumés come in, but Felicia was the first person to bring hers in person, along with a stack of pretty impressive writing samples—including a hilarious review of Burger World, with comments by her son, which she'd written specifically to set the stage for this interview. She's a go-getter, I'll say that for her. I like that. I like her attitude, too. She sounded quite confident and really interested in working here—not just because it's a job, but because she believes strongly in family. It's definitely a plus that she has kids. I'll tell you another thing: A lot of magazines like to hire young college graduates so they can train 'em up the way they want 'em. I'd rather have someone with a little bit of life experience under her belt—someone who's more likely to stick around for a while. I guess what I'm saying is, yeah, I liked her all right. If her interview goes as well as I think it might, I'd say she has a pretty fair shot at the job."

Brody grinned back at him. "That's great. That's exactly what I was hoping to hear."

The telephone on the desk let out an irritating buzz. Adam lifted the receiver to his ear, listened a moment, then covered the mouthpiece with his hand and looked at Brody with an expression of stunned surprise.

"You did say that you didn't want Felicia to know that you're involved in any way with this job opportunity, is that right?

"That's right."

"Well, I hate to tell you this, buddy ol' pal, but she's right outside the door at this very minute, waiting to meet me for our appointment."

"What?" Brody glanced at his cheapo watch again. It still read ten-fifteen. "What time is it?"

"A quarter to eleven." Adam's eyes danced. "She's a bit early," he said with a smirk.

"That's Fee for you," Brody grumbled, vowing to himself never to buy a cheap watch again. "She's like that. Punctual, I mean."

"How responsible of her."

"This," Brody said bitterly, "is no time for responsibility."

"Oh, really? And what is it time for?"

Brody shifted Gabe to a more secure position on his shoulder, grabbed the diaper bag, and scrambled back to stand behind Adam, where he could no longer be viewed through the door's tiny window. "This is a time for creative problem solving," he said.

"How is creative problem solving going to help you?"

"It's going to help me because it's going to keep Fee from knowing that I'm in your office. Now tell your secretary not to send Fee in. Tell her you'll be out there in a moment and that you're going to conduct the interview at her desk."

"But how am I going to—?"

"No *buts*," Brody ordered.

"I don't know about this. It doesn't sound like such a good idea to me." Adam shook his head and removed his fingers from the telephone mouthpiece.

Brody reached out with his free hand and clamped it over the place where Adam's hand had just been. "Do you want this woman to ever speak to me again?" he hissed.

Adam's whole round face lit up, making him look like a yellow Happy Face sign. "I knew it! I *knew* it!" he crowed.

"All I know," Brody told him, his heart in his throat, "it that it is *very* important that Fee not find out that I am in here."

"Mumm-mumm!" Gabe gurgled. "Mumm-mumm-mumm-mumm!"

Brody paled. Had the baby heard his mother's voice? Even worse, had Fee heard Gabe's? "Now tell the receptionist you'll be right out!" he whispered fiercely.

"Okay, okay. Don't get your tail feathers in a bunch." Adam did as he was told, then grabbed a pen and a manila file that had been resting on his desk and headed for the door. "But you are gonna owe me big when this is over, pal," he warned.

"What I'm gonna owe you," Brody growled, "if you don't get out there within five seconds—"

"I'm going! I'm going! Sheesh!" Adam disappeared through the door, leaving it open a crack behind him.

Brody counted to one hundred—quickly—to make sure that his partner had an opportunity to settle in at the receptionist's desk and get the interview started. Then he stealthily made his way across the room, Gabe cradled in his arms, and peeked through the tiny crack in the doorway. Adam was seated with his back to the office, so Brody could see only the back of his head. Fee was seated at exactly a ninety-degree angle to Adam; she would see Brody only if she deliberately turned and looked into the office window. Adam's secretary was nowhere to be seen. Brody turned his head to the side and pressed his ear to the opening.

"—appreciate your understanding," Adam was saying. "I know it's hard to believe, but a raving lunatic stormed into my office this morning, and…well, it's a long story. Let's just say we won't be able to use it for our interview."

"How terrible!" Fee sounded genuinely shocked.

"Isn't it though?" Adam clucked.

Brody crossed the room in three long steps, pressed some buttons on Adam's phone and waited. The ringer sounded several times in his ear before a male voice finally answered.

"Yes?" Adam responded, the slightest trace of amusement in his tone.

"Enough with the lunatic story already," Brody hissed into the phone. "Just stick with the interview!"

"Yes *sir!* I'm sorry, but I'm conducting an interview at the moment, *so I won't be able to take any more calls.* But I'll be happy to speak with you afterward." A click sounded in Brody's ear, and he crept back to his position at the door, dragging the telephone and its long cord after him.

"—was my boss," he heard Adam say. "Now, let's get started, shall we?" Brody listened for about fifteen minutes as Adam asked Felicia questions about her interest in publishing, her past experience, and why she thought she could do well in the proofreading position at *Child's Play*. All was going perfectly until he heard Adam say, "Well, Fee, I must say, you make a convincing argument for hiring you."

"H-how did you know my name was *Fee?*" Felicia said, sounding surprised.

Brody picked up the phone and dialed fiercely, making the receptionist's handset buzz repeatedly.

Adam ignored the sound coming from the machine next to him. "Um…I just assumed that was your nickname. I hope I didn't offend you." Brody stopped buzzing.

Fee shook her head. "No, of course not! I'm just surprised. Most people don't think to call me that unless they hear one of my friends or sisters say the nickname first. You're very clever to think of it. Please, *do* call me Fee."

"Thank you, Fee." Adam threw a smug little smirk over his shoulder, which Brody just barely caught before ducking, in case Felicia should happen to follow Adam's gaze. The interview went on for another ten minutes without incident, then he heard Adam utter, "All right then! I think that's all I need for now. It's possible I'll have an answer for you as early as tomorrow." And then the fatal words, "I'll just need to call your references and speak with Brody—"

"Brody!" Felicia exclaimed.

Brody began to pound on the telephone with all his might.

"—er, *Mr.* Brody. Mr., uh, Ethan Brody," Adam stammered over the loud buzzing coming from near his elbow. "Our accountant. He handles all our paperwork regarding new hires."

"I…see," Felicia said, but Brody could see through the crack that she was looking at Adam very oddly indeed.

"Mumm-mumm!" Gabe said proudly.

Feeling his heart skip a beat, Brody closed the door with a barely audible click and pressed his ear up against it.

"Was that a—?" Felicia paused.

"What's that, Fee?"

"Oh, nothing. Nothing." Her voice had returned to normal. "I thought I heard a baby." She laughed. "I guess I'm missing my little boy a lot. I'm actually imagining that I hear him! Isn't that silly?"

"Actually," Adam told her dryly, "I'm not surprised."

Heaving a heavy sigh, Brody let his head fall against the door with a tiny thump. "I think she bought it," he whispered to the child in his arms.

Gabe looked up at him seriously. "Dummm-dummmmm," he proclaimed.

Brody planted a kiss on the child's chubby petal-soft cheek. "For once, little guy," he said with a sigh, "I could not agree with you more."

Brody spent half the evening worrying that Felicia suspected the truth about him, the other half eating his heart out because her happy demeanor and warm interactions made it perfectly clear that she had not.

As much as he hated the thought of Felicia discovering that he'd lied to her, he found it almost unbearably uncomfortable to continue caring for her children—and her—under false pretenses. The strangest thing of all was, even if he could have been given a way out, Brody wouldn't have wanted to take it. The job that he'd backed himself into was turning out to be far more fulfilling than the work that had consumed the last five years of his life. He found more satisfaction in helping Dinah with her homework or tracking down Clifford's lost lizards or introducing Gabe to finger foods than he would in a lifetime of chronicling the adventures and misadventures of the spoiled and famous.

More and more each day, he was realizing what a terrible mess he had gotten himself into. Since Lucy's wedding reception, he had tried to resurrect the subject of Fee selling her story to the press only once more. But she'd given him such a look of disappointment that he'd apologized, dropped the line of questioning, and hadn't had the guts to bring it up since. His hopes for a painless and satisfactory resolution to the situation were becoming slimmer and slimmer each day.

The morning after her interview, Felicia remained at home until after ten o'clock, then announced that she was going out for a couple of hours to do her banking and grocery shopping. It was shortly after she left that Adam Bly called.

"Well, hello there, old man," he said when Brody answered.

"Hello, Adam." Brody tried not to sound too friendly. He was still holding a grudge against Bly for making the situation so difficult for him the day before. "What's going on? Why are you calling me here?"

"I'm fine, Brody, thanks for asking," Adam muttered. "And you?"

"I *didn't* ask," Brody reminded him.

"So I noticed. And I wasn't calling you, by the way. I was calling the person who actually lives there. You know, Collins, everything isn't always about you," he said with a dramatic air.

Brody chuckled. "All right. You're right. I suppose you're calling for Fee then. She's not here at the moment. Could I take a message? A very *detailed* one?"

"If you're pumping me for information," Adam told him coolly, "you're wasting your time. There's a sacred bond between an employer and employee."

"A what—?"

"The only person I would tell that Felicia did get the job is my boss. So there. You won't get a word out of me."

"Sorry. You're quite right." Brody tried to sound genuinely apologetic. "I won't ask again."

"See that you don't. Anyway, she left me a mobile phone number. I think I'll try her on that."

"Good idea. She'll want to know right away. And, Adam?"

"Mm?"

"Thanks."

Adam *harrumphed* something Brody could not quite decipher, but he knew what his friend was trying to say.

Feeling the need to celebrate properly, he spent the next hour fumbling around with a devil's-food cake mix and two jars of frosting he found in the pantry. From his high chair, Gabe cheered him on, crying, "Dummm-dummmm! Dummm-dummmm!" over and over. The night before, Gabe had repeated the phrase time and time again, and Fee had told Brody, blushing, that she thought he was trying to say "Daddy." Brody would have thought such a revelation would have made him feel anxious or claustrophobic. Instead, all he felt was pride.

When Fee returned at half past twelve, Brody was waiting for her, wearing his Kiss-the-Cook apron and holding out a sheet of chocolate cake covered in fudge frosting and creamy white letters he had sloppily stirred in with a knife: "Go, Fee."

"I wanted to write 'Congratulations,'" he explained awkwardly. "But I'm not that coordinated—and the cake wasn't that big. I'm afraid the letters blurred a bit too, because I didn't wait until the cake cooled off before I started working on the top."

"But," Fee said, dumbfounded, "how did you even know I got the job?"

"I-" *Dummm-dummmm!* "Um…your boss called here first, then said he'd try you on your cell phone. I guess I just assumed that you got the job. I mean…how could you not get it? I could have sworn you'd told me that you would hear from him by today. No? My mistake, I guess. Well, worst-case scenario, it would have been a chocolate consolation prize. As it is, it's a lucky guess!"

Fee seemed to take his explanation at face value. "You really thought I would get the job?" she asked shyly.

"I really thought you deserved to get the job," Brody told her, and meant it.

"You're very sweet, Brody," she said softly, then lowered her eyelashes like a veil. "Do you know that?"

"Well…" Guilt seared him like a flame. "I don't know about that."

"That's okay," she said, laying her smooth, long fingers on the rough skin at the back of his hand. "I do."

Abruptly, she turned away to admire her cake and cut them each a slice. And as she moved, Brody watched her and wished more than anything that what she believed about him was true.

Fee was scheduled to start work two days later, on a Saturday. Normally, she would have begun on Monday, she explained to Brody and the kids, but her boss had told her that her position had been left open for so long, things had gotten backed up. There was more to her job that just proofreading, she told them proudly. She had all kinds of responsibilities and would be in charge of organizing several of the departments and columns featured in the periodical. Adam Bly had asked her if she would mind coming in two days early to get her office and files organized so that she would be ready to go on Monday morning. Brody had called Adam shortly after that to ask why on earth he would make such a ridiculous demand—to which Adam had politely responded that if Brody wanted to handle his employees in a different manner, he was more than welcome to come into the office himself to do so face to face. After that, Brody had kept his suggestions to himself.

On Friday—his first day off from his childcare duties—Brody told Fee he had some personal business to take care of, left the house early, and headed straight for his office at *California Dream*. Even though he'd had Nicholas Fortunata's permission to take the week off to pursue the Tiffany Diamond story, Brody felt extremely guilty for having been truant for such an extended period of time. He half expected to find hammocks swinging from the rafters and Abby with a blender on her desk, serving piña coladas.

To his relief and surprise, the office looked much as he had left it.

"Hi," he said to his sister as he strode through the front door.

"Hello, sir," she said, staring at him blankly. "May I help you? Do you have an appointment?"

"Ha-ha. You're a riot," Brody told her with a straight face. "How's the fort?"

"Hasn't burned down yet," she answered cheerfully. "How's my pumpkin head?"

"Still on your shoulders, where it's always been."

"I was referring to the baby."

"Oh, *that* pumpkin head. He's fine. He's…uh…started calling me Daddy." Brody felt his ears burn.

"Oh, that poor child." Abby swung her legs out from under her desk and crossed them as she leaned back leisurely in her chair. "Come on. Out with it. Tell Abby the whole story."

"There's no story," Brody assured her and walked past her into his office. By the squeak of her chair and the click of her heels against the floor tiles, he could tell without looking that she was following him. He settled into the familiar comfort of his black leather chair without acknowledging her presence.

"You're wasting my valuable time by stalling," she complained and dropped into the seat across from him. "And you'll have my boss to answer to for it."

"All right," Brody said reluctantly. Abby could out-stubborn him any day. "What do you want to hear?" He reached for one of the yellow pencils in his cup and began to twist it between the fingers of his left hand.

"Does she know yet?"

"Who, Fee?"

"No, the tooth fairy. Of *course*, Fee!"

"No. She does not know. But I can't imagine that she isn't going to find out soon. I sort of helped get her a job over at *Child's Play*."

"Brody! Good going. It's only a matter of time until someone mentions your name. You can't exactly put a gag order on your employees."

The pencil snapped. "I know, I know," he said heavily and reached for another. "And even if she doesn't hear it from them, her sisters are due back from their honeymoon and business trip any day. One of them is sure to spill the facts."

Abby looked at him intently. "I don't remember ever seeing you look so terrible," she said bluntly.

"Flattery," Brody told her, "will get you nowhere." He ran one hand over his stubbled jaw. He'd been so caught up in taking care of the kids, he hadn't even remembered to shave since Wednesday. "I'm just tired, I guess."

"You're not just tired," Abby informed him. "You're miserable."

"I'm not miserable."

"Well then you, my friend," she said flatly, "are in love. Which essentially works out to be the same thing. At least for a while."

"Do tell."

"I am telling. I'm just not sure you're listening." She eyed him thoughtfully. "You know, that barracuda has been in here almost every day, looking for you."

"What barracuda?"

"You know, the one with caps on her teeth and hair like an enormous red rat's nest. Though why you'd want to wind up with someone like her is beyond me…"

"You mean Carmen?" Brody rolled his eyes. It was hard to believe he'd actually considered asking her out to dinner less than a week ago. What was he thinking? Why would he ever even consider dating someone like her, when someone like Fee—

His second pencil snapped. Brody flung the pieces to one side.

"All right, all right. You guessed it. I'm smitten with Fee," he confessed, the words coming out more like an accusation than an admission. "And there's nothing I can do about it. There. Are you happy?"

"Not yet," Abby said, wiggling her fingers in the air like a mad professor. "Nor will I be until we get you and your little lady friend together."

"Good grief." Brody glowered at her. "Isn't there anyone in this city who isn't a matchmaker? Forget about it, Abby. It's none of your business."

"Perhaps you're right. But it is *your* business. And I hope you intend to do something about it. If you're so smitten, you should tell the girl so. Declare your intentions."

"I can't do that. I can't say anything to Fee, not about this.

Not now. She doesn't even know who I really am." Brody knew he sounded desperate, but he couldn't help it.

"Didn't I tell you to come clean?" Abby scolded. Then, before he even had a chance to answer, "Never mind. There'll be time enough for me to gloat later. Right now, we have to concentrate on getting you back on the straight and narrow. I suggest—and now I realize this is a crazy, way-out-there proposition—that you tell her the truth. Hopefully, she's become attached enough to your ugly mug by now that she'll be willing to forgive you, and we can get on with planning the wedding."

"Sometimes," Brody told her, staring, "I cannot believe the things I hear come out of your mouth."

"Thank you," Abby said, nodding in agreement. "Sometimes, I amaze even myself."

Abby spent the next half-hour convincing Brody that telling Felicia the truth actually was the best plan of action and that there was a slight possibility that she might not respond to the news in a way that would result in his requiring months of hospitalization. Before she left at five o'clock, she poked her pert blond head into his office and elicited from him one last assurance that he would come clean with Fee when he returned home that evening.

When Brody got back to Felicia's around eight, however, she and the children were gone, and there was a note on the door to the guesthouse:

> *Dear Brody,*
> *The kids and I went over to Daphne's to watch a movie. We'll be back late—don't wait up. I confirmed with Adam that I need to work tomorrow, but you can have most of the afternoon off. Robert called and*

*said that he and Tiffany would be coming to pick the
kids up at around one.*

    Thanks again!

Love,
Fee

His lips set in a grim, thin line, Brody entered the guest-house and, with a heart like lead, began to dial the phone.

Eleven

Felicia came home with the children shortly before ten. Brody lay in the darkness of his room, still awake and fully clothed, and listened to van doors slam while Fee's soothing voice murmured crisp, indistinguishable injunctions to her offspring. After a while he heard the front door close. Then all was silent, and the evening still once more.

From his bed, Brody could see the lights go on upstairs one by one and, after some time had passed, off again. He squeezed his eyelids shut and tried to force himself to go to sleep. He threw up a quick prayer—one of several he'd made tonight. He reviewed in his mind several of the Scripture verses that had stuck in his head this week; he'd taken to reading Fee's old study Bible before bed each night.

Still, he could not sleep.

He knew he should get up and change into his pajama pants and close the blinds, to keep out the light that leaked in from the pale gray city sky. But he was depressed. He'd barely changed positions since throwing himself onto the bed after his phone conversation with Carmen. He'd tried two other photographers before calling her, but both were already booked. If Carmen already had plans for Saturday, she apparently didn't have any problem breaking them for Brody and had cheerfully pledged to be at Felicia's the next day by half past twelve.

He opened his eyes again and watched as a pale golden glow lit the window to the nursery. A shadow moved gracefully across his line of vision, then receded into the depths of the room.

Gabe must not be cooperating tonight.

Brody tried to ignore the ache in his stomach. His job at the magazine had caused him stress before, but never outright pain.

That's because you've never done anything this low and underhanded before. You ought to be ashamed of yourself.

He wasn't actually doing anything illegal, he reminded himself defensively. Carmen would be parked on the street, on public property, when she took the photographs. He wasn't invading anyone's privacy; they'd be in full public view: Robert, Tiffany Diamond, and the children...

The children.

The children, Brody told himself sternly, wouldn't even know that their photos were in the magazine unless someone pointed that fact out to them, and it didn't seem likely that any of their little playmates were subscribers to *California Dream*. And even if Clifford and Dinah did find out, they might not mind. Perhaps they'd enjoy seeing their faces in print. Children liked attention...up to a point.

Of course, that would be just the beginning of the media frenzy. Once the story broke, reporters and freelance photographers would swarm the Salinger-Kelley house like locusts. But...Fee could handle it. She was strong. It was her responsibility to protect the kids, and she knew and did her job well.

Then again, as the children's nanny, it was Brody's job to protect them as well. But that was a mere technicality. He was first and foremost the editor of *California Dream*; his primary responsibility was making sure they got the scoop.

Everything else was simply a means to that ends. He and Abby were both fooling themselves if they thought it could be any other way.

For more than two hours, Brody had been wrestling with his conscience, trying to figure a way out of the mess he now found himself in. If he thought there was a real chance of salvaging the situation with Fee, he would have been willing to scrap the story altogether and suffer Nicholas Fortunata's wrath. But there was no way Felicia was going to forgive him now. It was already too late. Truth and honesty were like water and air to her: She could not live without them. Yet since he'd met her at the wedding, nearly everything that had come out of Brody's mouth had been lies. There was no way she could trust him, and therefore, no hope for them to ever build a relationship with a solid foundation. She was going to find out the truth about him in the next few days, and there was nothing he could do to stop that from happening. Either he could lose Fee and lose the story, or lose Fee and gain the scoop of the year, bringing at least some good out of his disastrous week.

But, as Brody thought back on the events of the last seven days, he knew he would not have traded a single instant for the world.

Like a moth to flame, his eyes traveled again to the light in Gabe's window. The nursery light continued to burn. It looked as though the child was determined to stay up for the duration.

The Indiglo light of Brody's newest wristwatch revealed that it was ten-thirty-five: not an unreasonable hour to still be up, yet late enough that he knew his assistance might actually do some good. After tomorrow, everything was bound to change. The one thing he'd been longing to do would then be beyond his reach. It was now or never.

He slipped his feet over the side of the bed and jammed them into the loafers he'd kicked off two hours before. His khakis had reached a new state of dishevelment, and his straw-colored flannel shirt hung untucked at the waist, the button-down collar flopping loose on one side. Brody didn't even bother to right his appearance; he simply gripped between his thumb and forefinger the key he'd left lying on the desk and headed out the door into the night.

He took extra care not to frighten Felicia or the children—rapping gently on each doorway before stepping through. By the time he got to the second floor, he'd started humming "Baby Mine" from *Dumbo*. Fee had been singing it to Gabe the night before after watching the video, and it was the most nonthreatening noise he could think of. He did not hear a sound from Clifford's or Dinah's rooms. "Fee? It's just me," he said softly, pausing outside the nursery door.

"Brody?" Felicia peered out the door, her eyes wide and sleepy. She was draped in a heavy chenille robe tied over silk paisley pajamas that Brody could see sticking out from beneath the robe's hem. Not an inch of skin was visible beneath her throat, except for her hands, now wrapped around her baby's bottom, but Brody had never seen her look more desirable.

"Did I scare you?"

"No. I figured it was either you, or really large, musically gifted mice," she teased.

"I hope you're not disappointed."

"To see you? Never."

Brody's heart skipped a beat. "Good. I remembered what you said about those robbers, and I didn't want to throw you into a panic.

Fee flushed slightly and turned away. "What are you doing here anyway?" she asked, stepping back into the nursery. "Did you forget something?" She carried Gabe over to his crib and leaned over as if to deposit him inside. As soon as she did, his eyes flapped open like two tiny window shades, and he let out a sharp cry of protest. Fee sighed and straightened with him still in her arms.

"No. I was still awake, and I saw the light. I thought maybe you could use some help in getting the baby to sleep," Brody told her.

Fee paused, tilted her head to the left, and banged at her ear with one hand. "I'm sorry. Could you repeat that? I thought you said you wanted to help put Gabe down."

"That's what the man said." Brody reached out to take the child from her.

"Dummm-dummm!" Gabe cried, eagerly reaching out both arms.

"There is nothing dumb about wanting to help out a lady," Brody said sternly. "You might consider doing the same thing every once in a while."

"Isn't it a little late at night, and Gabe a little young, to be laying on shame that thick?" Fee laughed.

"You're just tired," Brody said sternly and nodded at the rocking chair in the corner. "Go on. Take a load off."

"Now I know I must be dreaming. But…at least I'm smart enough to know I might as well make the most of it." Fee lowered herself into the rocker and began to push it back and forth with her slippered feet.

For a good fifteen minutes, Brody paced the room with Gabe on his shoulder, Fee sitting in her chair with her eyes closed, a look of bemused contentment on her features. After a while, the rocker stopped moving, and Brody was certain that she dozed. A delicate snore escaped from her button nose, but this only succeeded in making her even more adorable to him.

He decided that Gabe was completely out and bent over to lay him in his crib. As when Felicia attempted the same thing, Gabe opened his eyes—though not as wide this time—and murmured in protest, "Mumm-mumm."

"Here, I'll take him," Fee said drowsily and slipped her hands under the baby's arms.

"Hey, you're supposed to be asleep." Brody hadn't even seen her rise. "I wanted to help." Reluctantly, he relinquished the child.

"Believe me, you're helping," she said, laying one hand on his arm.

"Not anymore."

"All right then," she told him, smoothing back the dark, baby-fine hair at the top of Gabe's head. "Sing him a lullaby."

"Then I really will scare you," Brody warned.

"Babies," she told him fondly, "are not music critics. And neither am I."

"Okay…" Brody let out a long breath. It was perhaps the last time he and Felicia would ever be alone like this. He could not bring himself to deny her anything she asked. "But don't say I didn't warn you."

He searched his mind for the words to something other than "Rock-a-bye, Baby." The only thing that came to mind was, again, "Baby Mine." He could not recall all the lyrics, even though he'd seen the *Dumbo* video just the night before. But what he had forgotten he simply mumbled over, and Fee did not complain. She only smiled sweetly and held her child close, while Brody lowered his face next to Gabe's screwed-up features and crooned:

"Baby mine…close your eyes. Hmm-hmmm-hmmmm-hm-hm-hmmm. You are so precious to me, cute as can be, baby of mine."

Fee smiled down at him, her eyes sparkling in the moon-light. Brody straightened, shakily drew one arm around her bundled-up shoulders, and pulled her and Gabe as close to him as possible. Without hesitating, Felicia laid the flawless skin of her cheek against the broad expanse of his chest and let it rest there.

"Lay your head close to my heart, never to part…baby of mine," he sang in a shaky baritone, swaying back and forth to the music in a sort of makeshift dance.

The beating of his own heart sounded loudly in Brody's ears. Instinctively, without even deciding he was going to do so, he dropped his chin and pressed his lips softly against Felicia's forehead. He felt her shudder for an instant in his arms, then relax against him.

Brody stiffened almost imperceptibly. *What are you thinking, Collins? Do you think she doesn't have reason enough to hate you already? Do you have to betray her even further by letting her think you're a decent, honorable guy—and allowing her to care about that guy? A guy who doesn't even exist?*

Tenderly, he unwound his arms. Felicia stirred, slowly, almost as if she was doing so in her sleep and cast Brody a wide-eyed, what's-going-on-here? look. When he did not immediately respond, she stepped back and laid the baby in his bed. This time Gabe went down quietly.

"I guess I'd better be going," Brody whispered. Felicia was several feet away from him now. He could not touch her unless he made a point of crossing the room and going to her, which he knew he could not do.

"I guess so." Fee turned back to him, her soft lips curving at him like a silent question mark.

"Well…" He knew there was nothing he could give her, no explanation, that would make everything come out right. *Felicia, there's something I've got to tell you. I'm not who you think I am…* Brody could not bring himself to do it. "Good night then." He paused at the door and threw her a weak, apologetic smile. "You're really quite a wonderful woman. Do you know that?" He had to tell her so, at least this one time.

The question mark curved up at the corners. "You know, I think I'm finally starting to believe that. Thank you."

"No. Thank you."

Brody paused with his hand on the doorframe, hoping his eyes were somehow communicating to her what words could not.

Felicia lifted one hand and gave a wobbly little wave, her expression unreadable.

Then Brody turned and made a hasty, heavy-hearted escape from the one person in the world he had absolutely no desire ever to leave.

Back in his room, Brody lay in the darkness—still wide awake, his heart racing now as he realized the significance of what he'd subconsciously chosen to sing for Fee. She was precious to him.

There was no getting around the truth. He was head-over-heels, out-of-his-mind, crazy-in-love with Felicia. He'd had no intention of loving her or anyone else, but that was exactly what had happened. With that love came an intense desire to protect her—as well as Dinah, Clifford, and Gabe. And, Brody realized with a rush of adrenaline, that was one desire that he could fulfill. Perhaps he could not make it so that she would ever love him. But maybe he could still stop a chain of events that was nearly out of control and would most certainly hurt her if he did not do something fast.

"Please, God," he whispered. It had been a long time since he'd allowed himself to place control of his life fully into someone else's hands. Ironically, he felt safer than he had in some time as he uttered the words, knowing that he was entrusting a situation that was hopeless into the care of one who actually *could* make the mess all come out right. "I've really gotten in over my head this time. I'm not even asking help for my sake. But if you could just help me fix things for Fee and the kids…"

He sat up straight and moved quickly to the desk, where he began punching numbers on a handset. On the other end of the line, the phone rang several times before someone answered.

"Hello, Nicholas? Brody Collins here. Look, I'm sorry to call so late."

"I suppose you have a good reason?" Fortunata's commanding voice boomed in his ear.

"Yes. Actually, I do. You know, I promised to have you something on the Tiffany Diamond story as early as Monday…"

"And you have it now? Excellent!" Brody could practically hear a cash register *chi-ching* in the background. "We'll get the designers to start working on the layout this weekend. I'll expect the text from you by Tuesday morning at the latest."

"Well…the thing is, I don't have it exactly," Brody answered slowly. "As a matter of fact, I'm not going to be able to get it, Nicholas."

"Things aren't going according to plan, eh? Well, fine. Whatever. If you can't get it to me this week, next week will be sufficient. Even if the story doesn't make our next issue, it seems that we will have scooped the competition."

"I'm sorry, sir." Brody cleared his throat. "I can see that I wasn't clear. What I meant to say was I'm not going to be able to get the story at all."

The silence that followed was nearly palpable. "Are you saying you can't, Brody? Or that you won't? Because I seem to recall you saying something the other day about sympathizing with this woman. And if your only reason for not getting the story is that you've gone soft, we have more than enough reporters and editors who would be capable of, and more than willing to, step in on your behalf." Brody caught the veiled threat lurking beneath Nicholas's words.

"I didn't realize that my job was on the line." Brody clenched and unclenched his fists at his sides.

"Yes. Well, now you do." Fortunata spoke in a low, threatening voice.

"Well then," Brody said heavily, sounding like a man clearly resigned to his fate, "I can see that there's very little left to say…"

When Brody arrived the next morning to watch the children, Felicia felt like a love-struck schoolgirl. She could barely look him in the eyes. After he'd left the night before, she'd been certain that she wouldn't manage to get even a single wink. But after tossing and turning until nearly four o'clock, she'd at last dozed fitfully, her dreams filled with diaper-wearing elephants with gargantuan ears and a familiar, handsome man holding Fee in his arms, whispering playfully, "Kiss the Cook!"

Brody, too, seemed almost embarrassed to meet her gaze. His abrupt departure from the nursery had been enough to confirm her suspicions that he was not yet ready to enter into a relationship with her. But the look of desire manifest on his face, the war of emotions played out on his features, and the tender kiss to her forehead had communicated blatantly that he felt something deeper than casual affinity or a mere working relationship.

It was not exactly the way she'd imagined a romance unfolding, Fee had to admit. This time around, she had hoped for something more like a fairy tale. Too many times as a teenager, she had found herself pining after young men who strung her along, but had no intention of actively pursuing her. If Brody was up to the same game, she thought fiercely, she wouldn't put up with it. She'd come to care for herself and her family too much to subject them to such a lack of respect and love.

But…her heart softened. She didn't think that Brody was the type of man who would treat her that way. And as long as she felt that he was at least honestly facing his feelings for her—good and bad—she was willing to hang in there and see what God had in store for them both.

Felicia was still daydreaming about the possibilities when she left the house at seven-thirty. It didn't even occur to her to mention what she would be doing during her lunch hour.

She'd arrived at work at eight and rendezvoused with Adam in the parking lot. After presenting her with a key, settling her into her office and getting her acquainted with her files, her boss had left, saying that he had obligations outside the office and would be back later in the day to check on her. At eleven, Fee had slipped her shiny new key into the glass outer office door and headed off to the airport.

At first she had worried about taking a long lunch on her first day of work. But Adam had seemed pretty relaxed about the situation in allowing Felicia to monitor her own hours. If she was unable to complete her errand within an hour, Fee figured, she'd simply work a little bit later that afternoon.

When she arrived at the airport at the designated time, her passengers were waiting at the agreed-upon place outside of baggage claim.

"Hey there, lovebirds!" She grinned and leaned across the seats to wave at them. "I mean, *Ciao*. How was Italy?"

"Expensive," Cam grunted and started to drag his and his wife's bags to the back of the minivan.

"Hey there yourself!" Lucy beamed, sticking her torso into the van to envelop her sister in an enormous hug. Her dark shoulder-length curls were tied up in a loose pony-tail, and her skin practically glowed. "Don't listen to him. Italy was lovely. He's just cranky 'cause we've been flying all night."

"I can't believe you're back already." Felicia shook her head disapprovingly. "Only a week? You call that a honeymoon?"

"Yeah, well…" Lucy shrugged. "It's spring, you know. My busy season. 'When a young man's fancy turns to love,' and all that. Cam's pretty backed up with his work at the university too. We're going to take another trip to New England in the fall." She stepped back onto the sidewalk and gave the van a double take. "Wait a minute. You're not Daphne. How'd you get this gig anyway? I thought Little Bit was going to pick us up."

"Daffy Daphne," Felicia told her, "is off on some ultra-romantic hiking trip with Elliott. The kids and I went to her house to watch a movie last night, and she begged me to take her place."

"She had to beg, huh?"

"Sorry. It's just that I'm a bit rushed today. I have a new job."

"Get out of town!" Lucy threw up her hand and caught Fee's in a high-five. "When I left you were just talking about it. And now you're already working? That was fast!"

"Yup," Fee grinned. "I am the new part-time proofreader and family-restaurant reviewer for *Child's Play* magazine. Can you believe it?" Cam slammed the back of the van shut and climbed into the backseat while Lucy climbed in up front beside her.

"I am soooo proud of you." Lucy settled back against the seat, arms folded, looking well satisfied. "I guess it worked out well to have Brody Collins help out with the kids, huh? You must have gotten a few free hours to work on your résumé—maybe taken advantage of some of his contacts?"

"I don't know what sort of contacts he'd have that could help me. But the time has sure helped. I've gotten more than a few hours out of him." Fee let out a hearty laugh. "I've been working the poor man all week long! I've barely given him time off to eat and sleep. I ought to lighten up; even prisoners get time off for good behavior. My job is only going to be part-time though. Once I get over this initial adjustment period, I expect I'll be able to be home quite a bit more, and Brody won't have to work quite so hard for his room and board."

Lucy snickered. "Room and board. That's a good one."

Fee blinked at her. "What is?"

"You know. Like Brody Collins would really need to work for room and board." Lucy slapped herself on the thigh. "Ha-ha-ha. Very funny, Fee."

"But…" A tiny furrow formed between her brows. "But he is working for room and board. That's the deal. He's staying in the guesthouse, temporarily anyway, in exchange for watching the kids. He's been there all week."

"What?" Lucy spun around in her seat and threw Cam a stricken look. He returned it with a startled one of his own.

"Uh-oh."

"What's the matter? 'Uh-oh' what?" Fee demanded. "What are you uh-ohing about?"

"Um…" Lucy bit her lip. "Wow. Fee, you are going to be so hacked at me."

"I," Fee assured her, "am already hacked, and I'm going to be a lot more so if you don't hurry up and tell me—*what is the matter?*"

"Well…um." Lucy pressed her body closer to the passenger-side door, as if preparing to make a quick escape. "I don't know what he told you. But the thing is, Brody Collins doesn't need room and board. He's rather…um…rich, I think."

"Rich?" Fee echoed stupidly.

"He's got one of the best-paying jobs in the city, I would imagine. He's the editor of *California Dream* magazine. You know, the one that focuses on the lifestyles of Hollywood celebrities?"

"I…I know the one." While waiting at the grocery-store checkout stand a month or two ago, Felicia had seen the cover photo of a besequined Tiffany Diamond at the Emmy Awards.

"Fee," Lucy said gently. "Brody told me at the wedding that he thought you needed help with the kids, and he said he'd sort of accidentally implied that he could give it to you. He asked me not to say anything to you about who he really was until he could clear up the misunderstanding. I said I'd agree if he promised to come clean with you within twenty-four hours. I thought he was going to maybe baby-sit for you that weekend and give you a break. Or maybe even take you out. You see, I thought…" Rarely did Felicia see her sister looking embarrassed, but for once, Lucy truly did have the sense to look thoroughly ashamed. "Well, I only did it because I kind of thought that Brody liked you and wanted to spend time with you again after all these years, seeing as how he's one of your old boyfriends and all…"

"My boyfriend?" Fee gaped at her. "He was never my boyfriend. I barely knew him. I just thought he was this nice guy from my yearbook class."

"Uh-oh," Lucy repeated, averting her eyes to look out the window.

"But…I don't understand," Fee said, staring blankly at the traffic in front of her. "Why would he even want to lie about something like that? What could he possibly have to gain?" She was so stunned, her mind was functioning at a mere fraction of its usual swiftness.

"Well," Lucy said grimly. "Where is he now?"

"At the house," Felicia said helplessly. "With the kids. I asked him to wait there with them until one o'clock. Robert and Tiffany just got back from Mexico after eloping and are coming by then to pick them up—" One hand flew from the steering wheel to cover her mouth. "Oh no!"

"He'll probably be there with that photographer," Lucy muttered. "You know, the redhead he brought to the wedding?"

"That was a photographer?" For a split second, elation flooded through Felicia's veins; she'd obsessed all week about whether the woman had been some sort of girlfriend to Brody.

Then her senses returned.

"That...that...phony!" Fee felt as though her heart had been crushed. It was a familiar feeling. But this time, the man had gone too far. He had come into her home. He had become an important part of her life. Worst of all, he had involved her children in his treachery.

Fee had had her heart stomped on before. But this time, she was ready to stomp back.

"I'm so sorry, honey," Lucy said soothingly, taking her by the hand. "Do you want Cam and me to take care of this for you and throw the bum out?"

"No." Felicia took in a long, deep breath and exhaled. Her eyes snapped. "I think I've had enough help for one week. This is one job I can handle *all by myself*."

Lucy later swore that on the way back to her house, Felicia had broken every law that was in the California driver's manual and almost certainly a few that were not.

Felicia never even tried to deny it. Her attention was so completely focused on protecting her children—on stopping their exploitation at the hands of her counterfeit nanny—that she had only the vaguest safety concerns in mind as she raced to get home before Robert and Tiffany were due to arrive at one o'clock.

The display on her dashboard still read 12:58 when she finally turned down the street that led to her cul-de-sac.

"Ha!" she cried, then raised one hand in the air and gave a little victory wave. "You'd better say your prayers, Collins, because here I come!"

"And there," Lucy broke in, her eyes following a snazzy red Miata passing in the opposite lane, "they go. Your kids, I mean."

"What?" Fee turned to see Clifford and Dinah waving to her from the backseat of Robert's convertible just before the car disappeared around the corner. "Oh *noooooo!*" she wailed. She turned into the driveway, where she found, to her horror, Brody and the red-headed photographer talking animatedly: the woman with her manicured hands on her shapely hips, Brody waving one arm dramatically in the air.

Felicia had barely pulled the van to a stop when she hopped out and stormed over to confront them.

"Well, hello there," she spat out. "Isn't this cozy? I'm so sorry to interrupt this lovely little *business* meeting of yours. But if it's not too much trouble, I'd like to speak to my employee. Or should I say, my Benedict Arnold? My Brutus?" Pausing to take a breath, she noticed for the first time what Brody held in his right arm. "Wait a minute. What are you doing with Gabe? *What are you doing with my baby?*" She seized the infant with uncustomary roughness, and the child began to cry.

Brody, who had paled at her use of the word *business,* shrank back in the face of her fury. "Robert said he thought he was better off at home." He looked at her compassionately. "He said he and Tiffany weren't really set up to handle a baby."

"They...oh, this is just great." Fee felt as though she'd been stomped on once more. Her heart welled up with anger on her child's behalf. "Well, fine. Gabe will do just fine without Robert, if he has to. I'll deal with him later. You, on the other hand, won't be getting off so easy. I'd like a word with you."

Out of the corner of her eyes, Felicia saw Carmen give her a slow feline smile. Dressed in a silver satin blouse and a short black skirt that reached barely halfway to her absurdly skinny knees, she looked like the media's idea of every man's dream come true.

Suddenly Felicia was aware of her own less-than-desirable appearance. Knowing that she'd be spending the morning on her hands and knees, sorting out files, she'd taken Adam's suggestion that she wear something casual to work that day. Her jeans were presentable, but not a particularly good fit, having come from the recesses of her closet where she kept several old, slightly too large favorites. Over her lumpy-looking jeans, Felicia had thrown a simple gray sweatshirt that did little to counteract the fashion nightmare that was her pants. Even her once-white sneakers had taken one too many trips through the mud puddles with Clifford to be considered anything less than grungy.

"I'll be brief," she said curtly, "and to the point. I know all about your real job, Mr. Collins. I know about everything, and I don't appreciate this little game you've been playing with me and my children all week. I told you that I wouldn't sell you my story, and so you decided to go ahead and take it." Her eyes landed on the thirty-five-millimeter camera he had slung over his left shoulder. It was too late. He had the photographs. "Fine," she said, blinking back the tears that threatened to rise to her eyes. "But I certainly hope you have a very good lawyer. Because you're going to need one. I don't intend to stand by and watch you hurt my children in this way."

"Look, Felicia," Brody said desperately. He reached out to take her hand, but she pulled away from his touch. "Sorry." He backed off and looked at her miserably. "I am *sooo* sorry about all this. Please, let me try to explain. I didn't mean for this to get so out of hand, I swear. I can explain about this nanny thing. And I can explain about *Child's Play*, too. I promise you didn't get the job just because I own it. You—"

"You mean there's more?" Felicia wailed. "That was all a lie too?" She felt she might burst into tears at any moment.

"Um…you said you knew everything…"

"Look, I don't want to hear it. I just want you out of here." She set her jaw and pulled herself up to the full height of her five-foot-seven-inch frame. Behind her, Lucy and Cam stood in front of the minivan, scowling, looking like a couple of modern-day suburban bounty hunters.

"Fee, if you'd just—"

"Go away, Brody."

"But if you'll listen, just for a sec—"

"No."

"It's just that—"

Looking into the serious face of the only male she knew who was more stubborn than her seven-year-old son, Fee had the ridiculous urge to start counting to three out loud. "Out," she said with all the authority she could muster. "And by the way: You're fired!"

"But," he said in frustration, "you can't fire me. *You* work for *me*. At *Child's Play,* I mean."

"Well then…," Fee stammered, her confidence momentarily shaken. "I quit!"

"You can't quit," Brody said helplessly. "You're my boss…"

"What? But—" Fee tried not to scream. He was trying to confuse her now. It wasn't going to work. "It doesn't matter what you say, Brody. Our relationship—whatever you call it— is over. You don't have much stuff with you; it shouldn't take you long to pack." She grabbed the diaper bag and the car seat that he had dragged out to the curb for Robert and began schlepping them back to the van. When Lucy and Campbell stepped forward, she passed the items off and spun back around to face Brody. "I'm going over to my sister's house for the afternoon. You can tell my 'boss,' Adam, if that's his real name, that I won't be back to work…ever. And when I get back here by four o'clock, I want to find you—and all of your things—gone. Have you got that?"

Brody nodded. He looked positively wretched. "You're right." He spoke so quietly she had to tilt her ear toward him to hear. "I don't know what else to say, except you're right. And…that I'm sorry."

Looking at him standing there, hands in his pockets, his once-bright blue eyes darkened by despair, Fee felt almost sorry for the man. Something in her made her want to go to him, to take him in her arms and tell him all was forgiven.

She set her feet firmly on the concrete driveway and resisted the urge with every ounce of strength she could summon.

"Good-bye, Brody." She turned away coldly and climbed back into the van. He made no move to stop her.

But as she retreated down the elm-lined street, watching his image recede bit by bit in her rearview mirror, she could not shake the nagging feeling that she was heading in the wrong direction altogether.

Having expended the energy it took to get completely wound into a full-fledged snit, Felicia decided to make the most of her wrath and called Robert at his apartment as soon as she arrived at Campbell and Lucy's.

When she got his answering machine, she spoke into the telephone as sweetly as she could and asked him to call her at Lucy and Cam's as soon as he could, please, if it wouldn't be too much trouble, thank you very much. Then she hung up the phone, pantomimed a violent choking impression, and proceeded to cry into her sister's afghan for a full half-hour without ceasing.

Despite her own exhaustion, Lucy was both comforting and nurturing—lighting candles, tucking Fee onto the couch under the soft wool-knit blanket, and making her a cup of her favorite orange-cinnamon spice tea. When Robert finally did call back an hour later, Felicia was considerably less emotional than she had been when she left her message.

She was, however, still thoroughly enraged.

"I realize," she bit out, trying to keep her tone from becoming shrill, "that you have a lot to deal with right now. But Gabe is your son. He needs to spend time with you too. Would it really have been so hard for you and Tiffany to take him for the afternoon?" To her surprise, she no longer found herself fighting a gag reflex when she spoke the woman's name.

"Sorry, Fee," Robert said easily. In the background, she could hear a woman's laughing; the sound seemed to be coming from another room. Closer was the sound of a television set blaring. She could barely distinguish the voices of the characters from Clifford and Dinah's favorite cartoon. "Tiffany just wasn't up to it. She says this is technically still our honeymoon, and she doesn't want to spend it taking care of *my* baby. I don't blame her, do you?"

Felicia counted to ten silently before responding through stiff lips. "Let's just say that Tiffany's well-being is not my greatest concern. I'm more worried about the kids. Speaking of which…were they very upset when they saw the photographer this afternoon?"

"What photographer?" Robert sounded alarmed. "What are you talking about?"

"The redhead." Felicia didn't believe for a moment that her ex-husband hadn't noticed Carmen. Noticing beautiful women was practically his full-time occupation.

"The one arguing with the nanny?" Robert no longer sounded worried. "She didn't have a camera. Now that I think of it, he did. But neither of them used it, as far as I could tell." He dropped his voice a notch. "You don't really think they took any, do you? Tiffany would have an absolute fit. She wants to announce our wedding her own way, through the publicist, all that…you understand."

"I…don't know." Suddenly, Felicia wasn't so sure what she thought Brody had done. The details about Robert's wedding announcement rolled right off her like water from a duck's back. "I'll let you know if I find out."

After she'd hung up, she turned to Lucy, who had curled up in a nearby armchair to await the results of the conversation.

"Well?" Lucy asked impatiently.

"He told me Brody didn't take any photographs. That other woman didn't either." Fee shook her head. "It doesn't make any sense. Why wouldn't he do it then? It was the perfect opportunity. No one was around to stop him."

"I don't know." Lucy gnawed on a thumbnail. "Unless…"

"Unless what?"

"Nothing." Fee's sister waved one hand dismissively. "It's too crazy."

"What?" Felicia rose menacingly from the sofa.

"Okay, okay!" Lucy raised her eyebrows at her. "Settle down, Lizzie Borden. I was just going to say maybe Brody didn't take the pictures because he decided he couldn't. Maybe he realized that his loyalty was to you first. If I recall correctly, that redhead didn't seem all that happy when we first got there. And it did sort of look as though he had taken her camera away…"

Fee plopped back down on the couch. Lucy was right. Now that she thought about it, it had looked exactly that way. But if he really felt so loyal toward her, why had he been lying to her all week? "I think," she said, feeling surprised to hear the words coming out of her mouth, "I'd better go back and

223

talk this through with Brody—if he's still there. I need to find out what's really been going on."

"Yeah," Lucy grunted. "So do I. So get your cute little self back to the house and call me as soon as you know something. I'll even watch Gabe for you. That's the kind of sister I am."

"You," Felicia told her gratefully, "are an angel."

"I don't want to be an angel," Lucy answered bluntly. "I want to be a bridesmaid. It's been a whole week since I've been in a wedding. So get on over there, already, and make up with that man!"

"You're an incurable matchmaker. Incorrigible!" Fee scolded, but the faintest glimmer of hope had been resurrected from the ashes of her heart. "You never give up!"

"That," Lucy told her without the slightest trace of vanity, "is what makes me so unbelievably *good*."

Twelve

All the way back to the house, Felicia worried that Brody wouldn't still be there, that she wouldn't know what to say to him if he was, that somehow he would hurt her again or, worst of all, that he was about to disappear out of her life altogether, leaving her even lonelier than she'd been before he ever breezed into her world.

"God," she whispered, praying furiously as she drove, "I know I don't trust you nearly as much as I should. But I know I need to now! Please show me how to handle this situation. Because I haven't a clue as to what is the right thing to do!"

She suspected that she probably shouldn't be opening herself up to Brody again. He'd probably just lie to her once more. Yet she couldn't shake the sense that she had to hear his explanation from his own lips. She needed to know once and for all why he'd done all that he'd done.

To her tremendous relief, the Falcon was still positioned directly beneath her elm tree, exactly where it had been parked when she left the house an hour and a half before. But as she drove past it into the driveway, she saw that the backseat was piled high with cardboard boxes, and a weathered suitcase made of a heavy-weave carpetlike substance was sitting on the curb by the Falcon's balding right front tire.

Fee threw the minivan into park and killed the engine. There was no reason to feel so morose at the sight of Brody's belongings being taken away, she reminded herself sternly. He was only doing exactly as she'd asked.

But as she made her way down the driveway toward the guest cottage, she felt as though a tiny hole had been poked into her life, allowing every last bit of joy to escape.

She was no more than five feet from the door when it opened and Brody stepped out into the warm afternoon, blinking at Fee as if she, and not the bright Southern California sunshine, were causing his pupils to dilate.

"Hi," he said, looking at her in stunned surprise. A large suitcase—a perfect match to the one at the street—was gripped in his right hand. The key to her guesthouse was clutched in his left. Brody held the small piece of metal out to her, and it glinted in the light like a jewel. Felicia took it from him silently, reverently, as if he were handing her a priceless gift.

"I'm sorry I'm not out of your hair yet," Brody said awkwardly, staring at his shoes. "I didn't start packing until just a little while ago. I thought you said you wouldn't be back until four."

"I did." Fee slipped the key into her pocket without bothering to lock the guesthouse door behind him. "I changed my mind." Brody looked up at that, and his eyes searched hers. "About hearing your side of the story, I mean," she hurriedly added. "Not about anything else."

"Of course." Brody nodded grimly. "That's awfully generous of you." With a look of resignation, he started walking toward the street with his suitcase. After a moment, Felicia followed.

She watched as he opened the passenger door and threw both suitcases onto the vinyl front seat. While she waited, Fee wandered around to the front of the car and sat down on the curb, resting her sneakered feet on a city sewer grate. When he'd finished, Brody slammed the car door shut and came around to sit beside her.

"First of all, I'd like to say," he began in a low voice, "that I didn't set out to deliberately mislead you. But that's what I did. My reasons were selfish, and I'm sorry. I've asked God's forgiveness, and now I need to ask yours." He kicked at a bit of gravel in the street. "The thing is, I lied from the very beginning," he confessed. "I am so sorry. It seemed harmless enough; it was just a little white lie, really, nothing more. I called Lucy to try to get her to let my magazine *California Dream* cover her wedding. She accidentally got the impression that you and I used to date, and...well, I didn't exactly correct her. I figured if she thought you and I were once close, she'd be more likely to let me have the story."

The blush of embarrassment started at his neck and crept up to the roots of his close-cropped, chestnut-colored hair. If he wasn't truly ashamed, Felicia reflected, he was at least making a good show of it. "Then I met you at the reception, and you told me about Robert and Tiffany. And that was an even bigger story! I was still trying to figure out how I was going to convince you to give *Dream* the exclusive, when you got the crazy idea that I provided childcare for a living."

"But, you said—" Felicia tried to remember exactly what Brody had told her.

"I said I'd made my living off of children for years. What I was referring to was the years I'd spent at *Child's Play,* which I founded and still co-own. You interpreted this as meaning that I'd been a childcare provider. When I offered to help you in a professional capacity, I was trying to gently lead up to getting you to sell me your story. You accepted, and it took a few moments before I realized that you wanted me to help out with the kids. Against my better judgment, I decided on the spot that I was perfectly capable of doing the job, and that if I helped you out, you might warm up to me and maybe we'd both wind up getting exactly what we wanted." The words spilled out nearly one on top of the other, as if he was afraid she might jump to her feet and vanish at any moment, before he'd had a chance to fully explain.

"I never wanted you to lie to me," she said bitterly.

"I know. I know." Brody looked at her as though he wanted desperately to take her in his arms, but didn't dare.

"And then you moved into my house."

"Your guesthouse," Brody corrected. "But yes. I did. I never planned that either. It just sort of happened. It seemed like you really wanted me there. And there was no denying that it was a better situation for me, with what I had planned. I knew it was stupid of me to even try it, but the next thing I knew, I had opened my mouth and agreed to it. There didn't seem to be any way out after that. I was already in way over my head."

"So then what? What did you have planned after that?" It sickened Felicia to think that he'd been lurking in her home all week, plotting his next move.

"I figured one of two things would happen," Brody admitted. "Ideally, I'd be able to convince you to sell your story. Worst case scenario, I'd be able to get the scoop without your permission, or at the very least come up with the photos I needed."

Felicia shivered. Despite the sun on her back, she suddenly felt chilled to the core.

"What I didn't figure on," Brody said quietly, "was what actually happened."

Time seemed to slow, and for an instant, it seemed as though her heart had stopped. "What *did* happen?" she managed at last.

Brody reached out and touched her fingers lightly. When she did not immediately snatch them away, he slid his underneath hers and held her hand as easily as if they were two schoolchildren waiting together for the neighborhood ice-cream truck. "I lost my nerve," he said in a steady voice. Fee looked at him and saw the intensity of his gaze. "And I lost my heart."

She drew in a sharp breath.

"I couldn't follow through with the story. Not after I got to know you." Brody squeezed her fingers tighter. "Don't you see?" He implored her with his eyes. "I couldn't do anything to hurt you, Fee!"

"But you did hurt me!" she blurted out.

"I know. And I'm so sorry." Brody looked at her helplessly. "I guess I should say, I wouldn't ever hurt you on purpose. You or the kids. How could I when I love you so much?"

Felicia's pulse began to race, and she could hear the blood rushing in her ears like the sound of the sea. "Love?"

"Yes. Love." For the first time, Brody's strong, full lips twisted up at the corners. "Don't you know by now that I love you?"

"Wh—?" Felicia caught her breath. "How could I?"

"You mean you haven't seen the way I look at you? Haven't noticed the way I've been transformed from a completely reasonable man into a perfectly ridiculous fool?" Brody chuckled self-consciously. "You can't actually mean to say that you haven't seen my heart beating out of my chest whenever you come within fifty feet of me?"

"No." Fee struggled to keep from smiling. "I think I would have remembered that."

Brody cocked his head to one side and looked at her curiously. Felicia suspected that he could tell that some inner shift had occurred within her, for the light had returned to his eyes, and the old familiar smile lines had returned.

"Well…Robert did say that you hadn't taken any photographs," she said, relenting. Now that she heard the whole story, she could see how things could have gotten out of control so quickly and could even recognize her own role in the ridiculous fiasco.

"That's true. And...I quit my job at *California Dream*."

"Really? Oh, Brody! You did that for me?" Fee felt her heartbeat quicken. "Well...I suppose I could be persuaded to give you a second chance," she said and gave Brody the tiniest of smiles. "I forgive you. Especially if you really, truly, *actually* love me."

Brody stared at her, wide-eyed with relief, then roughly pulled her into his arms and held her tight. "Oh, Fee. Sweetheart," he said. As she pressed her cheek against the comforting softness of his shirt and breathed in the scent of cotton and mildewed cardboard and man, Felicia had the overwhelming sensation that she had finally come home. "You have no idea how much I hoped to hear those words from you. I promise I will never lie to you again."

He pulled back abruptly and looked at her, dismayed, the twinkle in his eyes and smile lines fading away. "There's something else I have to tell you though," he said, sounding stricken.

Fee fought back the urge to jump back and run away. "I really wish you hadn't said that." She blinked at him. "I suppose now you're going to tell me that you're married?"

"No."

"You're a spy for the Russian government?"

"Absolutely not."

"You're really a woman?"

"Felicia!"

"Well what? I don't think I can handle any more surprise revelations."

"I'm not joking," Brody said, and she could see that he was telling the truth.

"All right then. What?" Fee wrapped her arms around her knees, steeling herself.

"Look, Fee. *Love*. You need to know that…I may very well be a carrier for Huntington's disease."

The words rattled around in her head; they meant nothing to her. "Huntington's disease?" A sense of foreboding overcame her. "Brody, you're *ill?*"

"No, no…" He reached out to pat her hand as she sat up in alarm. "I'm fine at the moment. But my father had the disease, and there's a chance that one day I will as well. If I do, there's a fifty percent chance that I'd pass it on to my children. I can get tested, and now I will. But I thought you should know before we make any plans. If I do have the disease, I've decided not to biologically father any children. And I know that you desperately want another little girl…"

"What?" Fee gave her head a little shake. "Where did you get that from?"

"When you were talking to me at the reception about your mother. You said that you wanted to give Dinah a sister and name her Anna."

Felicia looked at him in astonishment. "Well, I'm certainly not against the idea. I think it would be lovely, actually. But really, that's up to God. If it's meant to happen, he will make a way. If not, that's fine. I hadn't actually planned on having any more children anyway. I mean, if I were to get pregnant again it would be a lovely blessing. But"—she reached out both arms and draped them around his massive shoulders—"I would never want that to get in the way of any other dreams God wanted to make come true in my life."

Brody's eyes opened wide. "You mean—"

"Like you?" Fee leaned forward and planted a tiny kiss on his stubbled jaw line. His skin felt rough as sandpaper under her lips and smelled as tantalizing as spice. "Exactly."

Brody's eyes lit up with delight. "Well then, woman," he growled and pulled her tight against his chest once more. "Let me hear you say it!"

"Say what?" Fee tilted her chin stubbornly away and pretended not to know what he was talking about.

"I believe," he said patiently, "that when a man says 'I love you,' it's customary for the woman to say, 'I love you too.' That is, if she does. But then maybe I'm presuming too much."

Felicia turned back to him and gave him a stern look. "Bite your tongue! Of course I do!" She felt his chest expand as he took in a long deep breath and held it, waiting. Her long slim fingers smoothed back the frown lines that had moments before appeared between his thick dark brows. "Brody Collins, I love you." She bowed her head and gently kissed his muscular neck, just above the fabric of his collar.

"And I love you too," he murmured against her hair.

Fee snuggled even closer into his embrace. "Lucy will be so relieved!" she sighed.

"No more than I," Brody said with the voice of a sentenced man whose life had just been miraculously spared. "No more than I."

For the next several minutes, he and Felicia exchanged tender kisses and passionate declarations of love that would forever remain between just the two of them. Then Felicia shifted position ever so slightly, reached into her pocket, and pulled out something warm and familiar that she pressed into the palm of Brody's hand.

Recognizing the treasure immediately, Brody lowered his lips and whispered into the tiny shell of her ear. "Giving me back the key to the guesthouse, are you, my sweet?"

"Just think of it," she said, her heart brimming with love, "as the key to my heart."

Fifteen months later…

"I am…the fattest…bridesmaid in the world!" Felicia cried, glaring down at her steadily expanding figure, draped stylishly in an empire-waist gown of periwinkle blue.

"No, I am," Catherine interrupted, pointing to her own burgeoning belly.

"No, I am." Lucy shifted uncomfortably on top of the pillow she had brought along to place beneath her bottom. The three of them sat in a loose circle around the table provided for their portion of the wedding party, each precariously balanced on one of the modest-size, standard-issue folding chairs the party rental agency provided for receptions.

"I would have to say," Daphne declared, looking queen-like in ecru satin, "that it's an absolute tie." She raised one thin, dark eyebrow at the trio. Her hands rested on the back of Cat's chair, the morning sunlight causing her dark chestnut curls to shine. "And you three still maintain that you didn't actually plan to conceive at nearly the same time?"

Lucy rolled her eyes dramatically. "We do not exactly discuss our reproductive lives, O Suspicious One."

"Well, how am I supposed to know what married women talk about behind their single friends' backs?" Daphne grumped. She plopped into a free chair next to Cat, her voluminous skirts spilling out around her. When she crossed her legs, two feet poked out from her petticoats, and Fee got the clearest look she'd had all day of Daphne's glittery, ruby red slippers, a knockoff of the pair worn by Judy Garland in *The Wizard of Oz*.

"Guess you're gonna find out now," Fee grinned. "It was an incredible ceremony, Daph. You looked gorgeous. I thought for a minute there Elliott was going to start bawling."

"Jonas *did* start bawling," Cat said proudly, then looked around her. "Where is my husband anyway? And the groom?" she wondered aloud. "Come to think of it, where are all the guys?"

Fee let her eyes rove over the open sand to a group of four adults and three children not far away. Leave it to Daphne to have her wedding on the beach, less than a hundred feet from the ocean's edge, with only family and less than fifty friends present. It was the perfect day—intimate and infinitely memorable.

Nearby, the hired DJ fiddled with his equipment, and soon Sarah Vaughan's "You Stepped Out of a Dream" was rising forth from two gigantic speakers set up on the public beach. "They're playing Frisbee in their tuxedos," Felicia informed Lucy. "Can you believe it?"

"It wouldn't be so bad," Lucy grumbled, "if we could actually play too."

"Hey, I have no complaints; they're keeping my kids happy," Fee said, arms folded across the shelf of her tummy. She watched her husband throw a bright orange plastic disk dangerously close to Clifford's head, while nearby, Gabe in his sunsuit burrowed like a small animal in the sand. "I am going to be getting that stuff out of that child's ears for weeks," she mumbled.

"Nobody warned me I was going to get *this* big," Lucy complained, still staring at her stomach.

"Well Felicia got at least that big by seven months with both Clifford and Gabe," Cat reminded her. "Weren't you paying attention?"

"No, of course not. It was her stomach then."

The sisters were still trading pregnancy horror stories fifteen minutes later when Brody, Jonas, Campbell, and Elliott finally returned with Fee's children in tow.

"Hi there, doll," Brody said to Fee and knelt to kiss her stomach. "How's my Anna?" His eyes twinkled like stars when he uttered his daughter's name.

They were, in fact, having a daughter; this they knew for certain. Though the genetic testing they'd done had confirmed that Brody was not a carrier for Huntington's disease even before they'd become pregnant, he and Fee had agreed to go ahead and do an amniocentesis to put their minds at ease. This test had not only confirmed their baby's perfect health; it had removed any question about her gender.

One by one, the men pulled up chairs and settled themselves down beside their wives.

"Now this," Brody said with a contented sigh, "is what life is all about. The sun is shining. I've got the perfect wife, three amazing kids, and another one on the way. What could be better?"

"So I'm perfect, huh?" Fee asked with a wry grin. "Can I get that in writing?"

"You are the perfect wife for me," Brody said firmly. "And I've got the perfect family."

"Spoken like a true editor of a family magazine," Campbell observed. "How's work going these days anyway?"

"Couldn't be better," Brody grinned. "Fee's still working part-time at the office, as much as she wants. Adam's been letting me get more and more involved at the magazine. And I'm already two-thirds of the way through my book. What can I say? God is good."

Fee beamed at him happily. She was still amazed that in the aftermath of being fired by Nicholas Fortunata, Brody had made such an amazing professional comeback. Not only had he reimmersed himself in the operation of *Child's Play* with Adam's blessing, he had put together several nonfiction book proposals. He had been contracted to write, and would soon be finished with, one about planning family vacations in the state of California, for which Fee was writing the restaurant reviews. Due out the following summer, it would co-published by *Child's Play* and one of the most respected New York publishing houses, with versions on various states and regions to follow. On Brody's desk at their new home in Malibu, where they lived just down the street from Lucy and Cam, were three more proposals for children's stories he'd been tinkering with since the beginning of the year. She had no doubt that he would find a home for them and that his dreams would come true. Hadn't hers?

"God *is* good," Cat agreed. "And he's taken care of all of us, in very different, truly wonderful ways." She reached out and squeezed her husband's hand.

"That's true, isn't it?" Jonas nodded. "He brought Cat and me back together after being apart for twelve years, and we were married two weeks later. Felicia and Brody, you dated for...what? Four months before you got married?"

Fee blushed. "Seventeen weeks," she corrected, thinking it sounded longer. It might seem like a quick romance to the outside world, but she and Brody had known from the beginning where their relationship was heading. And with the kids loving him as much as they did, there hadn't seemed to be much of a reason to wait.

"Campbell and Lucy were together a whole year before they got married," Fee reflected.

236

"It took a while to plan that wedding, you know," Lucy said defensively. "And you and Brody should be glad we had such an elaborate affair, or you might never have met. Besides, look at Daphne! She and Elliott dated forever!"

Daphne stuck out her lower lip. Elliott just grinned. "We could have eloped, like Cat and Jonas," he reminded her. "Remember, we almost did."

"No, no," Cat broke in. "You waited, which was wise for you two. And I'm glad you did. Everything happened just the way it was supposed to. For each of us. God took care of us all, in very individualized ways, and I don't think any one of us has reason to complain."

"I know I certainly don't," Brody murmured, dropping a light kiss on the back of Felicia's hand. He cocked an ear as Sarah Vaughan's rich alto voice drifted off on a breeze and the DJ punched in a new disc featuring Bette Midler. "And now, my dear," Brody stood, then turned to Fee and firmly grasped her fingers. "I believe the man is playing our song."

The corners of Fee's mouth crept toward her ears as she recognized the recording, a remake of a classic Disney song. "Brody, what have you done?"

"Just a little bribe to the disc master." He bowed at the hip. "May I have this dance?"

Felicia nodded regally and allowed him to pull her—with some difficulty—to her feet, which proceeded to sink considerably in the sand.

"Baby mine, don't you cry…"

"From *Dumbo*, eh?" Fee's lips twitched. "Fitting, since I feel like an elephant and look like one too."

"Not to me."

Fee stepped toward her husband, ricocheted back as her stomach bounced off his, then tried two more times with equal success. Behind them, Daphne snickered.

"Rest your head close to my heart…," the legendary diva warbled.

"I don't think I can do that," Fee whispered loudly to her husband, her face burning. "I can't reach you."

"Never to part…"

"That's okay," Brody said, swinging his arms wide to encompass Felicia's gloriously developing body. "I'll come to you."

"Baby of mine…"

And that's exactly what he did.

If you haven't read Book Two in Shari MacDonald's
Salinger Sisters Series,
take a peek at what you missed!

A Match Made in Heaven

"Campbell Howard?" Lucy nearly dropped her pencil. "You mean, *the* Campbell Howard?"

"Well! It's not often that I hear a response like that when I introduce myself," the man chuckled. "But, yes, it's me, the infamous Campbell Howard. In the flesh." He beamed, clearly taking it all as one big joke. "I take it you've seen my 'Wanted' poster in the post office?"

"You're Campbell Howard?" Lucy repeated dully. "You are? As in: Alexandra Canfield's brother, Campbell Howard? The guy-who-stands-to-inherit-a-lot-of-money-if-he-gets-a-wife-in-a-month, Campbell Howard?" He blinked at her, clearly uncertain how he should respond.

This was the guy with the crazy sister? The one who agreed to a romantic match just so he could get his inheritance? The man who had sold out for money? Surely this was some sort of cruel joke. "But...but Campbell Howard is a geek!" she burst out, remembering the photograph she'd seen of him as a teen. How could this impressive specimen of a man possibly be the same person?

Once again, she was appalled at the words that were coming out of her mouth—even though she meant them. Her guest

239

appeared unfazed. "This is some sort of test, isn't it?" he asked in a dry tone. "This is to protect your female clients, right? You want to see how I respond to unexpected situations? See if I turn violent when pushed too far?" He looked around the room inquisitively. "Fess up. Am I on *Candid Camera*?"

"No, you are not on *Candid Camera*," Lucy answered testily. All feelings of affinity were gone. "But I did meet your sister this morning, and I'm afraid I can't help you…*Dr.* Howard."

"I see," Campbell said, though his furrowed brow expressed clearly that he didn't. "Of course, that's your prerogative. Might I ask why, though?" Lucy felt herself becoming grumpier by the minute. Didn't he get it? And why did he have to sound so infuriatingly polite?

She gazed at him levelly. "Why can't I help you?" *Because you're a user, a fake, a danger to women everywhere…including me.* "As I explained earlier, Dr. Campbell—"

"Dr. Howard," he corrected cheerfully.

Lucy sighed. Of course. Campbell was his first name. "Excuse me. Dr. Howard—"

"Please. Call me 'Campbell.'" His tone was friendly, easy.

Lucy hesitated. "Fine. Campbell. As I was saying—"

"My friends call me Cam," he suggested cheerfully.

"Dr. Howard, please!" Lucy glared at him. "As I said earlier, my goal is to help facilitate the matches that I believe are, well…preordained. I told your sister earlier, and I will tell you now as well: I don't force or manipulate matches that aren't meant to be. Certainly, in the past I've helped people find each other within a month. But I couldn't promise the same would happen for you. I couldn't go into this with that as my goal. And even if I found you the 'right one' within thirty days, I couldn't in good conscience support a decision to marry that quickly. It's…it's…."

"Insane?" Cam suggested.

Lucy sighed again. "Well, now, you would know that, wouldn't you?" she said, remembering that he worked in the mental-health field. She eyed him uneasily, unsure of how he would respond to her outburst. Anger, defensiveness, frustration, blame…all were possibilities. She was prepared for any reaction…except the one she got.

Laughter. It began as a chuckle and soon spread to a full-out bellow that filled the room.

"Touché," Cam grinned.

Lucy stared. "That's all you can say? Touché? I'm serious, you know. This isn't a game to me. I take my work very seriously." Even as she spoke, she heard the tone of her voice and envisioned herself as a little girl playing grown-up, stomping her foot to emphasize her point. As ridiculous as she sounded, however, she wasn't about to back down. "People sometimes think it's strange that I'm a matchmaker," she told him testily. "Like I should get a 'real' job. They don't take me seriously. But I assure you, this is my real job. I wouldn't be doing it if it wasn't important to me. And I'm not going to let you or anyone else take advantage of my clients. I can tell the difference between someone who's serious about finding a person to give love to and someone who's out to get his own selfish needs met. I assure you, Doctor, I'm no fool."

Campbell's eyes flickered automatically to her forehead, and he appeared to force back a grin. "Of course you're not," he said kindly.

"What?" Responding to the look, Lucy quickly threw one hand to her head. To her horror, her fingers met something stuck to the skin just above her left eyebrow. With a heart full of dread, she grabbed the offending item, lowered her hand to eye level, and slowly opened her fist one finger at a time. There on her palm lay a neon-green, plastic-coated paper clip.

Her mind raced as she searched for an explanation. How could a paper clip have gotten stuck to her forehead? Unless... She'd been absentmindedly playing with a pile of paper clips when Alexandra was in the office. A stray must have dropped to the desktop just in front of her, then stuck to her skin when she pressed her forehead to the desk. Had it been there the entire time she'd been talking to Campbell? Her heart sank. No wonder he'd been so amused when she'd been trying hard to appear the calm, composed professional.

He grinned, causing her anger to rise even further. "Uh— you have a little thing on your—" he began innocently, waving a finger at her forehead.

"Ha, ha. Very funny." Lucy threw him a murderous look. "You know, you could have told me."

"You're right." Cam's smile softened, and he gave her a look of kindness. "I should have spoken up. At first, I didn't want to offend you by saying something rude right off the bat. And after we'd been talking for a while, it seemed too late to say anything." The smile faltered. He appeared genuinely uncomfortable now. "I figured that sometime after I left, it would drop off and you wouldn't even notice. But you're right, there was no excuse for me not saying anything. I'd be pretty hacked off if I were in your shoes. How did it make you feel when you found that clip stuck to your head?"

"Well, I—" Lucy felt herself being pulled in by his warmth and charm. "Hey! I'm not one of your patients, you know," she grumbled. "I accept your apology. Now, let's just forget about it. There's really nothing else to say." There was no point in dragging this out any further. In a moment Campbell would get up and walk out of her office, and she'd never have to see the infuriating man again.

So why did she feel so awful...?

Barbara Jean Hicks
The Once Upon a Dream Series:
Classic fairy tales, retold in modern times—with a comic twist!

#1 An Unlikely Prince: A professor rents a quiet cottage in a distant town to accomplish his writing goals. Little does he know that his lovely neighbor is running a day-care center for seven imps straight out of Snow White!

#2 All That Glitters: Cindy Reilly launches a hilarious self-improvement campaign to win the heart of her chosen prince. Thanks to an eccentric "fairy godmother" and a disagreeably snooty stepmother, her campaign works—but not the way she'd planned!

#3 A Perfect Stranger: A beautiful woman is through with romance—until a mysterious pen pal unexpectedly trips up her heart. Then she discovers her sweet, sensitive mystery man is her miserable, undependable, utterly beastly ex-husband—and he wants her back! *Available Spring 2000.*

Annie Jones
The Route 66 Series:
Meet some incredible characters along historic Route 66—who'll steal more than your heart!

#1 The Double Heart Diner: Georgia Darling's mission seemed simple: Save the Double Heart Diner. But things have become more complicated since sophisticated Jett entered the picture. She likes him, maybe too much, but it's clear she can't trust him. Can she save the diner—and her own heart—before it's too late?

#2 Cupid's Corner: The feisty lady mayor of a small Kansas city on a stretch of forgotten Route 66 is trying to reestablish its title of Hitchin' City USA by staging a summer marriage-a-thon. Will the mayor and the editor of the local newspaper find themselves with their own irresistible itch to get hitched?

#3 Lost Romance Ranch: Built by a brokenhearted cowpoke years ago, the once famous dude ranch is now the subject of legal wrangling. When a separated couple are sent off on a treasure hunt along Route 66 to see who will win ownership of the land, can they find the love they've lost along the way? *Available June 2000.*